Venomous Craving

Eok Warriors1: Book One

Mary Auclair

Deliciously Dangerous Books

Copyright © 2023 by Mary Auclair and Deliciously Dangerous Books

Venomous Craving – Eok Warriors: Book One

All rights reserved.

No portion of this book may be reproduced in any form without written permission from the publisher or author, except as permitted by U.S. copyright law.

This publication is designed to provide accurate and authoritative information in regard to the subject matter covered. It is sold with the understanding that neither the author nor the publisher is engaged in rendering professional services. While the publisher and author have used their best efforts in preparing this book, they make no representations or warranties with respect to the accuracy or completeness of the contents of this book and specifically disclaim any implied warranties of merchantability or fitness for a particular purpose. No warranty may be created or extended by sales representatives or written sales materials. The advice and strategies contained herein may not be suitable for your situation. You should consult with a professional when appropriate. Neither the publisher nor the author shall be liable for any loss of profit or any other commercial damages, including but not limited to special, incidental, consequential, personal, or other damages.

ISBN: 9798871326442

Cover Design by QuirkyCirce

https://quirkycirce.com.au

ISBN: 9798874320485

Published and Printed in the United States of America

2nd edition 2023

Contents

	Fullpage Image	V
1.	Chapter 1	1
2.	Chapter 2	9
3.	Chapter 3	19
4.	Chapter 4	27
5.	Chapter 5	40
6.	Chapter 6	51
7.	Chapter 7	58
8.	Chapter 8	69
9.	Chapter 9	81
10.	Chapter 10	96
11.	Chapter 11	105
12.	Chapter 12	118
13.	Chapter 13	128
14.	Chapter 14	138
15.	Chapter 15	148

16.	Chapter 16	163
17.	Chapter 17	173
18.	Chapter 18	186
19.	Chapter 19	192
20.	Chapter 20	201
21.	Chapter 21	210
22.	Chapter 22	221
23.	Chapter 23	232
24.	Chapter 24	245
25.	Chapter 25	257
26.	Chapter 26	273
27.	Chapter 27	283
28.	Chapter 28	294
29.	Chapter 29	306
30.	Chapter 30	316
31.	Epilogue	321
	About Mary Auclair	325
	Other Titles by Mary Auclair	326

Chapter One

Rose

Rose looked at the tall, mottled-green male hovering over her. He was a Cattelan, one of the many alien races that plagued the Ring, looking for ships to plunder and goods to steal. This one's name was Arrik, and he was the captain of the largest pirate ship this side of the solar system. At least, that was what he said. Not that she cared.

His hand was still above his head, and his smoldering yellow eyes burned holes inside her skin. The entire left side of her face throbbed with pain where he'd backhanded her. It would leave a mark for sure. She'd be lucky if she only had a bruise in the morning. Rose swallowed and glared at him. The hatred she felt for the alien male was like a tidal wave of ice, digging through her internal organs, chilling the fear she should be feeling to a dull ache in the back of her mind. She was no match for his size and strength, but she wasn't a sheep to accept slaughter without a fight, no matter the consequences.

Still, the hand that reached for her throbbing cheek trembled. Some fights weren't meant to be won.

MARY AUCLAIR

Rose closed her eyes. One mistake, one little moment of inattention was all it took.

The Cattelan had captured her as she walked back from her hunt, a mere few hours from her house. Rose was exhausted and her feet and fingers were dull with the cold, but a string of three rabbits dangled from her hips. She was giddy with excitement at the thought of food, not looking around for signs of danger, as her father had taught her. As she had done countless times over the years.

It was her fault. Her fault the rabbits were thrown in the snow like garbage, like they didn't mean life or death for the four people waiting in the mudhouse. It was her fault their last hope for survival was now aboard a slaver's spaceship, leaving them defenseless and with no way of feeding themselves. They were doomed, and so was she.

Capturing her had been so easy.

It took Arrik only a second to jump on the opportunity, literally. As soon as he saw her, he leapt over the five feet or so that separated them and knocked her to the ground. The rest was history.

Rose was bagged and grabbed in a matter of minutes, and the world she knew had blacked out of existence. The next time she opened her eyes, she was inside a tiny white room, strapped down on a medical bed. The Cattelan had been there, looking over her body as if she was a unicorn sprinting out of the sea. He'd probably never seen a real life human before. Not many people had.

Cattelans were a merchant race involved in anything that turned a profit, including slavery. They would get more from the sale of Rose's body than they could spend in two entire lifetimes, the whole crew of them. But first, they had to deal with her human downsides. So, they fitted her with a top-of-the-line universal translator, embedded deep inside her brain, and proceeded to inoculate her against all illnesses humans were known to succumb to in the vast aggregation of planets known as The Ring. They performed every test imaginable, deemed her fit and healthy and, since then, she had been treated like an exotic pet—so precious and fragile it had to be preserved in a glass enclosure for its own protection.

That was about a week ago. Rose had spent her days since in a tiny cell under controlled atmosphere. She was about to go crazy in the confined space. She was used to the open spaces, and the claustrophobic living quarter made her want to scream and hit the walls with her fists until they bled.

Right now, she would happily replace the walls with the green bastard's face. Rose's stare locked with Arrik's and they exchanged strings of malevolence.

"Again, where are the other humans?"

"There are no others." She gave him what she hoped was an intimidating sneer. "I escaped from the breeding facility last spring, after killing my guards."

"You think I'm stupid, human?" He raised his hand again and Rose glowered at him, forcing herself not to flinch. "No specimen was reported missing from the breeding facility in the last twenty-three years. You're lying." An ugly smirk spread on his lip-less mouth, showing yellow teeth. "There are ways to make you talk."

Arrik stepped closer, his gaze sliding over her body, his intent as clear as the erection stretching the fabric of his pants.

"Get up." He tugged at his pants. "Take off your clothes. I've never had a human female before."

"If you touch me, you'll never have any other female, period." Rose glared at him. "I'll cut off your cock with my teeth if it's the last thing I do."

"Humans are supposed to be the best of all females." He pulled a long black belt from his tight gray pants. "Let's see if you're worth the fortune you're going to get me."

Arrik moved, his longer reach an advantage in the fight to come. It was easy to see that he didn't think she was a threat, no matter her earlier bragging. He wouldn't hurt her, though. Damaging merchandise as precious as Rose wasn't in his best interest, and Cattelans were experts at getting the best of their goods. Human females were worth fortunes, in any condition, but she was more valuable if she was pretty.

Still, what he had planned would wound her more than any blow.

"I'll kill you for that."

"A wild human female." A long, forked tongue lapped the air, tasting her pheromones. "I'll be richer than an Avonie duke."

With that last assessing look, Arrik leapt. His strong hands closed around her ankle and she was thrown on her back, too slow to react. He slammed his large body over hers, pinning her under his weight. He didn't even have to struggle with her, his nearly three hundred pounds were enough to render her defenseless. His weight was making it impossible to breathe, and all Rose was able to do was to gasp for air, opening her mouth uselessly as though she was a fish out of water.

As the seconds passed, her lungs burned and tiny spots of darkness grew in her field of vision. Panic took hold and Rose fought more fiercely, knowing she was using her oxygen reserves uselessly, but unable to control it. It didn't matter. Dying was better than the life the slavers had in store for her. As darkness invaded her thoughts, she summoned the features of her family, as they were before her father left. Her cousin Aliena, her twin brothers, even her mother's soft eyes, full of tenderness and love. Her father's easy smile, coming back from a hunt with a deer carcass on his back. Those were the things Rose wanted to see as she was dying.

Darkness grew and Rose felt her grip on reality slip.

Arrik grabbed both her wrists, brought them over her head, and pinned them together inside his larger hand, then finally lifted his crushing weight from her ribcage.

Rose gasped for air, gulping in the life-giving oxygen in large, greedy mouthfuls. The next second, the stench of the male's body hit her nostrils, a mixture of damp, rotting vegetables and acrid sweat. It was all she could do to prevent herself from gagging. Rose shut her eyes and focused. She needed all her strength to fight him off. Panic was just going to waste her energy, and she didn't have any to spare. Wasting precious seconds indulging in sensitivities such as smells wasn't one of her weaknesses, thanks to years of hunting with her father. When a girl knew how to gut a bear open, nothing could turn her stomach.

Without giving her time to recover, Arrik used one hand to keep her arms above her head while the other groped at her body. He squeezed her breast between his large, strong fingers so hard it hurt. Unable to restrain herself, Rose cried and twisted, but it was no use. He was so much stronger than her, she could as well wrestle with a boulder. Arrik's yellow gaze locked with hers as he used his knees to push her legs open, forcing himself between her thighs. A whimper escaped her lips, and tears stung her eyes.

She wasn't as strong as she thought. Not nearly strong enough.

"You're soft, and you smell like nothing else I've ever smelled." His voice was husky and bubbled with lusty violence. "I'm not even sure I'll sell you right away. Maybe I'll keep you for a while. You'll be worth less, but that kind of pleasure is priceless."

Rose's heart sank deeper in her guts. He was going to keep her for his personal pleasure. He would rape her, repeatedly, and she was sure he would take pleasure in inflicting as much pain and humiliation as possible. She had to think fast if she wanted to avoid that fate. Opportunities wouldn't come by the dozen, if they came at all. Then a plan imposed itself. It was a stupid, destined-for-failure plan, but it was the only one she could think of.

Arrik didn't have a choice. If he wanted to rape her, he had to undress himself and take off his clothes, too. Rose's pants and top were made of a light fabric, reminding her of cotton. Arrik could easily rip through them with his bare hands. His own clothing was another matter. He was wearing top quality synthetic leather, virtually tear proof. He had to withdraw from her and take it off if he wanted to do anything more than dry humping. And he did, without question.

Rose kept her eyes on Arrik as he let go of her wrists. He still towered over her, sitting with his knees between her spread thighs. His gaze didn't waver from her body as he started to fidget with his shirt. Her breaths rose in rapid succession as she searched for an opening, her mind racing. When Arrik's shirt was over his head, blocking his view for a few precious seconds, Rose didn't hesitate.

She rushed forward, head-butting him in the stomach. It had the intended effect and Arrik fell down on his ass, unbalanced. Summoning all her strength, she brought her knees high up on her stomach, then used her two feet to kick him square in the face. The kick hit its target squarely, jerking his head back with a sickening snapping sound. Arrik roared in fury, struggling against the constraint of the fabric, his arms still trapped in the shirt. Then the fabric came over his head and he glared straight at her. Two molten yellow eyes fastened on Rose, and she knew there would be no end to the male's retribution. Failure wasn't an option anymore.

With everything she had left, she brought her knees up high again and aimed her next kick at his groin. Her heels connected with the hard bulge of the Cattelan's erection with a muffled thump. This time, Arrik didn't roar, but let out a thin, choked sound of agony as he grabbed his sex with both hands. His eyes rolled in their sockets and he fell on his side, momentarily incapacitated.

Without losing another second, Rose jumped over his body and pulled with all her strength on the strong necklace that attached the universal magnetic key to Arrik's pants. It was sheer luck that Arrik was confident enough in his own superior strength that he didn't bother leaving it behind him. She would have had no means of opening the door without it.

As soon as Rose pressed the small, oval object into the depression on the side of the door, it slid up, and the hallway, with its long white walls, appeared. There wasn't a lot of time before Arrik regained his composure and ran after her. She looked down both ways, and sprinted to the left. There was no particular reason why she chose to go that way, she just made a quick decision because staying still, she knew, would mean defeat. She couldn't afford defeat. Rose ran along the corridor, searching the walls as she went.

Father had told her about spaceships when she was younger, but she'd never even dreamed she'd find herself on one. Rose silently thanked the man for his diligence in educating her, and kept searching. She scanned the long hallways for a round, red hatch, just big enough to let a grown man through. The escape pod was her only chance at freedom. Even death would be better than the life of a slave in the human female sex trade.

A shout traveled from the far end of the hallway, interrupting her thoughts. Her time was up.

Chapter Two

Rose

"You little bitch!" Arrik's enraged voice echoed off the walls.

Rose was too scared to turn back. She kept running, hot tears running down her cheeks. She wasn't even looking for the red hatch to the escape pod anymore. All her being was focused on one simple, meaningless task: to run as far away as she could from Arrik. She knew it was pointless. There was nowhere to go to inside the ship, nowhere she could hide, nobody who would lend a helping hand. Still, instinct pushed her legs faster, reaching the limits of her endurance.

Behind her, Arrik's footsteps were ever closer.

Rose tried, but in the end, it hadn't mattered. She had failed. She hadn't found the escape pod. She was going to be raped and sold, then raped some more, for the rest of her life. She wasn't even going to be allowed to die, she was too valuable for that. Whoever was going to buy her would keep her in optimal health for the duration of her long, hellish life.

She stumbled, her forces near depletion, but regained her footing at the last minute. The first of a long line of horrors was about to grab her, she could almost feel its putrid breath on her neck. At the last minute, she bolted in a wild turn, not caring to look out before she did.

Then it was there. The door wasn't round like Father had told her. It was rectangular, with a red circle painted in the middle. Inside the circle was another, smaller circle. It was the sign for the escape pod.

Fast, she pulled the lever and the door slid open. Rose rushed inside, and closed the door just in time to see Arrik's furious face slam on the small round window. He was beyond enraged. He looked mad enough to rip her to shreds with his bare hands. His nose was bleeding the gray blood of his race, and his lips were split. A vicious satisfaction sprung inside Rose at the idea that she managed to wound him. Hers wouldn't be the only blood spilled that day.

"Push the release button." A deep, masculine voice rose from somewhere inside the pod. "It's the round one, right next to your hands."

Rose turned around and tried to see where the voice was coming from, but couldn't make anything out in the near total darkness.

"Who's here with me?"

"If you don't push the button in the next five seconds, the door will be unlocked from the command center." There was a quiet urgency in the stranger's tone, and it made Rose's already racing heart skip a beat. "You won't get another chance."

The information raced to her mind and without another second of hesitation, Rose palmed around the door until she found what she was looking for. A large, round and flat button was there, right where the stranger said it would be. She pushed with all her strength with the flat of her hand. Nothing.

"I don't understand." Rose spoke, her voice small and shaky in the confines of the pod. "It's not working."

"Give it a second. It's the safety features sealing the ship's main air supply," the stranger said. He spoke with a calm and confident tone, like he was trying to reassure a small child. "It has to disengage the hydraulic pressure for the release."

There was a loud clicking sound as the seals cut the air supply. The air in the pod changed now that it was isolated from the main ship. Rose could almost feel the aseptic void of deep space on her skin. Of course she couldn't, or she'd be dead in a split second. Next, the anchors snapped free and the pod floated away, strangely small against the monstrous shadow of the Cattelans' ship.

The pod moved fast, using its high capacity boosters in a series of short bursts, as was its programming. She stared at Arrik's face through the small window as the pod accelerated. In less than a second, he wasn't visible anymore, and ten more seconds later, all that remained of the large slaver's ship was a tiny dot in the black immensity of space. A giggle rose in the small space of the pod, a sound of drunken relief. A few moments later, Rose realized it had come from her.

"You have to secure yourself." The unknown voice came back, full of tension. "Fast."

"What?" Rose was too drunk on relief to understand. "We're free!"

"This pod is going to jump into hyperdrive. You're going to get hurt if you don't secure yourself."

The words brought her back to reality. The voice was definitively male, and spoke with a deep roll of the throat, a bit like a growl. It was a good, reassuring voice, a voice she would have found sexy if she wasn't scared half to death. Whoever had spoken, he was right. The escape pod was about to undergo a series of accelerations so severe they felt like a single burst into the ungodly speed necessary for deep space travel. If she didn't secure herself, Rose was going to be hurled against the walls like a rag-doll. She would be hurt; bones would be broken. She could die.

"I don't see anything," she said, hating the shaking, plaintive undertone in her voice. "Where are the seats?"

"Walk toward my voice," the stranger said. "There's a seat right next to me."

Rose obeyed, walking toward the voice as he kept uttering encouragements. Her hands stretched in front of her, her heart pounding. She had no idea what was supposed to be inside the pod. She had spent all her life in Earth's wilderness, away from even the most basic technology. The only knowledge Rose had of all these things came from her mother and father, and the stories they and the other escapees told the children. She was clueless and defenseless.

Finally, her hands hit cold metal bars. A second later, strong, warm fingers wrapped around them. The stranger was on the other side of those bars.

"Good. The seat is on your left. I'll hold you, so you won't fall." The stranger's hands closed around her wrists. "You don't have long before the pod takes the jump."

"Okay."

Rose was thankful for the stranger's hands as she made her way to the side. She reached with one hand, the other still in the stranger's hold, and found the thinly padded seat. Reluctantly, she pulled away from the stranger and sat. Belts were attached to the back of the seat, and she fidgeted with them until they were secured across her chest in a crisscross pattern.

"Thank you. You just saved my life," Rose said.

"It's my pleasure, Pretty Thing," the stranger answered, his voice a low, humorous growl. "You just saved mine."

Rose opened her mouth to counter, but no words came to her mind, so she shut it again. How could he find the wit to call her Pretty Thing when their lives hung in such a precarious balance? And how would he know anything about her looks? The pod was pitch black.

Less than thirty seconds later, the pod shot into hyperdrive, blasting away from the main ship, the computer having completed its calculations to the nearest planet capable of sustaining life. The sudden surge of speed cut her thoughts short. Rose's head banged on the back of the seat as the pod surged forward, and darkness invaded her mind as she lost consciousness.

The last thing her mind registered were the stranger's strong hands, wrapping around hers.

Karian

What are you?

The small female's head lolled limply on her shoulders, long strands of hair covering her face in an avalanche of savage curls. Reaching between the bars of his cage, Karian lifted the curtain of curls from the female's face.

Her features were delicate and soft in a fragile way reminiscent of the just-born youngling, with large eyes framed by heavy eyelashes and plump lips that hung partly open. The bones underneath her silken skin were rounded and fine, giving her face an appealing, dainty appearance. Karian's gaze traveled down her body, strapped in the seat. She was slender, reed like, willowy, like a blade of grass on the plains of his homeland. She was a true enigma, more so than any other female he had encountered before, and he had visited half the worlds in the Ring. He inhaled deeply, tasting her sweet pheromones in the back of his mouth.

Midnight God! This female was arousing to no end.

Karian cursed the darkness that forced him to gaze upon the female with his infrared vision. The receptor cells in his eyes that allowed him to see even in total darkness were an invaluable asset in battle, but the landscape of red didn't allow him to catch all the subtleties he sensed in her, and it frustrated him. Strange that he attached so much importance to this female, of all the things he should be worried about.

But then again, after ten years in solitary confinement in a cage, he was starved for anything to keep his mind from spiraling into a pit of boredom bordering on insanity.

As the pod sped away to some unknown planet's surface, Karian let his thoughts wander back to the day he was captured by the Cattelans. All he could hope was that the others hadn't fallen into the same trap he did. Karian had followed a lead indicating the presence of an illegal slave market on one of the worlds controlled by the Eoks and rushed to stop the hateful trade. Eoks never permitted slave trade on the worlds under their jurisdiction, even if it wasn't entirely forbidden inside the Ring. Upon arriving at the market, Karian saw red and fought, killing the slavers until none remained. Or so he thought.

He should have waited for reinforcements; he should have planned better. It was his fault he was captured. His nerves had been on edge after leaving his brother Arlen's mating ceremony, and he was careless, his mind full of anger and distraction. He roamed the slave market, lost in his rage.

The Cattelans came from behind. He didn't even see them as they shot him with ionic charges. The extreme electric current ran through his body in a fraction of a second, before he could react or even formulate a thought. Only later did he take full measure of his mistake. He woke up in a Cattelan slave ship, in a cage, and already far away from home.

Another hour in hyper-drive and the pod was free-falling, victim to an unknown planet's gravitational force. Karian had no idea what the calculations had chosen, and could only hope for one of the many inhabited planets or moons in The Ring. There were plenty.

Even if that was the case, he'd still need odds-defying luck if the slavers decided to hunt him down. They wouldn't use all their fuel looking for him, but scouring one or two of the local moons and planets was a definite possibility.

As soon as the pod landed, he'd need to re-wire the distress signal and send for his home world. If the Eoks came before the slavers, he was saved.

For this, he needed to get out of that cage. The allurium alloy used to make it was the only metal strong enough to contain him. He was nowhere near strong enough to make a dent in it.

Karian glanced at the female's lolling head. She'd saved him, he couldn't deny it. It was a unique chance that she had chosen the very pod he was detained in to escape. How this fragile creature had summoned the courage to fight a male such as Arrik was beyond his comprehension. Yet, she clearly had, and she'd won.

He was going to repay the favor. A life for a life.

Karian winced. It would be hard to get the female to help him out of the cage. Being Eok had a lot of perks, but their reputation was not exactly enviable, especially with females. The fear was unwarranted, of course, but she didn't know that.

The female moaned, and her incredible scent penetrated his nostrils again. His attention went back to her wondrous features.

"What are you?" Karian asked her, reaching with his finger to pat a strand of silken hair away from her face. "Pretty Thing, you're like nothing else I've seen."

"Of course I am," the female answered, startling him. Her voice was musical and soft, even in her half-awakened state. "Humans are like unicorns and mermaids. Only fools claim they have seen one."

Her inviting lips stretched in a faint smile and she chuckled. Her eyelids fluttered, but remained closed. She fell back into oblivion, leaving Karian alone with the echo of her words.

Karian stared at the female's peaceful face while the pod dropped out of the unknown planet's sky. Confusion and incredulity mixed together as he studied her closer, then incredulity gave way to a deep amazement. The soft grain of her skin, the delicate features, the soft curves and the sweet smell coming off of her body in intoxicating waves, were all threatening to take him to the edge of insanity. Yes, she was human.

This changed everything.

The small female that lay unconscious, strapped in the seat beside him, was worth a fortune. She was a unicorn, a mermaid, and a golden goose if there ever was one. Karian swallowed, pushing hard on the knot that had taken hold in his throat.

Humans were extinct on their homeland of Earth. They had been hunted to extinction a century ago, decimated by other, stronger species' greed. The few specimens that remained were kept in breeding facilities under careful supervision, and when sold, reached prices of astronomic proportions. Wherever this one came from, she was worth more than a small world's yearly income.

There was no way the Cattelans would let her go without a fight. They would search for her relentlessly, plow the nearby planets and moons until nothing remained unsullied by their dirty hands. They surely already had a rich buyer for her—most probably the emperor reigning a few planets over—to finance the mission until she was found. Karian cursed his luck at finding himself in the pod with her. She had saved his life and was more intoxicating than any female had the right to be, but the human was a poison fruit like no other. Even when she was unconscious and in the dark, his body responded to hers, and his crotch burned with a stubborn erection.

No, she was definitively off-limits. He had more important things to think about than feeding his lust.

His thoughts stopped when the pod shook violently as it entered the unknown world's atmosphere. The human female's head started to jerk back and forth. Too fast and too harsh. It might hurt her, do damage to that fragile body Karian knew little about. A wave of protectiveness overcame him, and he reached for her beyond the bars.

She was so small, so fragile, with her soft skin and slender limbs, that fear shot through him at the idea of her being hurt. Reaching as far as he could, Karian cradled her head in his hands. He cursed the metal alloy bars that kept him away from her, stretching his own arms as far as they would go to touch more of her soft, warm body. Strands of her hair brushed his face and he inhaled her sweet, floral scent.

"You're a wonder, Pretty Thing," he whispered in her ear. "I wish I could claim you for myself."

The human female turned her head his way and blinked. He knew she couldn't see him, yet it was as if she saw through the darkness and deep inside his soul, where his most secret thoughts resided. Her full, soft lips stretched in a smile. She was not fully conscious, but the beauty of her face, the open trust of her smile, pulled him in.

"Thanks for saving me," she said with a voice like a spring breeze. "I wish you could claim me, too."

Then the human female closed her eyes and fell back into unconsciousness. Karian stared at her face, a knot of unprecedented feelings roiling inside his guts. Something shifted inside him, pushing his soul out of balance, and he knew nothing would ever be the same.

Chapter Three

Rose

The screech of an impact filled her ears, making them ring painfully. The sound rippled through the fog in her brain and reached her bones. Rose's eyes snapped open but the world refused to come into focus, swirling around like life in the eye of a tornado. Some remote part of her brain understood she was in the pod and that it was tumbling down as it hit the ground. Another sound soon joined the clanking of metal, and it took the burning in her throat for Rose to understand she was screaming. As if on cue, the coppery taste of blood filled her mouth as she bit her tongue, and pain joined fear in the chaos of her mind.

The only light came from the small round window, filling the tiny habitat of the pod with streaks of dusty orange rays. Strong arms held her firmly in her seat, preventing her head from banging against her chest and hurting her neck. It was strangely reassuring, even if she didn't know the man who was holding her.

His male smell permeated her panic: musky, deep and good. It soothed her, but not enough to stop the flow of the scream that scorched her throat. She used all the air from her lungs, pausing only to gulp more air, and screamed again until everything was spent. Gravity shifted, blurring her mind and making her lose all her bearings as the pod rolled wildly on the hard surface of the unknown planet.

For an endless time, there was nothing but the merciless movement of the pod and the stranger's grip, his voice hushing calming sounds into her ear like she was some kind of skittish wild animal.

A final, deafening blow invaded the pod, filling it with sounds and light, and her eyes shut in reflex. Air exploded on her face, heating her cheeks with abrasive dust. A sharp pain shot through her forehead and warm liquid poured over her cheeks, entering her open mouth and adding to the coppery taste that was already threatening to make her throw up.

As suddenly as the violence began, it stopped. Everything went eerily still. The world was an unmoving pit of darkness, the only sound the stranger's breath against her ear, calm and strong.

Her head hurt from the cut on her forehead and her throat was raw from screaming, but other than that, there was no pain. She allowed herself a few more breaths, then the soft brush of the wind on her face pried her eyes open. The stranger's hands pulled away.

Rose blinked furiously, trying to force her retinas to accept the sudden change in luminosity. After a few moments, her eyes adjusted enough to let her see the inside of the pod through the dust-filled air. There was a large gash in the opposite side, where the impact had ripped the metal open. It was a miracle they were still alive, even more so unharmed. If she hadn't buckled herself in in time... The thought made her shiver with horror. The stranger had saved her life twice over.

The stranger. She felt his hot breath on her nape.

"Are you okay?" His male voice again, deep and calm, vibrating down deep inside her. Then, with discernible alarm, "You're bleeding."

"It's nothing." Rose reached and patted at the small cut on her forehead. "A scratch."

She turned to face him, with all intentions to thank him like she'd never thanked anyone before. Her words stumbled on each other and were lost before they escaped her lips.

The first things her eyes focused on were the bars. A cage. The stranger, her savior, stared from the other side, his shining bright blue irises fixed on her like on prey. His appearance struck her across the brain like a blow.

He was completely bald, and his ear-less head was smooth and round. The features on his face were sharp and angular, with prominent cheekbones and brows, accentuated by a straight nose marred by three ridges. His was a sensuous face, direct and challenging, the face of a man used to the reaction of others to his superior strength. His mouth was stretched in a superior smile, and Rose's eyes caught on his full, fleshy lips, parted to show a row of pearly white teeth. And fangs. He had two long, sharp fangs where humans had merely harmless canines. His midnight blue skin shimmered in the dusty light, and as the air cleared progressively, so did the fog in Rose's head.

Her eyes traveled across the landscape of tiny scars marking his skin in a regular pattern over his cheeks, forehead, and along his jaw. He wore pants, but no shirt, and his exposed torso was a tangle of lean muscles, bulging with strength going down to his waist. He was a fine man, with power and raw testosterone leaking from every pore of his being. Supremely masculine, attractive to no end, and definitively not human.

Oh, my God.

She knew *what* he was.

"You're Eok." The words stumbled from her lips in a whisper, as if she spoke them any louder, they would bite her tongue.

"And you're human." His eyes traveled up and down her body in a slow assessment. "A pretty sight, and a surprising one too."

Rose stared at the formidable creature and had never been more grateful for a cage in her life. Eoks were the most feared warrior nation in the Ring—and beyond. Monsters, that was what they were. Killers, merciless and cold-blooded, leaving entire towns empty of life wherever they set foot.

Too close, she was way too close to him. She scrambled to undo the belts holding her in place in the seat and fell down on the ground on all fours as the restraints clicked free. In a few ungraceful steps, she was far enough that her racing mind was able to formulate a rational thought. Slowly, Rose turned to face her companion again.

The Eok stood there, boldly intimidating. His long, well-muscled arms were folded across his torso as he watched her with unruffled calm.

Her cheeks burned with sudden shame at her brutal and somewhat childish reaction. Rose wiped her palms on her pants, taking a few seconds to collect her thoughts before scrambling to her feet, her dignity heavily battered. She had reacted like a scared little girl, not exactly what she wanted to project. She couldn't afford to show weakness, not ever. Not to him. Again, Rose lifted her gaze and studied the Eok.

He was wearing pants made from the same material as Rose's tunic and pants. He was a slave, then, like her. That was reassuring because if he was a slave, the cage had been built for his spectacular strength and it would contain him. The insidious possibility of the cage being compromised by the impact crawled under her skin, but she pushed it away. If the Eok ever got out of that cage, she was as good as dead—at least, if she trusted the Eok stories.

Rose stared blankly at the Eok, trying her best to hide the undercurrent of terror that still crawled under her skin. Weakness made her angry and she welcomed the familiar feeling, hoping it would quench her impulse to run away screaming.

"Scared of me, are you?" The Eok's lips twisted upward in an arrogant smile.

"You're the one in a cage." Rose crossed her arms on her chest, and wished she could smack the smirk from his lethal, handsome face. "Maybe you're the one who should be scared of me."

"Oh, I'm terrified." His smile widened, and damn her if she didn't feel a stirring in her stomach. And maybe lower, too. "Pretty Things like you are creatures of nightmares."

Rose snorted and chose not to answer. Pointedly ignoring him, she tore her eyes away from the Eok and stared at the blazing sunshine that poured inside the pod from the impact point. She had other things to do that were way more important than arguing with him.

"Do you know where we are?"

"No idea." He shrugged, and the muscles on his chest rippled with strength. "They kept me in this cage for a long, long time. I have no idea what part of the Ring we were in when your charming feet stepped into my prison."

Her mind ran wild with the information. He was locked up in that seven by seven feet cage, alone and in the dark. There was no way to know what a long, long time meant, but by the way he said it, she knew it was long enough that she would have gone mad by now. Her heart broke for him, to think what torture it was for a force of nature such as him to be trapped inside the confines of a cage. A single week of the cell in the Cattelan's ship and she had been ready to rip someone's throat out.

He must want out so badly it hurts.

Rose swallowed, breaking her dangerous train of thought. She didn't have time to think about the Eok's feelings.

"Are the Cattelans going to be able to find us? Will they even try?" She hated the uncertainty in her tone but she couldn't help it.

"The pod was programmed to go to the nearest planet capable of sustaining life." The Eok spoke calmly, but his blazing gaze never left her. "As for locating the pod, the slavers are scanning every nearby planet as we speak. They're not going to let their ticket to ten lifetimes of riches get away without a thorough search. They *will* find us, sooner or later. Sooner, probably."

"We're screwed, then." Her shoulders slumped. "I'm not getting caught again. Not alive."

"There's another way." The Eok leaned against the cage, his muscular forearms resting between the bars. "I can disable the locating chip inside the pod. It won't mean they're not already on our trail, but it's a start. No signal, no locating the pod."

"Okay, sounds like a plan." Rose tried not to sound too eager. She couldn't have him thinking she needed him, even if she undoubtedly did. "What do I need to do?"

"You're not doing anything." The Eok lifted his chin. "You're going to help me get out, and I'll disable the signal."

"Like hell you are." She chuckled. How stupid did he think she was? "Nice try, but you're going to stay right where you are. Tell me what to do."

"There's no way they trained you on micro-computronics." His smile turned feral, all the warmth drained from his expression. "Guiding you will take too long; we don't have that kind of time."

"I wouldn't even know where to begin to open that cage." Rose opened her arms and lifted her brows. "You have no choice but to tell me what to do."

"Get out. Bring me a rock." The words were sharp and unyielding. It wasn't a request; it was an order. "I'll take care of the rest."

"Fat chance." Rose shook her head and forced herself to sustain Karian's smoldering glare. "I'm not letting you out."

"You need me." His brows set in a straight line, and his eyes reduced to fiery slits.

"And you're on the wrong side of those bars. Guess you don't have all the leverage after all."

"You're feisty. I like that."

The Eok's smile stretched, but turned cold and deadly, revealing a perfect row of sparkling white teeth with two sharp, elongated canines. A shiver of fear skittered across her backbone. She had an inkling he knew exactly what he was doing, exposing his fangs like that. And even if she hated admitting it, it worked pretty well.

"What's your name, Pretty Thing?"

"My name's Rose, not Pretty Thing." She carefully stepped over some shrapnel and turned to the caged Eok. He was still leaning on the bars, his alien eyes unreadable. "What's yours?"

"Karian, son of Enlon, of the Erynian tribe."

"Well, Karian, son of Enlon, consider yourself my prisoner."

With one last look at the Eok warrior, Rose turned and walked outside the pod.

Chapter Four

Rose

Rose walked back toward the shining surface of the pod, sweat pouring down her back between her shoulder blades, the blazing heat of descending twin red suns hammering on her body mercilessly. As the shadows grew, so did her thirst, dehydration making her mind muddy.

Her situation was dropping from shitty to all-out-disastrous by the second.

The pod had landed in a vast plain of what appeared to be an endless desert. Looming like the jagged teeth of some ancient, long dead monster were tall, cylindrical looking peaks of rocks, sprouting from the ground in every direction. A steep mountain hovered nearby, casting its inviting shadow towards the pod. It seemed close, but Rose knew that was only a false impression, and the distance separating her from the potential refuge was huge, the road deadly. They were lucky to have landed in the plain, for if the pod had hit one of the mountains, the impact would have killed everyone inside.

From the dry, wrinkled dirt grew shriveled-up shrubs, poking from the pale sand in round bushes, their wiry, intricate branches screaming of thirst. The vegetation was sparse and vast, with only a few tall shoots, round and yellow, breaking the monotony of the shrubs. Needing a break, Rose stopped in front of a group of shoots to study them. They looked like wild wheat, but were at least six or seven feet tall, depending on the maturity of the plant. Their stalks were a good three inches in diameter, and topped with bushy crowns of spidery, wicked needles. Carefully, Rose snapped a particularly tall and wide stalk with her knee, discarding the top on the ground. It was hard, but not as hard as wood, and it was so dry that it broke easily when she bent it.

Disappointment filled her as she inspected the stalk. She had hoped to find moisture in it, but it was dry and its center was hollow.

At least it's going to make a fine walking stick, she thought. *I could even sharpen it into a spear.*

The thought was a good one, but it didn't cheer her up as it should have. As she walked back, carrying her find, her feet crushed ageless clumps of dry earth, sending clouds of dust in the windless air, making it even harder to breathe. The red suns above her head were cruel and hot, radiating waves upon waves of dry, scorching heat on her head. Her clothing offered little protection from the elements, and she longed for her old clothes. Her forearms were red, and Rose knew she would be in agony from sunburn by nightfall. She shouldn't have walked so far from the pod, not without protection. But she had been desperate, and walking helped calm her mind.

When she finally stepped into the shade of the pod, Rose blinked a few times until her eyes adjusted to the darkness. Her body welcomed the immediate relief from the suns' relentless heat, but thirst still scorched her throat. The pod was cooler than the outside desert, but not by much. The Eok—Karian—was still standing, leaning on the bars of his cage. He watched her with a despicable, arrogant smile on his handsome, despicable face. She wondered if he stayed like this, unmoving, like a reptile waiting for wandering prey. His glowing eyes reflected the little light that penetrated the pod, and he didn't miss a single one of her movements. Or maybe it was only the stress of the situation that made her paranoid.

It's not because I'm paranoid that the man locked in a cage in my escape pod isn't out to get me.

To possibly eat her alive, or whatever devious, violent things Eok warriors did. Rose chuckled at the thought, and Karian raised his brows in question. She cast him an assessing look, then sighed with resignation. Dangerous or not, he was her only companion, and ignoring his presence was pointless.

"We need water, and fast. Food, too, but it can wait a few days. And medication for sunburn, if we can find any." The list of their needs made her heart sink. They needed so much, and she had no answer for any of them. She stared blankly at the sterile expanse of the steel ceiling panels. "We're in a desert."

"If you'd bothered to ask, I could have told you as much." Karian's tone didn't leave much doubt about what he was thinking. He thought she was a fool.

"And how did you figure it out?" Rose raised her eyebrows, too curious and too desperate to take offense.

"The heat and lack of humidity made it clear." Karian shook his head. "Don't bother trying to find the population, either. It's an uninhabited planet. Escape pods aren't designed to be discreet. If there were people in a five-hundred-mile radius, they would have been on us in the first two hours."

"Well, then, I guess I made sure of it." Rose was maybe desperate, but his patronizing tone was getting on her nerves.

"It was reckless. More than that, it was stupid." Karian scowled, the gesture transforming his features into a fearsome mask. "Don't do anything like that again."

"You're not exactly in a position to order me around." She scowled back, ignoring the fluttering of fear in her stomach at the sight of Karian's anger. "And there I was, about to think you had a good side."

"Pretty Thing, you have no idea how good being by my side can be." He smirked that awful, arrogant smile she was beginning to be familiar with. "Come closer, and I'll show you."

I'll wipe that smirk off your face, you'll see.

Not that she would be reckless enough to get close to him.

"Not a chance. You can keep your deadly hands to yourself."

Karian chuckled, unfazed by her answer. This male was as arrogant as he was handsome. He towered over her, watchful as a mountain lion ready to pounce. Great. Her luck kept getting better and better. She was stranded on a desert planet, with no way home, and the most dangerous being in the known universe was caged in her only shelter. All she had was a dry stalk she could fashion into a spear to protect herself.

"You don't have to go out there by yourself." His words came, soft and dangerous like his voice. Seducing. "If you help me out, I'll take care of you. I owe you for freeing us."

Rose stopped and stared at him as hard as she could. The thought of him roaming free around the pod sent shivers of fear across her spine. Yes, she did save him, but only because she needed to escape, a fact they both were aware of. She couldn't rely on his sense of honor for her survival. Eoks might not even have a sense of honor.

"It's an escape pod. That means people planned to be stranded in here for a while," Rose said. A slow smile spread on her lips. Yes, that was right. "There have to be some supplies in here. Water. Food. Maybe even weapons."

She spoke aloud, more because it helped her think than anything. Karian was her involuntary audience. Too bad for him if he didn't like it. She scanned the pod with a new set of eyes. The cubic habitat had six seats lined up against the walls. Those seats were the only things that could be used to hide something in the bare space. Except for her new friend's cage, but she doubted the Cattelans hid emergency rations in a prisoner's cage. So the rations had to be hidden somewhere inside or under those seats.

She started right away, looking under each seat, pulling the cushions out, throwing everything around carelessly. She was a hurricane, leaving only destruction in her wake. Soon, the pod's floor was a mess of shredded fabric and filling. Still no traces of food or water. Nothing.

"It's not possible," she whispered, more for herself than Karian. "There has to be something."

This was an escape pod. There had to be emergency supplies stashed in there, at least a few days' worth of water, and some food. Frustration welled into her as time went by and she found nothing. The dryness in her throat turned to a scorching heat and her tongue felt swollen in her mouth. Her head hurt and her eyes were itchy. She needed water, and she needed it now.

In his cage, Karian tilted his head to the side, but the rest of his body remained still.

"What about you?" Rose turned and glared at him, lifting her chin in defiance. "You need to drink and eat, too. It's in your best interest to tell me where to find the supplies. I'll share whatever I find with you."

"I can survive without water for five weeks, a month at least. Food, I can go without for six months." His voice was neutral, but his words sent shivers under her skin. "What about you, Pretty Thing?"

She stared at him, blood draining from her face. He could outlive her by months. She searched, but there was nothing she could find to justify not telling him the truth. She had nothing to lose.

"I have three days, probably less in this heat. I'm already dehydrated." Then it dawned on her. "If you have any idea where the rescue rations are, you'd better tell me. I die while you're still in the cage, and you're no better off than me."

"I'll make a deal with you, Pretty Thing." Karian gave her a wicked, sexy smirk. "You go back out and grab a rock at least as big as your head and give it to me so I can smash my way out, and I'll tell you where the rations are stocked. It's a win-win situation if there ever was one. You gain your survival, and I gain my freedom."

"Like hell. What's going to stop you from doing the same to me as the Cattelans were planning?"

The words hung in the air between them. His sapphire blue eyes never faltered. He kept studying her, staring, searching for a weakness. She had a full buffet of them, he could just pick and choose. Rose chuckled, a low, sarcastic growl deep in her parched throat, and walked to the only remaining seat, the one beside the Eok's cage. She should have planned better, but there it was: she had torn every seat from the walls except that one. Maybe her subconscious just remembered how safe she had felt in his arms before knowing what he was.

How she longed for that feeling again, the warm embrace of those arms around her. Those fingers on her face, so gentle. So soothing.

No. Stop it, stupid girl. It's the dehydration that's making you crazy. He's dangerous.

Rose raised her head and stared at Karian's face. He hovered over her, exuding agile strength, with lean, hard muscles wrapping around his frame like a fit predator. Her gaze wandered to his broad, muscular chest. It was as hairless as his head, but that wasn't what made her eyes widen. How could she not have noticed before? Her mind must have been mush.

The Eok's chest was covered in scar marks, arranged in a swirly pattern, just like on his face. Dozens upon dozens of small incisions created bumps, decorating his flesh in a flashing display of the agony he had endured. It was the first time she stopped to really see him for what he was. He wasn't just a force of nature. He was as deadly as any predator ever created, and probably as cruel. She shivered, deep inside, where all her fears lived. She was nothing but a mouse in front of him. Defenseless and insignificant.

"Those scars." Rose pointed at his chest and face. "Where did you get them?"

"An Eok warrior marks his own body during the Rite, before the ancients of the Warrior's Guild."

Karian stepped to the edge of the cage and extended his powerful forearms through the bars, rotating them so she could see the dozens of scars running along his flesh. It was hard, but she held still. Inching away would be a display of weakness, and she couldn't afford to show more than what she already had. It was too much as it was. Karian lifted his jaw in a proud gesture.

"I have more marks than any other males in three generations. Five-hundred-and-seventy-nine."

The words shook her to her foundation. He had done this to himself, cut into his own flesh a staggering number of times. This time, Rose did inch back.

"Why?" Her voice was a high-pitched child's song. "Why would you hurt yourself like that?"

"To prove my worth to the Warrior's Guild and to my clan. Pain has to be mastered if one aspires to become a warrior. I can endure more pain than any other living warrior of my clan." His eyes flashed in the darkness of the pod. "What about you, Pretty Thing?"

"I already asked you to call me Rose, not Pretty Thing. And no, I guess I can't. Enduring pain isn't one of my pastimes. Too bad for you I'm the one on the outside of the cage."

For now.

The thought insinuated itself on her, dangerous and strangely appealing.

Karian's confident smirk melted some, but not completely. She still had the advantage, but barely. Rose leaned against the thin padding of the seat, allowing the desperation to settle deep inside her bones. After all she had done, she was defeated without those emergency rations. Giving way to her frustration, she kicked a loose metal panel, sending it flying across the pod with a dead, hollow sound.

Then she saw it.

Small, oval and metallic—she had forgotten all about it. Arrik's universal magnetic key. Rose picked it up and flipped it between her fingers, then her eyes went back to the cage. There was a similar indenture in the central panel that ran the length of the cage, about midway. The key fit right in. Her gaze locked with Karian's. He was holding his breath, glaring at her with those unsettling eyes. The balance of power had just shifted and he didn't like it. Not one bit.

"Open the cage." His tone was pure ice. It was a command, given by one used to ordering warriors thousands of time stronger than she was. "Open it now."

"No." She sustained his gaze, flipping her hair out of her face with a defiant lifting of her chin.

"Let me out of that cage and I will protect you, I will provide for you. You will never want for anything."

"Maybe it's me who will provide and care for you." She couldn't help the mocking tone of her voice. She'd had enough of being treated like a weakling. It was just so incredible that he would think she was stupid enough to let him loose. "From *inside* the cage. Who's going to be a Pretty Thing now?"

Karian's mouth reduced to a thin, cruel line and his eyes flashed with anger, but he kept silent. He didn't answer, didn't lose his temper, but began pacing in his cage. He could only walk three steps before reaching the bars, but he kept pacing relentlessly. Three steps one way, three steps the other way. Back and forth, back and forth. His eyes never left Rose, those blue flames shining like pieces ripped from a summer sky. A dark, mindless fear crept inside her mind at the sight of him.

By then, the twin suns had almost completed their descent in the alien sky and darkness was invading the pod at a racing speed. She wouldn't be able to see a thing in a few minutes.

Looking away was against all her survival instincts but she did it anyway. She ignored Karian pointedly as she got back to her wobbly feet and started arranging the cushions from the seats in a semblance of bed. She couldn't afford to lose time worrying about him. If he ever got out of that cage, she was as good as dead. He might not have killed her before, but now he was sure to take revenge. She might as well concentrate on her other problems. Taking a slow, burning breath, she decided to push the Eok out of her mind.

She was dehydrating faster than she had calculated. Rose didn't have the two to three days she originally thought she had. She was going to be dead by this time tomorrow if she didn't find water.

The next day, by the end of the morning, Rose sat down on her makeshift bed, holding her head in her hands, trying to massage away the headache that dug deep inside the folds of her brain. The Eok hadn't said a word since she'd refused to open the cage. That was right before sunset the day before, when she still had her mind intact. After a long night of teeth-shattering cold, she wasn't sure she had all her marbles anymore.

Her lips were cracked, and she could feel the dry, leathery skin when she passed her sticky tongue over them. The heat was rising again, and this time Rose was going to be dead before the cold of the night came down again. It was such a sad end to her heroic escape, so tragic, she would have laughed if she wasn't so damn tired.

"Give me the key, Pretty Thing." Karian's voice broke the emptiness of the pod. It wasn't his usual mocking tone, it was full of concern and warmth. "I'll get the emergency rations out. You need water, bad, you're just too stubborn to admit it."

She turned her head and gazed into dazzling blue eyes. She could see the pattern of the scars for what they were, now. It was impressive, and forced respect. She wondered how old Karian had been when he had marked his flesh like that. There was so much she didn't know, so much she wished she'd learned about him.

You're losing it. Focus.

Rose shook her head, and was rewarded with a flash of white hot pain searing through her vision. This creature wasn't her friend. He was a predator, and she would do well to remember it. His attractiveness was the pretty colors on a venomous snake, or the softness of a mountain lion's fur: a lure, a disguise to hide how deadly he was.

"I'm not giving you the key."

Karian glared at her, his blue eyes shining and his jugular veins pulsating with fury. His jaw twitched with anger but he remained silent. He was a closed-mouth son of a bitch when he wanted to be. She was counting on his anger, hoping it would make him reckless, desperate.

If he called her bluff, she would lose. Rose wouldn't let him die in the cage. There was no sense in wasting both their lives. He didn't need to know that, though. Not yet.

Her best hope was to convince Karian that his survival was tied to hers. The Eok knew where to find the supplies. The only thing he cared about was getting out of the cage. That key was her only leverage, and she twisted it between her palms, taunting him, trying to lure him into giving the information away.

"Don't be foolish, little human." Karian spoke with an even voice, but the anger lying underneath was almost enough to make her crumble and give up the key. Almost. "You'll never survive without me."

"And you will shrivel up, little by little, if I don't let you out. It will be a long, lonely, agonizing death." Rose managed a smirk, even if it hurt like hell to stretch her lips and all she wanted was to curl up and die. "I don't envy you your superior strength."

This got to him. He roared and punched the bars of his cage but they didn't even rattle. It was the first time he gave way to his temper. Rose turned her head away, allowing her hair to hide her face. Her smile remained, truer this time. She had done it. She'd won her bluff. After a while, her smile faded and she lifted her gaze to him again.

Karian resumed his pacing and pursed his lips, exposing his fangs. The clear display of hostility was scary enough to make her scramble across the floor, as far away as she could from him. He was even more formidable when he was angry, his muscles rippling with aggression. Every inch of him was screaming lethal force, and Rose suddenly became his target.

A few more turns, then he stopped. His irises reflected the light, and when he shifted his body to face her, Rose couldn't help but tremble. So much power, he could break her in a snap.

"The ceiling." He talked with resentment, the words harsh. "Behind the central panel, the one with the three triangles engraved in one corner. That's where you'll find the supplies. Use your key to open it."

"Thank you."

Rose sustained his gaze for a few seconds, then struggled to her feet. She had to blink a few times to force her eyes to focus, then she saw them. Three triangles, engraved in the sterile gray of the ceiling panel. Standing on the tips of her toes, she reached as high as her arms could. The panel was too high; she couldn't reach it. Frustrated, she looked around. The pod was mainly empty, there wasn't much she could use to step on to reach for the panel. Then her eyes landed on the seat, the only one she hadn't destroyed. Yes, that would do. Rose walked over to it, and pulled it right under the panel with the carved triangle.

"You'd better pray I don't break my neck."

With one last look at Karian, Rose put one foot on the unsteady seat, and then the other. She almost lost her balance, then regained it at the last minute. Karian gasped, but kept silent as she used the key to unlock it and proceeded to push the panel sideways until it tipped out of balance. It clanged on the floor with a metallic bang. Water, bags and bags of water were neatly piled on one side of a large storage space, while on the other side were stored packs of labeled food rations.

"We're saved! There's enough food and water for weeks!" Rose turned to Karian, who was staring at her with an undecipherable expression. "Don't you see, we're not dead yet!"

Chapter Five

Rose

Rose sat on the floor in the mounting heat, draining her third water ration, then threw the discarded synthetic envelope away. Guilt washed over her at the knowledge that she was using up her meager rations too fast, but she couldn't help it. She was so thirsty; water was being sucked up by her dehydrated body like a sponge. Already her lips felt soft, her tongue less raspy. She stopped herself short of picking up a fourth bag and crossed her arms over her chest. She needed to control herself, or she was a walking corpse with a brief relief.

Her eyes wandered to the opening in the pod's wall. The light was fading again.

With trembling hands, she began to sort and count the food and water. It wasn't nearly as much as she'd thought. Not nearly enough. She had maybe three weeks' worth, and that was only for her own needs.

Rose's eyes found Karian's gaze, across from her in the pod. She held his intense stare, refusing to break the contact first. With his size, this reduced the rations by more than half. She gulped. They had a week, maybe two if they were careful.

Then her eyes widened and guilt bit at her. She had forgotten all about him. He had endured the days of heat without demands or complaints, but he had to be as thirsty as she was.

Rose tore her eyes from Karian's mesmerizing gaze and looked at the pile of water rations. Seconds passed, and she bit her lower lip. When she looked up again, Karian followed her gaze to the water. He didn't need to say anything. Shame burned up her cheeks, and she hated herself for the hesitation.

Without waiting, she reached for a single pouch, then added two more and got to her feet. She felt steadier already. The water was flooding through her body, hydrating her parched flesh. The relief was only one more reminder that Karian needed water as much as she did.

"Here, take this." Rose approached without thinking and handed the water to the Eok. "Let me know if you need more."

He reached out, fast as a snake, and wrapped his powerful hands around her smaller wrists with an iron grip. As soon as his skin came in contact with hers, an electric shock traveled up her arm, making every hair stand on end. His fingers were strong and rough in a pleasant, masculine way. A flash of those hands, running along her body, came to her mind, but she pushed it away as fast as it came. She didn't have time to reflect on how good his contact was. She had been reckless, and now she was at his mercy.

A wave of panic surged inside her and Rose struggled to get free, but it was useless. He was too strong. She stopped struggling. No need to lose precious energy fighting a losing fight.

"You won't survive as long if you share with me." Karian's gaze bored into hers. He narrowed his eyes and studied her face for a reaction. "Why?"

"Because no creature deserves to die of thirst and hunger. Take it. No need to thank me." Rose shook the rations in her hands, still holding the bags. "But just a warning. The key is on the floor, by the rations. I don't have it on me. If you kill me now, you're stuck."

"What makes you think I have any intention of hurting you?" He smiled and pulled her closer through the bars of the cage. "There are much more enjoyable ways of spending my time with you."

"Try, and you're not going to find them so enjoyable."

But from the way her guts twisted and her stomach fluttered, Rose knew it was an empty threat. There was no mistaking her attraction to the Eok. As dangerous as he was, she began to suspect there was more to the handsome warrior than pure violence and savagery. She let him pull her closer, tilting her head up to sustain his gaze, her heart hammering against her ribs and her breath coming in increasingly faster succession. She didn't allow her stare to falter, answering challenge for challenge. Soon, too soon, she was standing so close to him that his breath brushed her lips.

He looked down at her, his mouth slightly open. She could see the tips of his fangs, and it sent a shudder along her spine, tingling every one of her nerve endings with unwelcome arousal. His grip on her wrists softened and his fingers brushed up her arms. His touch was gentle and warm, and when he pulled her again, heat flared inside her, burning up her lips and spreading heat down lower in her belly. They were so close, her cheeks touched the metal bars.

Karian's gaze slid to her lips.

He kept his eyes open as he lowered his head, his eyes locked with Rose's. She gazed into the majestic depths, feeling like heaven was coming down on her. His lips closed on hers, and she shut her eyes under the shock of the contact. His lips were firm and supple, and he massaged Rose's with a gentleness that surprised her. His tongue slipped between his lips and caressed hers, asking for permission. A wave of passion replaced the fear she once felt and she gave way willingly, greeting his tongue with hers. His taste invaded her mouth and a wave of warmth spread between her legs.

Karian took possession of her mouth, wiping away any thoughts she had that weren't about him. He replaced them with a desire that burned so hot, she dissolved under it. His hands moved along her arms and slid up her elbows, circling her waist. He pulled her closer until her breasts touched his hard chest, crushing her into him through the bars. He owned every bit of her, and she melted into his kiss. A wild desire shot through her, and she found herself wishing he would rip the clothes off her body and lay his hard flesh upon her.

Then heaven withdrew and Rose was cold, her eyes closed and her mouth open.

His hands released her, and she opened her eyes. A single water ration was pulled from her fingers, and he kept his eyes on her as he ripped it open with his fangs. Karian drank the whole pouch in one long sip, then threw the bag on the floor of the cage.

"Don't you want more?" The question was honest, and she blinked through the fog of passion that still held her in its embrace. She wasn't even sure if she was talking about the water or the kiss. "I'll give you more if you want."

"No, I have enough for a while." Karian looked at Rose in that strangely intense way he had. "Thank you."

She nodded, then stepped back. She turned her face away, unable to sustain his gaze any longer. She would be lost if she allowed herself to be swallowed by those deep, shining blue eyes. There was something in them, something soft and full of need under the heavy blanket of steel. It tore her heart apart. There was danger there, in more ways than she could count.

He's trying to trick you. You stupid, stupid girl.

Rose couldn't trust him. If she did, he was going to be the death of her.

In a daze, she walked back to the pile of rations. She had to forget that kiss. Survival was all that mattered, and she would do well to remember it. And to remember that her Eok companion was a threat, and not to be trusted.

Rose grabbed two small pouches of food rations in translucent plastic. Studying the gray sludge, she grimaced, then tossed one to Karian. She ripped hers open and stared as a drop of gray goop dropped on her fingertip. This was supposed to be food, but it didn't look like it.

She turned the pouch around in her hands and read the claims on the label. This gray sludge was a protein, mineral and vitamins complete meal, enhanced with meat stew flavors. She brought it to her nose and smelled. Disgusted, she pushed the pack away from her nose. She had no choice, she needed the nourishment. There was no space left for the faint of heart in this life. As long as it didn't make her ill, Rose would lap up every drop of it.

Mother and Father had often talked about the food that was served in the breeding facility. She pulled her finger to her mouth, and immediately wished she hadn't. The nutritious sludge was overly sweet, with a nauseating metallic under-taste. It was nutritive, with exactly everything a living being needed on a daily basis, but it was a horrible way to feed. She shivered, thinking about her parents' life in the breeding facility, the boredom of the claustrophobic existence. It was a long, hellish existence, one she was thankful she didn't remember.

The pod reminded Rose of the tales of that life, and it chilled her despite the searing heat.

"It's awful, but it's going to give us strength." She spoke, more for herself than the Eok. She took a sip of the slop and felt her stomach rebel, but held it down. "Tomorrow, I'll go out again. Maybe I'll find food this time."

"You're losing your time, and mine." Karian eyed the nutritious sludge, distaste obvious on his features. "I could hunt much better food, regardless of where we landed. If you let me."

"I don't need you to hunt for me," Rose answered with a chuckle. This didn't sit well with him. Karian watched her with squinted eyes. She knew it angered him, but she didn't give a damn. She'd been a huntress all her life, she didn't need his patronizing. "I've hunted scarier beasts than you."

Now that was a lie, and a big one. Rose had never even seen anything scarier than the Eok, never even imagined anything that terrifying could exist.

"And where would a Pretty Thing like you have learned to hunt?" Karian scoffed. It was clear he knew how intimidating he was, and that nothing she had ever seen compared to him, not even a bit. "Did they show you movies in the lab? Gave you a stuffed animal or two to practice? Your future owner would have thought it *adorable*. A tiny, harmless, trained huntress to play with."

"I'm not from the breeding facility." The words slipped from her mouth, and she immediately wished she hadn't said them. The existence of the wild human community was a secret. Her entire family's existence depended on its secrecy.

"You're a wild human?" Karian looked at Rose with renewed interest. "I thought you were long extinct."

"That was the whole point," Rose answered bitterly. "We hid, all these years. No one was supposed to know we existed."

"A wild human female, not trained to be docile and meek." He said the words like they were candy melting on his tongue. Karian and Rose's gazes locked, and she was swallowed in the strange beauty of his eyes. "Do you have any idea how valuable you are? The Cattelans are never going to stop hunting you."

"I'm never going to see my family again." As she said the words, a blanket of sadness wrapped itself around her shoulders. The weight of what she had lost settled on her mind, and she fought the enclosing panic. "All that matters now is that I stay out of their hands long enough for my people to leave, to get far enough that no one will ever find them. Arrik was right about one thing. There are ways to make a person talk, and he's greedy enough to do whatever it takes to make me betray them. In time, even I will break."

It chilled the marrow inside her bones, but it was the truth. Arrik had more tricks up his sleeve than taking her body by force. Torture wasn't above the Cattelans' arsenal of tools, and Rose was lucid enough to understand that past a certain point, she would do anything to stop the pain. Even give up those who were worth more to her than her own life. For that reason alone, she couldn't allow herself to be captured again. Not alive, anyway.

"I'm sorry for your family." At first, she thought he was only mocking her, but when she lifted her gaze to him, there was no mockery in his face. Karian's strange eyes glowed, and she didn't know if it was only in her mind, but she thought she saw genuine sadness in him.

"I was stupid, and I'm paying the price. Now everyone I ever cared about is in danger." She shook her head in negation.

"How were you captured?"

Rose thought about the event leading to her capture. She didn't know why, but she wanted to tell the Eok what had happened. Maybe it was because he was a slave, like her. Maybe she was stupid to yearn for his company, for his conversation, but she did. She yearned for him in all the wrong ways, and that kiss hadn't helped. If anything, it made the yearning more unbearable.

"We had a blizzard that lasted four days. We ran out of rabbit meat by the second, and by the fourth, we were so hungry we started to eat the bark from the nearby saplings." Rose closed her eyes and allowed the memory of her family, hollow despair marking their faces, the flame playing cruel tricks on the protruding bones in their skeletal faces in the darkness of the mudhouse. "Aliena was sick. She was going to die without food. I couldn't wait anymore, I had to go on a hunt, at least make the run to check my snares. Mostly, I was just scared and angry. I couldn't stay and watch her die, doing nothing."

Silence settled between them. Karian didn't talk, didn't try to pry more from her. He let her continue at her own pace, allowing the painfulness of that day to come back.

"I was on my way back with three rabbits." Karian's blank face told Rose that the name of the animal didn't make sense to him. "They're small animals, good prey, plentiful. I wasn't paying enough attention. We had been hungry for so long, all I could think about was the faces of my little brothers when they saw the food. By the time I saw him, it was already too late."

"You risked your life for them." The concern in Karian's voice was too close to being genuine. It threatened everything she fought to believe. "You shouldn't carry that weight on your shoulders alone. Let me help you."

Rose paused, closing her eyes against the images that imposed themselves in her mind. The faces of her loved ones came to her mind, painfully clear. Aliena; her brothers Dunkan and Illian; her mother. She was never going to see them again. The pain was almost too much to bear. It took all her willpower not to allow tears to come to her eyes. Betraying her feelings wasn't going to make things any easier for her, it was only going to make her appear easy prey in the eyes of the Eok.

"I'm past help." For maybe the first time, she allowed herself to say what she felt deep inside, past the survival stubbornness that kept her going. "My only chance at a free life was on Earth."

A long silence stretched. Rose forced herself to open her eyes. She lost herself in Karian's eyes, wondering what feelings were brewing under the iridescent shine of his strange stare. Did he care, or was he indifferent to her suffering? She couldn't read anything on his alien face.

"They'll starve now," she said in a whisper. "There's no one left to hunt for them."

"No Eok mate would have to hunt to survive. If there are no males left in a family, others provide for the widow and children, as is only honorable." Karian scrutinized her face, searching for answers she couldn't give. "Doesn't your species have males to hunt and protect you?"

"We had my dad." Her voice broke, but she held her head high.

"What happened to him?" Karian asked, with a voice softer than she thought he was capable of.

"He left to raid the breeding facility with other men from the village." When Karian frowned, Rose felt the need to explain her father's actions. "When they escaped, my father had to leave his sister, along with her children. That day, he chose to save my mother and me, leaving them behind. He wanted to go back ever since. He left nine weeks ago and didn't come back." She closed her eyes again. The very thought made her stomach churn and her guts twist in angry knots. "In the beginning, Aliena and I managed fine. She's every bit as good a huntress as I am, but she got sick. I was the last one who knew how to survive."

Tears rose up in her eyes, and even if she had wanted to keep talking, she couldn't. Her throat was clamped shut, and all of a sudden, the fear, the anger, all those emotions she had been able to keep in check, drowned her. She let them wash over her like a tide, swallowing everything in their wake. Rose rolled her legs up to her chest then wrapped her arms around them, curling in a tight little ball, then hid her face on her knees, letting her curly hair fall on each side of her head like a curtain.

Then she cried. She cried for her lost freedom, for her lost family, for everything that would happen to her loved ones and that she would never know about.

A long time passed in silence as she wept, but eventually, the tears dried up and fatigue rolled over her. She hadn't slept more than an hour at a time since her capture, and not at all since the pod landed. As her mind drifted into oblivion, she barely registered Karian's hands reaching through the bars of the cage, petting her head gently as she drifted off.

Chapter Six

Karian

Rose slept on the seat beside him, her head in her hands and her long brown curls cascading over her shoulders, hiding her face. She snored softly, the sound regular and as sweet as she was.

He liked her name. Rose. It fell off his tongue like a caress, reminiscent of things fresh and fragile. He should really make an effort to use it instead of calling her Pretty Thing. She didn't like it at all. It angered her and, truth be told, that was one of the reasons he used it. She was even more attractive when she was angry, with her gray eyes shining like a storm sky and her cheeks flushed and red. She looked like a flower. Karian closed his eyes, remembering the feeling of those soft, pliable lips under his. How much sweeter would it be to have them against his skin, down his body? The thought made his seed stem stir and swell against the light fabric of his pants. Rose was every bit as delicious as a human female was fabled to be.

Get a hold of yourself! You're worse than a youngster before his Rite.

The human was off-limits, no matter how much he wanted her. In fact, she was off-limits because he wanted her too much. He wasn't going to allow his unnatural attraction for this female to rule over what reason dictated to him. He couldn't let his lust blind him, make him lose sight of what really mattered.

She was so stubborn and unyielding. She refused to release him from the cage, even though he gave her every reason to. That she was so spirited should make him angry and less attracted to her, but it only made her more desirable. A surge of frustration overcame him and Karian kicked at some nearby debris, sending it flying across the pod. He had to get this female to release him from the cage, and contact his Eok brothers.

That didn't mean he wouldn't repay his debt. No, Karian was going to help that courageous, helpless human and repay her for the life she saved.

Her generosity surprised him. Rose shared the little food she had found in the pod with him, a perfect stranger. More, a feared warrior. She even gave up her water rations, a resource her soft, pliable body needed desperately. There was steel in that soul, and whatever strength her body lacked, she made up for in her mind. She was a skeleton of steel wrapped in a cover of soft, lush flesh. It left him awed. It left him aching for her like nothing else before. Never had he felt such admiration for a female.

She would make a strong mate, and a fierce mother.

No. I have to stop. What is wrong with me?

His eyes slid to the corner where she had left the key. It shone softly in the low light, taunting him. After ten years, freedom was an itch he couldn't scratch, just inches from his grasp. Karian had been imprisoned for so long, he almost forgot what it felt like to walk outside, feel the sun on his face, let it warm his body to the bones.

He could feel what Rose had given him coursing through his body, making him strong again. He hadn't realized how weakened he had become before drinking that water, eating that food. Karian's flesh was a sponge, his veins filling with the added supply of new blood, and his muscles quivered in anticipation, rejoicing in the energy from the tasteless sludge of nutrition.

An hour had passed since Rose fell asleep. He let her take as much rest as they could afford, but time was out. Karian had to disable the distress signal and re-wire it for Eokim, or the Cattelans were going to come for them. There would be no second chance. Once Rose was in their hands, she was never coming back. The idea of losing her made his insides churn with bile. He wasn't going to allow anything bad to happen to her. On his life, he wouldn't.

"Rose, wake up." Karian trailed his finger down the round fullness of her cheek.

Midnight God, save me. Her skin is soft, so soft.

"There's not much time left."

The human groaned and whimpered, then she lifted her face to him. She blinked, shedding the sleep away, becoming instantly aware. She looked right through him with those big, stormy eyes, so deep they made him think he could touch the sky by kissing her lips.

"Our time is up. Give me the key, now." When Rose pressed her lips together and the soft gray of her eyes turned cold, he sighed with impatience. Didn't she see he was only trying to be reasonable? "If I don't re-wire the distress signal right away, you'll have escaped for nothing."

She looked at him, her face closed off and unreadable. A hand went up to her hair in an instinctive gesture, trying without success to tame the mass of curls.

"What makes you think I've changed my mind?"

"Don't be stubborn, human. I've let you have your way long enough."

"Just because the slavers find the pod doesn't mean I'm going to get caught. I'm not the one in a cage."

She smiled at him, in a way no female dared smile at an Eok warrior. It made him want to grab her delicate little neck and kiss those mocking, full lips. It made him want to lay atop her, make her his in all the ways that mattered. It made him want to see those eyes darken with desire and heat. It made him want to be savage and tender at the same time, and make her whimper in ecstasy.

With a supreme effort, Karian pushed the dangerous thoughts away, aware of how obsessive his attraction was becoming.

"If I wanted to hurt you, I would have done so already." Those lips. Karian's eyes refused to look away. He wanted to kiss them again. "For both our sakes, let me out."

Rose looked at him a long time, the smile gone from her face, the fatigue and danger of their situation making her brows crease with lines of worry. She put her head between her hands again, shielding her face away. When she looked up, her gray eyes were lined with steel.

"I'll let you out. You win." She bit her lower lip, hard, then licked the blood pearling where the skin had broken. Her pink tongue appeared and disappeared, and his seed stem stirred once more. "But I warn you, Karian. Betray me, and I'll kill you. Even Eok warriors have to sleep sometimes. I'll bide my time, and I'll kill you."

VENOMOUS CRAVING

She staggered to her feet and walked to where the key lay. She picked it up and played with it between her fingers for what felt like an eternity, her back turned to him. Her threat hovered in his mind. She dared threaten him, an Eok warrior, ten times superior to any other race in the art of combat? No, no other female was comparable to this one. So brave, and so foolish, too. What did she think she could do against him?

When she turned again to face him, something pulled at him, deep inside, where the primal urge to take a female resided. In his mouth, he felt an unfamiliar tingling where his tongue touched his fangs. Bewilderment gave way to amazement as Karian passed his tongue over the sharp tip of his fang. A sudden surge of heat dashed through his body as the drop of potent venom penetrated his bloodstream. Understanding slashed through the lust, and he swallowed, working hard to contain his instincts.

He knew what it was. This was the Mating Venom, a unique compound secreted by an Eok warrior's body in a purely instinctive manner when he encountered a female he wanted to make his mate. In all his years, Karian had never had the Mating Venom come to threaten to take his sanity away.

It shouldn't surprise him, though. Not with the way his body responded to her.

Blinking the confusion away, Karian realized he had been staring at her the entire time. Rose swallowed, and Karian stared at that movement, all the way to the swell of her breasts. A savage rush of lust traveled up his limbs, running faster than adrenaline in his veins, compelling him to take the female, make her his. With a control few males could maintain, Karian held still, fighting the basic urge of the

Mating. He couldn't afford to allow the compulsion to take control over him.

"I will let you out on one condition." Rose squared her slender shoulders and looked at him, her gaze unwavering. "If we manage to escape the Cattelans, you have to help me get back to Earth."

"Why would you want to go back?" Karian frowned, not liking where the conversation was leading. Why did she want to go back to a place where she starved and was cold, unprovided for? Another insidious thought crept into his mind, one he feared would only grow to become more important in the near future if his body continued to produce the Mating Venom. Would he be able to let her go? Trying his best to hide his reluctance, he talked. "I owe you. I will provide and care for you forever. A life for a life, that's the honorable thing to do."

"I don't want you to provide for me. I want to go back home so I can save my family, my village." She lifted the key to eye level, extending her arm to show it to him. "It's my offer. Take it or leave it."

Karian stared at Rose for what felt like an eternity. She was infuriating, unreasonable. He wanted to shake some sense into her and, at the same time, her strength forced his admiration. He hadn't met many people, male or female, who forced his admiration. It stirred emotions deep inside him, in a part of his heart he'd thought long tamed and docile. He'd been wrong.

That's only the Mating Venom speaking. I'll be back to normal soon enough, as soon as she's safely home and far away from me.

Karian nodded, as much to his thoughts as to Rose's words.

"I, Karian, son of Enlon of the Erynian tribe, swear to protect you and your family from all harm, lest I forfeit my life to the Midnight God."

Rose stood still, her stormy eyes piercing his soul as surely as an ionic blade. Did she even know what he was swearing to her? Karian had said the sacred words, those an Eok only gave to a female if she meant more to him than his own life, only if she was about to become his mate. The words had slipped through his lips, unbidden.

Midnight God help me, I mean it.

Chapter Seven

Rose

They were stuck together. For better or worse, she had tied her survival to Karian.

She kept silent as he stalked free of the cage and stopped right in front of her. Her breath caught and dread filled her bones. This had been a terrible, terrible mistake.

He gazed at her for what felt like a lifetime, his blazing eyes reflecting the low light inside the pod. Karian took a single step, closing the distance between them. His face was unreadable, betraying nothing of his emotions or his intentions. His smell filled her nostrils, masculine and wild, evoking images of touching flesh and hot, breathless nights. It pinned her in place. Even if she wanted to avoid his contact—which, for better or worse she didn't—she couldn't have. She was mesmerized.

The steel panel behind her seared the flesh on her back with cold, contrasting with the radiant heat from Karian's chest. Her breast touched him at each one of her breaths, making her breathe faster, deeper. She was absorbing him through the pores of her skin, through the air in her lungs and open lips. She couldn't have enough of him. She was trapped, and the only sound that filled the air was the beating of her heart, pounding like a stampede against her ribs. His considerable height forced her to tilt her head back to gaze into his eyes, and her head swam at the thought that he would kiss her again. His lips were pulled together tightly, forming a hard line.

It was as if he was fighting with himself, and losing his battle, fast.

As if on cue, he brought his arms up on each side of her shoulders, bracing himself on the steel panel, surrounding her body with his. His head lowered until his breath caressed her lips, making her ache for his contact. His nostrils flared, and his blazing eyes became heavy lidded and dark like a midnight sky in summer. Lust filled the air around them like a palpable being. Heat spread between her legs, and Rose couldn't help but wonder what his large, rough hand would feel like on her body. Pinching her nipples, gliding down her waist. What would those large fingers feel like, entering her, spreading her heat up and down her folds?

There and then, she knew. She would not resist him. If he wanted to have her, she would happily let him.

Karian's gaze flickered like cold fire, but he didn't kiss her. On each side of her head, his hands clenched into fists, but they didn't touch her. He swallowed, then shook his head once and stepped back. He turned away from her and walked to a steel panel on the far side of the pod, near to where the door had stood before the crash.

"We're lucky it wasn't damaged during the crash." He didn't turn, focusing his attention to the control panel. "It'll be much faster to work on if I don't have to repair it first."

"Great."

Rose wished she had something else to say. Something smart, or stinging, to make up for being so weak in front of him, but her mind was a blank. All she could think was how badly she wanted to touch his muscled back, with his large shoulders and sleek waist, all the way to his perfectly round ass. He was a perfect male, the most attractive she had ever met. He certainly was the most dangerous, too.

Now that he was free, she would find out soon enough if she had made a mistake in trusting him.

Karian didn't turn back. He ran his fingers over the cold metal, searching for something that eluded her completely. Finding what he'd searched for, he yanked the panel free of the wall and put it down, revealing a landscape of blinking lights, electrical wires, and strange clumps of metallic composite. With a care she didn't think him capable of, he began to pull on some wires and the blinking lights slowly died. Without pausing, Karian knelt in front of the panel and worked on re-wiring the signals.

Not knowing what else to do, Rose came to stand beside him. She watched him work, and a new feeling loomed over her. She was helpless and ignorant, and it made her feel worse than the terror of the capture or the torture of the thirst. This was a different kind of fear, the fear of the unknown. She was able to fight, and to endure pain. She had spent her entire life fighting the harshness of the vast wilderness of Earth, but even the most basic technology eluded her.

The only knowledge she had of the rest of the world and the wonders of technology was from her mother and father's mouths, and as subjects of the breeding facility, that was restricted. They had never traveled the Ring. They had never met with other races like the Eoks or the Cattelans. They only knew the breeding facility and how to escape it.

In the face of what Karian was doing, Rose's knowledge was sorely inadequate.

Who am I kidding? I'm fucking useless.

It was true. As much as she wanted to deny it, she was useless when it came to this. Well, she was useless for a lot of things, thinking about it. She needed Karian as much as she feared him. There was no way she was going to escape this planet without him. As much as she refused to allow herself to depend on anyone, especially a male, she wasn't a fool, either. This time, and only until it was absolutely necessary, she had to rely on him. The thought made her squirm with unease.

Hours passed, and Karian kept working. The first sun was gone behind the horizon and the second sun's light was fading fast. The light inside the pod was so low Rose could barely see his fingers running along the panel. Finally, as the last rays of light melted, he turned to her. His expression was grim and his blue eyes shone in the darkness.

"I didn't finish." He sounded frustrated, and when he sat on the floor, he let his weight fall with a heavy thump. "There are a lot of safety measures to prevent the re-wiring. Those bastards know what they're doing."

"Can you do it?"

"Yes." He turned his face to her and smiled, but it was a joyless smile. "Tomorrow, I'll finish, but I'm afraid it won't be fast enough."

"When do you think your kind will come for us?" Rose chewed on her bottom lip. She had pushed the threat of the Cattelans to the back of her mind, but now it loomed heavy. She hadn't escaped from that fate, not really.

"I can't be sure." Karian kicked the remnants of some seat stuffing with his foot. It flew and rolled away outside. "The signal should reach Eokim—my home world—in about two weeks at the most, if we are on the Eastern Quadrant of the Ring. Any passing Eok ship should also receive this frequency, but we would have to be beyond lucky for one to receive it. It's not like my nation has many trading ships wandering around. We're a nation of warriors, not merchants."

"What will we do if they don't come?" This was the real issue, wasn't it? Not only if they came late, but came at all. "The Cattelans will take us again."

"They will come." Karian spoke with assurance. "You don't need to worry. Eoks never leave one of their own behind."

"Seems to me it's a lot of resources for only one person."

"They will come." He looked at her with unreadable eyes. "The Commander in Chief of the Eok armies is not just any warrior."

Rose didn't answer. She swallowed heavily, taking in the importance of what he had told her. So, she had been right to think he was accustomed to giving orders. He was the Commander in Chief of the Eok armies, nothing less. A great warrior, someone of importance for his people. And he had made her a promise that could save her family, her people... If only they could reach the other Eoks in time.

Everything hung in the trust Karian had in his people, and the trust she had in him.

"Well, we should eat and sleep, then. Nothing else to do."

"Yes, we should." He turned to the hole in the pod. "But first, I want to feel the free air on my face again."

Rose came to stand beside Karian. The remainder of the light faded to give way to a moonless sky illuminated by a blur of stars and planets she had never seen before.

Even the sky isn't the same.

She watched, feeling farther away from home than she had ever thought possible. After a long time, she turned to look at Karian.

Standing like this outside made her take the full measure of his size. He was tall, perhaps a hair under seven feet, her head brushing just under his shoulders. His stature was intimidating, but she was beginning to find it more attractive than threatening. Rose glanced at his upper arms, bulging with muscles. The swirling pattern of his scars played with the faint light of the stars. He had the body of a warrior, all the way to his rugged, weathered features. Captivity must have been torture for such a creature.

His eyes were shining in his midnight blue face as he gazed on the wide, open space of the unknown planet.

"What's your world like?" Rose asked softly, so as not to disturb the strange peace of the moment.

"Eokim is a beautiful world," Karian answered, his eyes far away, looking at the landscape of shadows. "It's a harsh world, not unlike this one, but it's filled with so much beauty, it's as if the planet wants us to forgive her for creating a hard place to live for her children."

His words made her pause. She didn't know what she had expected, but it surely wasn't this.

"What about your Earth?"

"My village is hidden in a dense forest, with trees as tall as a hundred men, with trunks so wide it takes four people holding hands to reach across. If you climb a mountain, you'll find the forest stretches as far as the eye can see. We have lakes and rivers filled with fish, and a week's march away is the sea." Her voice broke talking about a home she would never see again. "It can be cold in the winter, but it's never dry."

"Your world sounds like a good one to live in."

"Yes, it was." Rose hesitated, then put her hand on his arm. A deep shudder ran through where her fingers touched his skin, as if a current of electricity traveled from her fingertips to him. "How long were you a prisoner?"

"By my count, it has been more than ten years since I breathed free air."

There was so much longing in those words, so much they didn't say. Her fingers traced a slow arch, up his arm to his shoulder, barely caressing the smooth blue flesh. The texture of his skin was different than a human's, it was smooth and firm, like fine leather, and much more resistant. It was strange, but not unpleasant. No wonder he didn't need as much water as she.

The small patterns of his scars were raised under her fingertips, smooth and complex. Beneath his skin, his strong muscles rolled as her touch traveled up to the nape of his neck. Rose hesitated, then let them slide further up his bald skull. A long shiver rang across his body at her touch, but still, he didn't move.

His breathing was deep and fast and his features were taut, but he was otherwise as still as a statue. Rose knew he was hanging on to every movement she made.

"I believed you," she whispered, and a ripple crawled under his skin where her breath warmed it. "When you said you will not hurt me."

"Never."

Karian turned his face to hers, ever so slowly. They locked gazes again, and even though it wasn't the first time, it took her breath away. Memories of the kiss they'd shared rushed through her, and her chest heaved.

She had every reason to fear him. He was Eok. That was reason enough in itself. They were Death unleashed. They ravished females, capturing them and bringing them back to their homeworld to live as captives. Trusting him was going to be the death of her, and yet, there it was. There was something noble in him, something that appealed to her.

Despite all she knew about his kind, she couldn't deny the way he made her feel. She didn't truly fear him, not anymore. What she felt was more complex, and much more dangerous than fear. He made her feel protected from the world. He made her long for him, for protection and strength. He made her long for the very thing she had sworn she would never come to rely on.

She wanted him. God help her, she wanted him on her. Inside her.

"What is it that you want from me, Pretty Thing?" Karian tilted his head so his lips were inches from hers.

That was the real question, wasn't it? If only she had the answer. She didn't understand herself when it came to him.

"I'm not sure. The only thing I know is that we're stuck together tonight. Tomorrow, we might be dead, or wish we were. We might as well make it a night to remember."

There it was, the truth she was searching for. It had been a long time since she'd had this, a night of complete safety. Karian gave her that.

"Rose," her name fell from his lips like a caress, "I can't."

"It's okay. You don't have to." She stepped back, away from his searing heat. Her heart constricted. Didn't he want her? She was so sure he did. Maybe he had someone waiting for him back home. A beautiful Eok female, as proud and strong as him. "You have someone waiting for you back home, don't you?"

Karian stared at her with unreadable eyes. "Yes. At least, I hope they do."

"She's lucky, your Eok mate," Rose said, trying her best not to show how the idea of him being with another female left her aching and empty. "She must love you very much."

"Eoks don't have females." Karian stared at her, his face as handsome as it was mysterious. "This is why we always take mates from other species. We are a race of males, and only male younglings are born."

"So you really are stealing females and taking them back to your world?"

"A long time ago, perhaps." His mouth slipped into a humorous grin. "Now, all matings are consensual and the Eok nation has many powerful allies who are more than willing to have their female offspring mate with our warriors. Our days of pillaging are long gone. Eoks embraced diplomacy and the laws of the Ring over a century ago."

Rose nodded. It made sense. Her father and mother's stories probably dated back to a time when humans were free. To the time when women were captured and sold by the hundreds of thousands to the flourishing slave markets. Before the Human Genetic Preservation Act that made her ancestors prisoners of the breeding facility. In those days, many women were probably captured by Eoks. Maybe those had been the lucky ones, if they spent their lives with mates such as Karian.

"Oh, so you have a mate waiting for you, back on Eokim?"

"No, Pretty Thing, I do not have a mate waiting for me." Karian's face lost its grin and his eyes darkened. "To take a mate, an Eok warrior's body must recognize her, first."

She lifted her fingers from him, and missed the contact immediately. So she had been wrong. His words were kind, but crystal clear. His body didn't recognize her, whatever that meant. She shouldn't be so disappointed about it. He was a total stranger, and she had a plethora of problems to concentrate on that were more pressing than a little romance, but there she was, burning cheeked and hollow hearted like a scorned teenager.

Karian kept his gaze locked with hers, furrowing inside her soul, pinning her into place. It took all her strength to break the stare and turn away. Her cheeks burned and her heart beat a crazy rhythm, shame and confusion pushing together inside her mind. Rose took a step away, back toward the shelter, then another. A hand closed on her upper arm, stopping her from going inside the pod.

"We have to keep our focus on the Cattelans." His voice was husky, without the usual mocking tone. "We can't let anything distract us."

"We don't need to make promises." She hated herself for pleading with him, but damn it, she wanted him, and he wanted her, too.

Close, he was so close, and yet, she wanted him closer.

"One night doesn't mean more than it needs to."

She turned her face and there he was, her new companion, her new torture. Karian's heat seared through her. His hand on her arm slid down and long fingers intertwined with hers. It felt more natural than it had any right to, this simple gesture. Rose lifted her surprised gaze to him, not even trying to hide her confusion. The entire universe wanted to possess and use human females, had hunted them to near extinction a century ago. And yet, she was flinging herself at the most powerful race of warrior in the Ring, and he didn't take what was offered.

"Why not?"

"Because, Rose, I don't want to take you for a night. I want to make you mine. Midnight God help me, there is nothing I want more, and it will damn us both if I give in."

His hand left hers, and a long shiver skittered across her skin. Without talking, he went back inside the pod.

Chapter Eight

Karian

A fool, he was a fool.

Rose stepped inside the pod right behind him. Her sweet smell of arousal invaded his nostrils, threatening to push him to the edge. Karian dug his claws into the palms of his hands to prevent himself from turning around, ripping the clothes off her back and taking her right there. Pearls of blood fell to the floor at his feet, and he let them. Perhaps some of the heat from his blood would leak into the cold floor and he would regain his sanity.

What was he even talking about? His sanity was long gone. It had been gone even before he had tasted those lips. She truly was like a flower, her smell pure and light, and her taste like honey. It made him want to lose himself inside her, forget everything that was not her.

The Mating Venom still rushed through his bloodstream, dripping inside his mouth in a constant trickle of sexual urge, strong and intoxicating. Now that it was happening to him, he understood. It was a pure chemical urge, as addictive as any drug on the underbelly of the Ring.

Now I understand why no warrior ever resists.

He usually held his control in a steel hand, allowing nothing to get in the way of his goals. With no other female had he felt the urge to make her his mate, no matter how attractive.

He could afford not the slightest distraction to affect his better judgment when both their lives hung in the balance.

Later, when we're safe.

Karian shook his head against the intrusive thought, knowing it was the mating urge speaking.

"I'm so thirsty," Rose said from somewhere at his back. The need in that voice tugged at his organs, made him want to provide everything she ever needed. She didn't deserve to be thirsty, or hungry, or cold. She deserved to spend every minute of her life cared for and cherished. He wanted to be the male to provide this for her.

A fool, again. He was such a fool.

"I shouldn't take more, but my head hurts," she added.

"Take as much as you need, there's no point in depriving yourself of anything."

Karian didn't trust himself to turn around. If he saw need and want in those stormy eyes, he was going to melt, and everything was going to be lost. "I'll set off in the morning to find fresh supplies."

"What makes you think you're going to succeed where I failed? There's nothing for miles around. No water, no prey to hunt, and no edible vegetation. Nothing."

"If the pod landed on this planet, then it's capable of sustaining life." Karian shrugged her objection away with a wave of his hand. "There's no mistake in the programming. You just haven't been able to find it."

"And you will?" Her tone was mocking again, with an undertone of irritation. "You're so full of yourself."

"It's not arrogance when you know you're the best."

Karian moved away from Rose again, intending to sit by the opening of the pod to keep watch while she slept. As he took his first step, Rose scoffed at his back, and a bag of water landed on the back of his head. He swung around, and locked his gaze with a desert storm in those large, beautiful eyes. Her cheeks were flushed red and she crossed her arms on her chest, making her round, full breasts puff up in two soft mountains. How he would love to run his tongue along those soft mountains, suck on the nipples in the middle until they were hard and ripe.

Stop. It.

"Well, I guess we'll see about that." She lifted her brows in challenge and reached for another pack of water, then drank it in two long gulps. "That's your plan for tomorrow? Scavenging and hunting? Good, I'm in."

"What do you mean, you're in?" His mind was racing. Did she really mean it? She thought he would allow her to go out there, in a desert they knew nothing about, and roam free to get killed, maimed, or worse? "You're not going out again. I'm going to find us another shelter, food and water, and you're going to stay here, where you're safe."

"No way." She had the nerve to shrug his objection off. "I'm going with you, whether you want it or not."

"I will not allow you to put yourself in danger."

"You're going to make me stay here?" She smiled that mocking little smirk that perked her nose up. "You and what army?"

Karian glowered at her until she squirmed, standing first on one foot, then the other, but still sustaining his gaze. Damned stubborn female—she was provoking him, but he wouldn't give in. She wasn't going to put herself in danger ever again. He wouldn't be able to bear it if she was hurt.

"It is settled." Karian showed her his fangs, and this time, she had the good sense to shrivel under the command of his superior strength. "You will stay in the pod while I venture outside. That's an order."

Rose narrowed her eyes at him but didn't argue. He watched closely as she bent and picked up another pack of nutritious sludge, then proceeded to gather some of the stuffing from the seats and make a primitive bed out of composite foam. She sat cross legged and started to suck the foul liquid, her face twisted with disgust, but thankfully silent.

Karian was grateful for the end of the argument. She had a way of making his blood boil, and he was close to walking right over there, pulling her into his chest, and kissing her adorable mouth shut.

I'm losing my mind. I'd best start thinking with my head, not my seed stem.

Rose finished her ration and threw the package away, then lay down on the makeshift bed. Karian watched her turn and toss until she fell asleep, a drop of saliva dangling from her slightly open lips, her body limp. He finally relaxed. The battle to keep her alive was nothing compared to the battle he had to wage with himself to control his urges.

He stared at the sterile panel of steel as the hours went by, one after the other, in the small shelter of the pod.

Rose's sleeping body tormented his every breath. Her offer to share her body tantalized him, kept him awake through the silent hours. The way she had touched him, the feel of her fingers, had been almost impossible to refuse.

Almost.

Males took females, a tale as universal as life.

Then why don't you take this one? She's willing. You're an idiot.

The urge to take this female and mark her was overpowering. He had almost given in twice. The first time he'd kissed her, he'd been so grateful for the cage, he could have kissed the bars that held him.

Her taste made him stir, the feel of her tongue, the way she opened her mouth for him, so eager, so hot, full of passion. When he'd pulled her soft, fragile body to his and felt those plump breasts against his chest, he'd nearly given in. He could have taken her, even with the cage.

He was a fool to even think about her that way. It was a waste of his time and energy, one he couldn't afford. He had too much to do to think of taking a female.

The sooner she was out of his sight, the better.

With a monstrous effort of will, Karian brought his focus back to the current situation. The signal had gone off for too long, the Cattelans were sure to be on their way soon—if they hadn't already found their location. There was no way to know when Karian's people would get the signal. It could be days or weeks from now.

There was nothing to do about it. Worrying about things out of his control wasn't the Eok way, so he pushed it out of his mind. He had plenty of things to take care of in the meantime.

Rose used too much water and too many food rations. Even if he refused to use any, she didn't have more than a few days' worth. The pod was too hot in the day and too cold during the night.

Tomorrow, he was going to find a better shelter. Tonight, he had to resist the lust.

Rose

Rose opened her eyes to the early morning's soft blue light. Her head still hurt, but the pain was a low pulse in the back of her skull, a remnant of what her body had endured the days before. She looked around, expecting to see Karian asleep in the far corner of the pod. She frowned, puzzled, then irritation took hold. The pod was empty. Karian must have left some time before without waking her, just like he'd said he would. Muttering unladylike curses about pig-headed males, Rose scoffed, then sat in the makeshift bed.

What an arrogant asshole.

The Eok warrior wasn't what she had expected, in more ways than she wanted to even think about. Yes, he was arrogant and high handed, and thought that he had every right to order her around like some brainless doll. He made her want to claw his eyes out sometimes—most of the time, actually. If only he were always unlikable.

But he also had a sharp sense of humor, was as smart a man as she'd ever known, and had a body to spend her nights dreaming about.

Shame burned her cheeks at the memory of the way she had flung herself at Karian. Well, she wasn't going to make that mistake again, sensual dreams or not.

As Rose picked up another pack of food, she paused, then added one of water as well. She ate and drank, looking at the pod's paneled walls, her mind going back to her family and the looming threat of the slave trade. Steel walls and nutritious sludge mixed together in a soul-sucking facility where their only jobs were to produce children. This was going to be the lives of the people she loved if she didn't succeed in saving the small human settlement. Panic compressed her chest, and it took her a long time to be able to breathe again. The nutritious sludge stuck to her tongue, coated her throat in a thick, repulsive chemical taste, but Rose forced herself to eat. She was going to need every ounce of strength she could get.

A plan had formed inside her mind during the night. She had come to realize that now that their existence was known, there was no going back. The human village was going to be the object of a hunt so massive that no matter where they hid, they were going to be found. It could be sooner or later—maybe even years down the road, when Rose was old and tired—but they would be found. Gaining protection for her family was no longer enough. She couldn't protect them without protecting the entire village. And what they needed wasn't anonymity anymore, but protection. They needed allies and protectors.

The Eoks were the strongest race of warriors inside the Ring. If she could secure Karian's help, maybe he would help her obtain the

Eok nation's support for her entire race. For this, she needed to talk to Karian as an equal.

The first step to prove her worth to Karian was by contributing to their immediate needs. She wasn't going to allow him to shoulder the sole responsibility of their survival. If she caved in to his domineering ways now, there was no telling what he might do. He might never intentionally hurt her, but he would deem her unable to provide for herself, unable to choose for herself.

Rose slid the water ration into the elastic band of her pants. Now all she needed was something to hunt with. With a frown, she studied the contents of the trashed pod. A smile spread on her lips. There, in a corner, lay the broken stalk she had taken the first time she ventured outside. She picked it up and looked at it. After a good sanding on a rock, she would have a nice sharp tip to use as a spear. Rose flipped her newfound weapon over in her hand, assessing its weight and feel. After a few minutes, she headed out into the desert. This time, she wasn't going out unprepared.

As her face met a warm, early morning desert wind, resolve poured like iron down her veins. If she listened to Karian, there was life in that desert. She had an inkling he was right. He might be arrogant and controlling, but he was a survivor. Rose would do good to learn from him and she wasn't foolish enough not to try, even if he was being an ass about it.

She felt a wild smile spread on her face. With a bit of luck, she would show him. The best thing she could do would be to succeed where he failed and bring back a kill from her hunt. Whatever animals lived in this desert should be at their most active in the early dawn. If things went her way, she would find some prey to roast for breakfast.

After about half an hour, she spotted a furtive, scurrying movement behind a cluster of vegetation. Smiling, she stalked closer to her prey. The animal, whatever it was, was behind the long, yellowing shoots, digging in the sand with its front paws. She couldn't see precisely what it looked like, just that it seemed vaguely reptilian.

The animal's head came into view as it emerged from the vegetation, chewing on the dry, hard grass. It looked like a harmless small beast, with leathery, hairless skin and long claws perfect for digging the hard dirt. Its head was round with a short muzzle framed by long, square teeth. It hadn't seen or smelled her, thanks to the wind blowing upward from the animal to Rose.

Holding her breath, Rose brought her shoulders way back, arching her back in the tense fashion her father had taught her. The shoot was lighter than the wooden spear she was used to, but it went flying through the morning air with blazing speed and accuracy. The animal looked up with large, fearful eyes. Comprehension came a second too late, and the spear pierced the soft skin of its abdomen. A pathetic cry flew through the peaceful air, and the creature convulsed a few times, then went silent. Rose stood still, a smile spreading across her lips.

She had done it!

With a spring in her step, she approached the animal, retrieving it from the ground. It was a strange creature, definitively leaning on the reptilian side. Its body was covered in a thick, smooth leather, completely hairless and without scales. It had a snub nose with three large nostrils, and a long, forked tongue hung from its open mouth. It was small, slightly bigger than a wild cat, but its plump body seemed fat enough to make a good meal.

Rose pulled the spear from the creature's body and hung it by its hind legs to the piece of string holding her pants, like she did for birds and rabbits back home. At this rhythm, she could have a handful of these before Karian came back. Just as she was about to turn around and walk away in search of more prey, something attracted her attention. She looked again, and a flutter of excitement grew in her chest.

She bent down where the creature had been digging, and pulled on the long, tubular root still semi-buried. Another drop of water leaked from the root, pure and crystalline. With a giggle, Rose brought the root to her mouth and sucked. She was rewarded with a small but sustained trickle of fresh, sweet water, filling her dry mouth with moisture. This was even better than the kill. They needed water badly, even with Karian's minimal requirements. She had only ten pouches left, barely enough to cover the next two days comfortably.

Rose sucked on the root a long time, closing her eyes and savoring the sweet flavor of the sap. The sound of vegetation moving broke her concentration.

She opened her eyes to look directly into two large, yellow irises slashed by vertical pupils. The animal staring at her was large, at least the size of the cougars that haunted the woods where she used to live. It looked strangely like a cat, but with the same leathery skin as the creature she had just killed. The animal, definitely a predator, fixed its yellow, malevolent stare on her, obviously trying to decide if Rose was a threat or prey. There weren't any other options.

After a few more seconds, the creature seemed to come to a conclusion, and it let out a long, furious hiss in her direction. Doing so, it exposed two wicked, sharp fangs dripping with a suspicious milky fluid. Her brain resonated with a single word, one that brought with it the worst kind of fear. Venom. This large, powerful, feline-like predator had venomous fangs, to boot. As if it needed anything more to tear her claw-less, fang-less and venom-less self into tender mouthfuls. The only thing she had on her side was the spear.

It felt both futile and harmless between her trembling fingers.

Without waiting, the predator leapt, fangs and claws at the ready. A piercing sound ripped through the unmoving air, and Rose realized she was screaming. She fell on her back, holding the spear in front of her body in the hopes that the animal's momentum might help impale it. As its long, curved, sharp claws came closer and closer to her face, she realized her mistake. The spear was a good idea, but she had overlooked the most important aspect of it. It wasn't long enough. She would be shredded to pieces before the beast could impale itself.

As the claws were about to penetrate her skin, the beast was knocked over to the side. A large, midnight blue form rolled into the sand, clawing and hissing in concert with the creature. Karian and the predator rolled and fought, each beast's viciousness rivaling with the other. Rose stared, paralyzed with fear, as the Eok and the predator fought. Finally, with one mighty slash of Karian's talons, the beast's head was ripped from its shoulders and rolled to the ground, cut clean off. Karian stood slowly, his chest heaving in fast, deep movements as he looked at the dead creature.

"Are you okay?" Rose's voice cut the eerie silence.

Karian's head snapped her way, and she recoiled at the blue fire in his eyes. His face was twisted with an expression she didn't recognize, something between the savagery of a berserk beast and the cold stare of a lion about to pounce. In a strange way, he was the scariest of the two monsters she had encountered that day.

"You disobeyed me," he hissed, his fangs exposed and his talons fully extended into deadly weapons, made to tear flesh into ribbons. "YOU DISOBEYED ME!"

Fear shot through her in a surge of adrenaline, and Rose turned on her heel and ran.

Chapter Nine

Rose

Rose ran with death on her heels. Her mind was blank and her lungs burned, but she pumped her legs through the fire. All those years in the wilderness as a huntress hadn't prepared her for becoming prey. All her training was useless.

She simply wasn't fast enough.

The dry, cracked dirt sent clouds of dust into the air as her feet battered the ground in her desperate attempt at escape. In her crazed mind, she had a flash of empathy for the poor creature she had just killed. Rose understood how he—and all the rabbits and partridges she had hunted in her life—felt. Being thrown to the other side of the mirror in the prey-predator relationship sucked big time, and as she ran, she reflected on how terrible it was to be the small, fragile creature about to lose its life.

Behind her, a gravelly, deep sound filled the abrasive air. She was out of time.

A long shadow stretched beside hers, with sharply angled shoulders and long, curved talons extending from ghoulish hands. Panic rippled through her nerves like wildfire, sending tiny bites of electrical shots through her muscles, giving her added strength and speed. She rushed forward, her feet unable to sustain the speed at which her legs were pumping. At length, Rose lost her footing.

The ground rushed to meet her face and she screamed, putting up her hands to protect herself. Strong arms closed around her waist as Karian threw his considerable weight over her shoulder, sending them both to tumble on the hard sand. She was going to be crushed underneath him. Bones were going to be broken, skin torn and bruised.

It didn't happen that way. Just before the packed dirt met her face, Karian flipped onto his side, taking the brunt of the impact on his shoulder. Sand flew in her face, and she choked on the dry, irritating dust. Her eyes were filled with the particles, making her blink furiously under the sharp pain, but she was otherwise intact.

"What's wrong with you?" Large hands gripped her shoulders, talons digging into her skin but not breaking it. "Will you stop!"

"Let go of me!" Rose flapped at his arms, trying to free herself from Karian's grip, but it was useless. "You bastard!"

"Are you insane?"

"You're hurting me!"

Her shoulders were freed and Rose stumbled back a few steps. Her first instinct was to pat the dust from her eyes. As she blinked, a looming shape appeared through her tears. Karian's shoulders were heaving up and down, and his eyes were blazing with a light from within. His hands were scythes, tipped with wicked talons. He was a creature of nightmares.

"You wonder why I ran?" Her voice shook with unshed tears. "Look at yourself. You're a monster."

Karian straightened, and a long, deep shiver ran across his body. His eyes stopped glowering and he retracted his talons to small stabbing knives. He wasn't reassuring in any way, but he wasn't a monster straight from her most feverish nightmares anymore.

"I told you to stay in the pod." His voice was controlled and even, but there was no mistaking the heat underneath.

"And I told you I was going out on a hunt."

"How am I to protect you if you disobey me? You were almost killed. You were lucky I was close enough to come to your rescue."

"Well, I wasn't." Her voice was sharp, sharper than she intended. Sharper than what was wise. Anger flared inside her. This was his fault. "It wouldn't have happened if you'd let me come with you."

"It wouldn't have happened if you'd stayed put, like I told you."

Rose slapped her thigh in anger, and her hand met the cold, limp body of her kill. Following her impulse, she grabbed the beast by its two hind legs.

"I caught us lunch." She flung the creature at Karian and it landed on the sand at his feet. It had been battered by the run and fall, but was still more or less intact, if less appetizing.

"You hunted this creature?" He picked up the dead animal and studied it a while. His brows drew closer together, and he pursed his mouth. Food, real food, that was what those eyes were saying. "This won't last long."

"You're welcome." Rose put as much scorn as she could in her answer.

"It wasn't worth risking yourself." He stared at her, his eyes hard and his face closed. "You should have obeyed my orders."

"Your orders? You're delusional if you think I'm going to come to heel like a dog. I'm not one of your soldiers, or your—"

"Don't disobey me again." Karian cut her off and started to walk, going past her with the creature Rose had killed in his hand, not sparing her a single glance. "I won't repeat this."

Acid boiled cold and hot through her blood at the same time. Rage at the injustice of his reaction flared through her, sending her caution to the wind.

"You don't own me."

Karian spun on his heels, turning to her with a frown on his fearsome features. He was getting mad, but so was she. Anger made her reckless, and she didn't care if he was pissed.

You'll see just how much I'm going to listen to your stupid orders.

"Do not test me, Pretty Thing. I am the one in charge."

"Fat chance. If you want a pet, I suggest you buy one." She folded her arms and held her ground. He wanted her to follow like a dog? Well, he was in for a surprise.

"I found something else we need." She flipped her head to one side and pursed her lips. "I found water."

"You did?" He blinked a few times, apparently surprised at the sudden change in conversation. Good, this was exactly where she wanted him. The frown disappeared from his face and he glanced around at the dry, barren landscape. When he paused, she knew she had bested him.

"Where? I have scoured the land for fifteen miles around."

"Two points for the *adorable* huntress, then." She made a face and walked up to him. Too bad she had dropped the root when she'd run from him. Rose pointed to a clump of vegetation to their right. "It's those plants. The long, spiked ones. The animal was digging up the roots when I hunted it. There's sweet sap in them. You have to suck pretty hard to get it, but there's enough for both of us, for as long as we need."

Karian glared at her but kept silent. She couldn't tell if he was confused, embarrassed—or both—that she had found something he'd missed. By the way his shoulders were stiff and his eyes skimmed the landscape, glancing at the large, heavy clumps of vegetation surrounding them, it was obvious. He didn't like being outwitted by a female.

"Show me," he said grudgingly.

Rose stalked past him, her head high. She kept her face as slack as she could keep it, knowing it would do no good to gloat over her success now. She had won, and that was it. As soon as Karian was safely behind her, she let a triumphant smirk spread on her face. Sweet, sweet justice.

It wasn't long before Karian knelt beside her and dug for the fat, tubular roots. In a matter of seconds, he was holding a large clump between his taloned hands, staring at the clear fluid with a relieved smile. Without pausing, he brought it to his mouth and sucked hard enough that his cheeks were hollowed. After a while, the root shrunk to a dried-up shell and he threw it away, smacking his lips together in apparent delight.

"Why didn't you take more water at the pod if you needed it so much?" Rose asked. "I took more than I needed."

"You are more fragile than I am." Karian glanced her way, then proceeded to dig up another big clump of roots. "You needed it more. I can go a long time without it if necessary, but that doesn't mean I like it." He paused, his talons deep in the dirt. His gaze settled on her, steady and direct. "It was smart, finding water the way you did."

She smiled, a true one this time, then helped him dig until they had a healthy supply of fat roots, dripping their sweet sap into the moisture-starved ground. Without words, Karian and Rose got to their feet and walked back toward the pod, sucking on the roots side by side until their stomachs were full of fluids. The silence between them was a comfortable one, the kind Rose was used to when she walked back from a hunt with her father. It was a good silence, a silence of trust and satisfaction.

They weren't out of trouble, not by a long shot, but for now, they were safe. Together and safe.

Suddenly, Karian stopped walking and she bumped into his large back, then landed straight on her ass. Karian hissed silently, exposing his fangs. She opened her mouth to spill a good piece of her mind at him but stopped short. His body was tense, and his talons were fully extended, curving in lethal weapons at the end of his fingers. One hand was extended her way, the palm open flat. He wanted her to wait, or to hush, or both.

Rose obliged him, scrambling to her hands and knees, ready to pounce or run as soon as he gave the signal.

Karian ignored her completely, his eyes fixed on the distance ahead. He crouched, the roots forgotten in the dust. Rose's gaze followed Karian's. Her veins coiled in tangles and fear cramped her stomach, threatening to make her throw up the precious fluid.

The Cattelans had found them.

Karian

"What will we do?" Rose whispered. He heard the edge in her voice, the raspy choking just beneath the surface, ready to break.

"Keep silent!"

He snapped his head her way, ready to bully her into silence. When he saw her terrified wide eyes, his anger melted and he shook his head in a silent plea. Still shaking, she nodded and kept quiet, but inched to his side, so close, her cheeks brushed his jaw. He was painfully aware of how close she was, and it infuriated him that he wasn't able to focus one hundred percent on his task.

Up in the distance, a good two miles ahead, the Cattelans were moving and speaking, inspecting the pod and its contents. Anger and frustration flared inside him at the speed with which the Cattelans had found them.

It's my fault. My obsession with Rose made me weak.

He should have disabled the distress signal sooner. They had lost precious time while he was in the cage. Still, he couldn't blame her. He blamed himself for not pushing her harder to release him. He had been so hell bent on making her see him in a favorable light that he'd forgotten that danger was looming ever closer.

He needed to think, plan with his usual cold logic if they were to remain free.

"We're going to crawl back behind those rocks." He spoke in a whisper, jerking his chin in the direction of a cluster of boulders. "Follow me, and don't make a sound."

He waited until she was safely on her way before moving as well. As soon as he was away from the Cattelans' line of sight, he turned to lock gazes with Rose. Her face was serious and closed, and she was biting her lower lip.

"It's me they're after." She talked with a toneless, dead voice. "There's no sense in you dying for me. Go, save yourself." Striking gray eyes locked with his. "But keep your promise. Save my family."

"Mark my words, Pretty Thing," Karian said, rage flaring in his mind like fire on the grasslands. "I'm never going to leave you behind. For better or worse, we're together."

When she didn't answer, he crouched in front of her, his face inches from hers. His eyes met hers, the link he felt already running bone deep, even without a mating bond. How he wanted to convince her, soothe her fears into submission. He reached for her, cupping her cheek in his hand, retracting the talons so as not to hurt her fragile skin. Rose closed her eyes at the contact, exhaling a shaky breath. He ran his hand against the silk of her cheek, sliding his thumb down her jaw, running it across her lips. So soft, so inviting.

It was as if he was drowning in her touch. Without realizing he was doing so, his lips closed on hers. This wasn't the all-consuming, hungry kiss of before. This was a kiss filled with tenderness, with the taste of home. It filled him with a savage need to protect her from all harm. When he finally withdrew, she was staring at him, her gray eyes shining with an emotion he feared to contemplate.

"Okay." Rose took a deep breath. "Okay. I'm with you."

Karian gazed into her eyes once more, making sure her soul was tethered to reality before breaking the bond. He crawled to her side and sat, his back against the stone.

"They've disabled the signal." Karian clenched his jaw. "I can see the transmission panel on the ground. They caught up with us too fast."

"How many are there? They're too far for me to see."

"I counted three but there could be more."

"It's not too many." Rose's voice was more alert, calmer. Deadlier. "We can take them."

"This is a recon team." He glanced up to the cloudless sky. "Now that they've found the pod, more will be on their way. Fighting won't be an option."

He waited while Rose kept silent. He could almost feel her thirst for the Cattelans' blood. He shared her hatred and anger, but this wasn't the way to go. He would give her revenge if he could, but the priority was to get as far away from the pod as possible. There were enough caves and hideouts on this planet.

"I finished the rewiring this morning. The signal should reach Eokim within two days at the most. All we have to do is wait until then."

Rose's head snapped his way. Her sharp eyes glimmered.

"How do you know?"

"I know where we are," he said with reluctance. It wasn't good news. "We're on Saarmak. It's a small moon close to one of the worlds controlled by the Eoks."

"Why do I get the feeling you're not happy about it?"

"It's a dangerous planet," Karian explained, trying his best not to frighten her. She had enough to worry about as it was. "I recognized the animal that attacked you. It's an aakvan. The one I killed was just a juvenile. There will be more if we walk farther into the mountains, where there's plenty of prey for them."

A long silence stretched as Rose assessed the measure of their predicament.

"Nothing is as scary as you," she joked, poking his shoulder playfully. "I was only kidding when I said I've hunted scarier beasts than you."

"Well, these might just be. They are not only huge, but poisonous. A single bite is all it takes."

Rose fell silent again, and Karian turned to study her. She had a stubborn expression on her face that he was starting to recognize. As long as she had a glimmer of hope, she was going to keep fighting. He nodded his approval and she lifted her gaze to him. A tacit alliance was being sealed. She was there for him, too, said that face.

Emotions came to him, and he looked away. Eoks didn't need protection, least of all from a female. Still, there was something there, something he recognized as a true partnership. She was ready to give where nothing was expected from her.

"We can stay here until dark. We move out when they sleep, kill them, take their transport, and get as far away from the pod as we can."

Rose nodded, then seemed uncertain. "How will your people find us then?"

Karian smiled. "They will. We are good trackers, the best. For now, you have to sleep."

A few hours later, Rose held her knees up to her chest with her arms to ward off the frigid desert night, but from the sharpness of her breaths, he knew the cold still slithered from the sand and slipped into her body, depleting it of much needed warmth. Her biosynthetic cotton clothes were sorely inadequate and offered no protection. He knew she couldn't stand much more of this cold, but he didn't trust himself to touch her.

If he did, there was no telling where he'd stop. And when the Mating was sealed, he wouldn't be able to think straight. He would be nothing but a lust-crazed fool for a few days, and those were days he couldn't afford to spend.

Her teeth began to chatter and long, bone-deep shivers ran through her body. Guilt riddled each cell in his own body, and Karian turned to her. By fearing to lose his control, he'd let her get dangerously cold.

What a poor protector I've been. Look at her, she's freezing.

"You're losing too much heat." He got up and walked over to Rose, then sat at her side. "Let me warm you."

"It's okay." Her voice shook, and guilt lashed at him in blazing strokes of shame. "I'll be fine. Keep watch."

"You're not fine." His arm circled a shoulder of ice. "Midnight God, Pretty Thing! Your body is about to shut down."

Karian grabbed Rose's shoulder and pulled her into the cradle of his body. She made a face at his possessive gesture, but didn't protest. She needed the heat too much. She was so small against him, her body made of subtle curves and secret places.

Lust came, unyielding and imperious. He had known it would, and ignored the tingling of the Mating Venom on his tongue. There was no way around it, the venom slipped through, entering his bloodstream.

I would warm her faster if we were both naked.

No. This was the Mating Venom talking again.

His hand reached up a goosebumps-covered arm, kneading the soft flesh, massaging his own heat into it. Rose moaned and hid her head in the crook of his neck, nestling her body closer to him. Heat flared from deep inside his body and he squeezed her closer, breathing in her intoxicating scent. His hands were animated by a will of their own as they explored her small, female body, running across her legs to grasp her firm, shapely thighs.

Rose's breath on his neck turned raspy as she molded her breasts to his chest, leeching every sparkle of fire from his contact, sending his desire into overdrive. Karian's blood turned to a flow of lava and he was remotely aware of his fangs, trickling with the Mating Venom, pushing the boundaries of his control just beyond his reach. Each second that passed made him more intoxicated, more lost in the lust for this female.

Her cold, full lips closed on the skin of his neck and a deep shudder traveled through his body, ending at his crotch. His seed stem was so hard it hurt, and when she pressed her firm ass on it, he could barely contain his impulse.

"You're playing a dangerous game, Pretty Thing." Karian nipped at the taut skin of her neck, then licked where his fangs had pinched her. His grasp on the Mating Venom was becoming thinner by the moment, and what was worse, he wasn't sure he cared anymore. "Are you sure of what you're asking?"

"No," Rose said truthfully. "But we might die in a few hours. It seems to me like there's no point in overthinking it. If I'm about to die, then I'd rather die with your taste in my mouth."

He held her chin between his fingers and turned her head to him. Their gazes met and melded together. They were trapped inside each other's souls.

Gazing into the gray depths of her eyes, Karian wasn't sure where the female ended and where he began. His life before her, his impressive rise to the highest rank of Eok military and his years of relentless dedication, seemed empty and void of meaning in the face of what he felt now that he had her in his arms. Maybe she had always been there, somewhere in a corner of his mind, waiting.

"You have no idea what you're asking of me," Karian said. "You have no idea—"

He didn't finish what he wanted to say. Rose closed her now warm mouth on his in a hungry kiss that lay waste to his sanity. Grasping her, he turned her around so she faced him and she wrapped her firm thighs around his waist, pushing her hips against his crotch. Karian tore his lips from hers, then covered the supple, soft flesh of her neck with his mouth, kissing every inch of skin deeply.

He stopped at the curve of her neck, his jaws opening and his tongue flicking over her quivering skin. A trickle of Mating Venom dripped from his fangs, the slick drug covering her tender flesh. Over his ear, Rose moaned and pushed her sex harder against his. The smell of her arousal invaded his nostrils and his burning erection throbbed, imperious with need.

Far in the back of his mind, a small voice suggested: *Take her. Take the female. She's yours.*

His hand slid to her breasts, kneading them softly until her nipples perked, hard and needy, through the fabric. His fingers rolled the hard knobs of flesh and she arched her back, whimpering in pleasure, making her breasts protrude even more.

"Pretty Thing, you don't know how I hurt for you."

"Then don't hurt anymore. Take what you want." She managed to talk through the panting. "I want you, too."

Karian's lips landed on her throat with all the hunger of a long held starvation. The impulse rushed through him and he opened his jaw to enclose the fragile flesh, fangs at the ready. Mating Venom coursed through his veins, veiling his thoughts with the need to make her his, to seal the bond with the bite. His jaw tightened and the fangs pushed against her skin, piercing the membrane slightly. The taste of blood entered his mouth, coppery and salty. It made the rage all the more urgent, the possession all the more pressing. He had to take her. He had to make her his mate.

"Are you going to hurt me?" Rose's voice came, shaky but still laden with desire.

Her words reached him through the dense fog of lust. She was afraid. She should be. He was seconds away from giving in to his instincts to bind her life to his irremediably. Without her approval, without her knowledge.

He should be ashamed of himself.

With a supreme effort, he opened his jaw, releasing her throbbing throat. His breathing was fast and jagged, and his entire body vibrated with frustrated need.

I resisted this time, but I won't be able to resist much longer.

As soon as the thought formulated, he knew it was true. He had no idea how he was able to resist the Mating Urge, maybe it was the fear in Rose's voice. Maybe it was because he knew it was wrong to mate her without her approval. Whatever the reason, he managed it this time. He wouldn't be able to a second time.

With firm hands, Karian lifted Rose away from his body. She disentangled her legs from his hips and sat in the sand beside him. Holding a shaking hand to her neck, she then brought her fingers up and watched with wide eyes as the black stains of blood were revealed under the light of the stars.

She bit her lower lip and swallowed. He could smell her arousal mixed with her fear, the potent mix of pheromones threatening his tenuous hold on the Mating Urge.

He had to get away. He had to go now.

"Time to set the plan in motion." His own voice was alien in his ears. How could it be so cold, so controlled, when his mind was prey to a hurricane of desire? "Stay hidden until I come back with the transport."

Chapter Ten

Rose

Rose blinked and searched the desert landscape for Karian's silhouette, but her night vision was poor and he was too far away. All she could to do now was wait for him to return with the transport so they could get far away from the pod—and the Cattelans.

As she waited, rubbing heat into her goosebumps covered flesh, Karian's face hovered in her mind. No matter how much she tried not to think of him, the stubborn obsession came back, each time a little stronger. She had to face the truth; getting away from him was going to be much harder than she thought.

The more time she spent with him, the more the Eok warrior surprised her. His gentleness, first of all, but also his selflessness. That was perhaps the most perplexing of all. She was at his mercy, he could do whatever he wanted with her, yet he hadn't taken her. He wanted her, she was sure of that—both his body and his words told her so, over and over again.

Then why doesn't he just take what he wants?

He was a mystery. One minute Karian was a cool warrior, calculating and ruling with an iron fist over whatever he decided to rule over, particularly her; the next minute, he was all over her body, kissing her with a burning passion, making her feverish under his touch.

As the night continued to unfurl, Rose took comfort in her memories of Karian's touch, how warm she felt when he kissed her, when his hands ran all over her body. She craved him at least as much as he craved her.

Behind her, the sands shifted, tearing her away from her daydreams.

She turned, still rubbing her arms. He was back faster than she thought, but then it was hard to keep track of time in this desert. A quick glance at the sky showed her the night was still young. Rose frowned, then her eyes locked on a tall figure standing between two rocks, black hair shining under the starlight and a cruel smile spreading across his mottled green face.

He stalked toward her with slow confidence until they stood merely ten feet apart.

"We meet again," Arrik said, licking his lips. "No escape pod for you to run to now."

Rose was paralyzed, her eyes wide and her limbs frozen as Arrik stepped ever closer, his unhurried gait a telltale sign that she was doomed. Finally, she broke free of the curse and backed away from him, pushing the dirt with her feet.

"Keep your dirty hands away from me or you will lose them." She muttered the empty threat, backing up until her back brushed the cold of a giant rock. Out of desperation, she raked the ground with her eyes, hoping against all hope to find a weapon to defend herself.

Her gaze landed on the makeshift spear, lying on the ground between two shriveled husks of vegetation. She grasped it, holding it between fingers slippery with a sudden cold sweat. She wasn't going to best him a second time. She could see it in the dangerous, hateful glint in his eyes.

Her hands squeezed the frail spear so hard her bones hurt. She lifted it in front of her like a sword, feeling every inch of its useless, pathetic length. Again she was reminded how defenseless she was. Arrik was trained in combat and twice her size. Last time she'd fought him, her only advantage had been the element of surprise, but now she had nothing going for her.

"Stupid, stupid human *whore*," Arrik said, passing a long, forked tongue over his yellow teeth. "I'm going to fuck you until I tire of you. Then I'll give you to my crew to enjoy until I deliver you to your new owner. He's going to be pissed you're damaged, but he'll forgive me when I give him a whole village of humans to compensate. Who knows? Maybe he's even going to give you to me in compensation."

The words sent a shiver of horror down every single cell in her body.

Arrik's hateful eyes narrowed and a ripple traveled down his long, bulky limbs. She saw the tightening of his muscles, and the moment of absolute stillness in his body. He was going to jump her, and she knew the outcome. She was no match for him.

Despair gripped her in its cold embrace, ripping away every hope of warmth. There would be no salvation. There would be no more of Karian's hot, blazing touch on her body.

No, she thought. *I won't allow it.*

On the edge of her broken hope, she brought the spear to her neck, just under her chin, where her jugular vein pulsed a crazy rhythm. Her breathing became a threadlike wheeze as the tip of the weapon pushed against her flesh, the throbbing of the vein like a drumbeat, counting the remaining seconds of her life. It was one thing to say she wasn't going to allow Arrik to capture her alive, that she was going to sacrifice herself to protect her family, but it was another to do it. "I'll die before I allow you to take me."

Arrik froze, his eyes going wide.

In that instant, the balance returned slightly to her side. It was shitty leverage, but she was worth nothing dead. Her fingers tightened on the spear. If she killed herself, he was screwed. In a flash, she wondered just how screwed he would be.

"How much do you owe him, huh? The male who bought me?" Rose smirked, tears gliding down her cheeks. "My guess is that if I die here, so do you. You're in way over your head."

"Don't do this!" Arrik's face was a mask of pure terror. "We can talk this over. Lower the spear."

He lifted his hand toward her, his fingers spread out wide, then took one more step.

"Stop!" She pushed on the spear and a sharp pain burned under her chin where the wood pierced the skin. A warm trickle of blood slid down her throat and hot wetness spread on the light fabric of her sweater. "You're not touching me."

"You don't have it in you." His eyes were two deadly slits, but he lowered his hand and took a single step back.

"Don't test me." She did her best to sound detached, like she didn't care about pushing the wood deep into her own flesh. Like she didn't care about lying there on the alien sand while her life gushed from her throat.

Her gaze locked with Arrik's and they were both immobile. They were stuck there, then. He wasn't letting her get away, and Rose wasn't fast enough to outrun him.

Her only hope was to stall him long enough for Karian to come back.

Long minutes passed while Arrik and Rose faced each other in silence. The wind blew over the desert sand, and the moons shone as they faced each other. There was a strange kind of intimacy in this, like their lives were tied together in a perverted way.

A humming sound rippled through the night and Arrik's eyes slid to her side, in the direction of the pod. The sound could come from nothing else than the transport.

Elation filled her. Karian had done it! He had killed the Cattelan guards, taken their transport, and now he was back. They were safe.

"You're dead." Rose enjoyed every bit of the savage smile that spread on her lips. "Karian will kill you."

"Is that so, human?" Arrik straightened, his face a mask of strange satisfaction.

Rose paused, confused. The Cattelan should be terrified of a confrontation with Karian. She didn't have time to reflect on Arrik's response. The transport glided through the air past Rose and stopped at Arrik's side. She watched as two tall figures threw a limp, muscular body on the sand. A whimper escaped her lips and her hands started to shake.

"Karian! What have you done to him?"

Arrik smirked an ugly, hateful grin, exposing his yellow teeth. Rose barely registered the two other Cattelans moving out of the transport to stand on the ground on each side of Karian. All she was able to focus on was Karian's unmoving form, flat on his back. His face was turned to her, his eyes closed. Her eyes slowly glided down to his chest. She didn't see it moving.

Oh, God, no. No, no, nonononono.

Her mind was lost in a whirlwind of denial.

Her strength wavered and the spear lowered by an inch. From the corner of her eye, she saw Arrik take a furtive step in her direction. Rose snapped the spear up instantly, harder than she meant to, and blood gushed down her skin. She had cut herself good this time. It wasn't just a warning nick, it was nearly enough to pierce the vein, and then she would bleed out in seconds. Arrik couldn't bring her back from that.

The Cattelan froze, his arms extended toward her, his wide eyes shining in the starlight. She snapped her head to him.

"Is he dead?" Her voice filled the night with fury, stronger and more savage than she thought possible. "I swear I'll have your life if he is."

"You care about this animal?" Arrik tilted his head, his eyes glinting with calculation. "He's not dead yet, but he will be if you don't lower your weapon."

Arrik snapped his fingers and the two Cattelans unsheathed their weapons, pointing long, shiny blades at Karian, one at his head, the other at his chest.

"Don't hurt him." Rose heard the edge of panic in her own voice. "If you kill him, I'll plunge this spear into my neck before you can stop me."

"I'll make you a deal." Arrik lifted his chin and pursed his lips, his gaze never wavering. "You come to us without harming yourself, and we let him go. I'll even throw in a bonus. We won't touch you."

Arrik's words penetrated her mind, one syllable at a time. She knew even before he finished that he had won. She would never allow Karian to die for her.

"He's going to die if you leave him here." Rose cast a quick glance around the shadow-filled desert landscape. How many monsters lay in wait there, ready to pounce on defenseless prey? "You have to bring him back to the pod."

"He's Eok. He'll be fine. And if he's not, the universe will be a better place without another one of those animals in it."

Arrik spit on Karian, and with a rash of viciousness, kicked him squarely in the ribs. Karian didn't even stir.

"Think fast, human, my patience is not unlimited."

"Okay," Rose breathed. "Just don't hurt him."

She opened her fingers and the spear fell to the sand at her feet with a muffled hollow sound. Arrik didn't lose a second, he jumped, and she was tackled to the ground so hard her ears rang from the shock. She was flipped onto her stomach, a knee digging into her back. She screamed in pain but he didn't change his stronghold on her body, instead clasping her wrists tightly.

He jerked her to her feet, and her back throbbed where his heavy weight had dug his knee. Rose knew there would be a bruise there, and the side of her face was battered, bloody and raw where she had hit the ground.

The ugly Cattelan's face came to her side and his putrid breath licked her skin.

"You're mine." Arrik pulled her in to his body, his arousal digging into her back. A wet, raspy tongue slid along her throat, from the base of her neck up to the corner of her lips. Rose couldn't fight the whimper of revulsion that escaped her. "Now I'm going to fuck you until you wish you'd slit your delicious little throat."

"You gave me your word."

Rose hated how her voice shook. How stupid she had been. She choked back a cry, despair and fear washing over her at the same time. Then her eyes landed on Karian, still unmoving on the ground. She could see it now. His chest moved up and down in a slow, steady rhythm.

A strange calm overcame her, washing away some of her despair. Whatever happened to her, some good was coming out of it. She had saved him. Karian would live.

The crazed panic tearing through her ribcage slowed. Rose turned her head to Arrik, returning his glare. The yellow, glowing eyes slid to her fallen companion, then back to her. A predatory smile stretched his lips, and she knew.

She had lost everything.

"Farnick, Azil, kill him," he whispered softly, not looking away from Rose, as though he were murmuring loving words into her ears. "And make him suffer."

Rose's wordless screech filled the night. She writhed and fought like a banshee, but to no avail. Arrik and the other two Cattelans laughed, the cruelty of the sound filling her with a new kind of emotion, something she had avoided all her life. No matter how harsh or painful her situation had been, she had never felt bloodlust before. Now she knew how it felt. In a way, that made it possible to understand how her father felt about the breeding facility and those who ran it.

The desire for violence was a fire that consumed her until nothing was left, and now she truly wanted to end the Cattelan's life. She would kill anybody who hurt Karian, with a hate spawned from the pit of the darkest corners of her mind.

Arrik dug his fingers into her wrist, hard enough to leave a string of bruises in the pattern of his fingerprints on her skin, while the two others kept laughing, looking at her with cruelty in their eyes.

"Did you let him fuck you? Did he taste that sweet, sweet little pussy and ravage it? Did you like it?"

Arrik's left hand slid over her breast, while the other yanked her wrists higher up behind her. She cried out in pain and arched her back. His finger pinched her nipple, hard, sending a shot of pain all the way to her brain.

"You're so soft, I can't wait to know how you feel inside." Arrik rubbed his erection against her, underlining his intention. "I bet you're every bit as good as they say you are."

The hand left her breast and slid down her stomach, an inch at a time, kneading her supple flesh with unbearable anticipation. A choking sob escaped her throat.

"The best." Arrik licked her neck again. Despair washed over her like a wave, depriving the world of oxygen. "I bet you're going to bleed when I fuck you."

Then a flash of glowing blue eyes ripped through the murky despair of the night, and a male scream filled the air.

Chapter Eleven

Rose

The first thing she was aware of after the initial scream was Arrik's hand deserting her flesh. The relief that rippled through her body was enough to make her head spin, but she held on to consciousness like a drowning woman.

It's him. He's alive.

Karian was awake, and his retribution would know no bounds. Arrik was petrified against her back, his erection melted from the fear.

Karian was magnificent. Even half-starved and injured, his body moved with speed and accuracy through the air, slashing at the Cattelans with his talons fully extended. Blood spilled under the blue light of the stars in a strangely beautiful dance, the glowing droplets catching the starlight in a deadly ode to the night. One Cattelan soon lay on the sand, his throat slashed in Karian's initial attack.

"Azil!" Farnick called the name of his fallen comrade. "You killed him!"

There was a lull in the fight. The remaining Cattelan watched his companion's lifeless body while a pool of blood spread underneath it, disappearing into the thirsty ground.

Slowly, like he wasn't sure he wanted to fight anymore, Farnick turned to face Karian. His face was a mask of fear and despair. He knew Karian was the better warrior, and that he was going to die. Rose almost pitied him. Almost.

Karian and Farnick circled each other, the Cattelan holding his weapon up between them. It was a long blade, sizzling with a strange array of electrical sparks. An ionic blade, Rose's brain screamed. One touch and Karian was dead, killed with a million volts of electricity, searing through flesh like mere air.

She wanted to scream, to tell him to be careful, but she didn't dare make a noise.

They kept moving. For the first time, Rose noticed Karian was walking with a slight limp, favoring one leg. A long gash ran along his thigh, dark blood running black under the star light. His face was a landscape of hatred, the face of nightmares on the battlefield, his body a weapon every bit as lethal as the ionic blade.

"Get him, Farnick!" Arrik yelled behind her. "Kill the bastard!"

Farnick turned his head to look at his master. That was a mistake, as Karian jumped to the ground, head first, rolling under the menace of the blade. As he straightened, Karian thrust his talons up with both hands, deep into the Cattelan's chest, embedding them to the wrist.

Farnick's eyes grew wide, and he opened his mouth as if to say something. A gush of blood ran out, and the ionic blade fell to the sand, useless. Karian roared and yanked his hands out. Between them were the twin hearts of the Cattelan, still beating in panic, dripping with blood. Farnick stared at the hearts, his eyes filling with the terrible knowledge, his mouth open in a silent scream. Then he fell, his body limp.

Karian's war cry invaded the air, and the sheer power of it sent waves into the very fabric of the night. Karian's terrible warrior face was drenched with the blood of his enemy, his fangs exposed and bloodied. He wasn't a creature of nightmares. He was the creature nightmares were terrified of.

That creature turned its wrath to Arrik.

Rose felt the trembling in the Cattelan's body, along his limbs and down his hands on her.

"Let her go." The words were almost lost in Karian's growl. "Get your hands off her."

"If you move, she dies." Arrik brought his free hand to Rose's neck. His voice was high-pitched and unsure. He was terrified, and well he should be. "Don't take another step."

"I swear on the Midnight God guarding the souls of my ancestors, I will rip the hearts from your chest and eat them while you watch."

A long shiver rang through Arrik, and Rose felt every terrified ripple of it. His hand on her neck lowered with his panic. This was her chance. On instinct, she brought her head down to her chest and yanked it back as hard as she was able to. It connected with Arrik's nose with a sickening wet sound of crushed eggshells, and white streaks of pain shot through her head. The sharp pain resonated through her skull, but she had succeeded, as Arrik's hold loosened by a thread.

Using the last of her strength, she kicked wildly behind her, hoping to hit him straight in the knees. Rose missed, but the movement yanked her free. She stumbled, losing her balance and rolling in the sand.

A heavy, booted foot hit her kidneys, and she yelled. Rose rolled, backing away from Arrik. He was going to jump her again. She was his only chance at survival now, and she knew it. Her hands clasped frantically at her sides, searching for anything to defend herself with. Finally, her fingers closed around a small wooden stick. Without pausing to think, she grasped it tightly, realizing it was the spear. Arrik's face was misshapen by rage as he rushed down on her, murder in his eyes gleaming like a flame. Rose brought her hand up, slashing at the Cattelan's face with fury.

A gush of hot, coppery liquid washed over her face, blurring her vision. Arrik stumbled backward, holding the left side of his face with his hand. Rose fell back on the sand, away from the threat.

"You took my eye!" Arrik yelled, his voice a howl of fury. "I'll kill you for that, whore."

But Arrik didn't attack. His head snapped up to where Karian was, then he ran to the transport. Soon the air hummed with the sound of the engine. Rose watched as the transport hovered away at a blazing speed.

"Rose!" Karian's face floated over hers. He was a vision of horror, with blood all over, his eyes blazing with a light from within and his fangs exposed in a hiss. He was the most beautiful thing she'd ever seen. "Are you hurt?"

Karian pulled her to her feet. Strong hands turned her around and ran over her skin. She could have purred under the contact.

"No," she said, rubbing her eyes to get rid of the sand. "I'm fine. What about you?"

"Nothing more than a scratch."

"That's not true." Her eyes slid down his leg, where the fabric of his pants was ripped to shreds and the exposed flesh was a mangled mess. "This is serious."

But Karian didn't pay any attention to her. He was staring in the direction Arrik had left. His face was closed, and his body rippled with unshed aggression. Rose reached for his shoulder, and as she touched him, he shook the contact away.

"We need to leave, now." He snapped his head to her. "He's going to be back soon, and this time, he won't have only two guards with him. He's going to bring his entire crew."

"Oh," she breathed. "Right."

His hands clenched on her shoulders. His lips were pressed together in a tight line, and she thought she saw him flinch under the pain, but he didn't complain. He didn't need to. They both knew his injury was serious, and they also both knew there was nothing they could do about it. Not while the looming threat of an army of Cattelans forced them into a hasty retreat.

"Where are we going to go?" She looked around, but found nowhere to hide. They were out in an endless desert. No matter where or how far they went, a hovercraft could find them.

"To the west," Karian said. "Into the mountains."

She didn't have time to answer. Karian walked away without waiting, and she watched him take the next few steps. He stopped, then he turned his head slightly to the side. The message was clear. She had better follow him, it said.

In that moment, he wasn't the warm, darkly humorous Karian who made her blood boil and her stomach flutter with need. He was the warrior, the leader she'd met that first day in the pod. The giver of orders, the survivor who would drag her through the sand kicking and screaming if he thought it was the best thing for her.

She started to follow, then stopped. A shining, curved object shone in the sand, not far from Farnick's body. The ionic blade. Rose reached down and picked it up.

"Leave it," Karian ordered. "It's going to give a heat signature for them to follow. We don't need to make it easier for them to find us."

"It's the best weapon we have." She flicked the blade through the air. "We might need it."

"I'm the best weapon we have."

"Maybe, but I'm still bringing it."

Karian turned to face her. He was deadly and serious, imperious in his authority. She didn't give a shit.

"I said leave it."

"And I said I'm bringing it. I'm not like you. I need a weapon to defend myself."

"You have me." Karian talked in a definitive, short voice, but there was a concession in that tone. His face twisted in pain, and he wasn't fast enough to hide it. Rose had an inkling he knew she might be right, but couldn't say it. "I will protect you to my death."

"And what happens when you can't fight anymore?" She nodded her head at his wound, but kept her voice soft. She didn't want to push him to a defensive stance. He was all male pride, and no good could come of ruffling his feathers. "You can tell me it's just a scratch all you want, I know better. We're losing good time. Now, are we going to leave, or what?"

He glared at her for a few more seconds, then nodded. There was no way to tell what part—if any—of what she had said he agreed with, but the main thing was that he let her keep the blade.

As they walked under the rising light of the early morning, its metal felt like death in her palm.

Hours followed hours, with the sun high in the merciless sky, hammering over Rose and Karian's heads with a renewed hatred. Karian wasn't slowing down, walking three steps ahead of her, not turning back, not talking.

Rose's head was swimming in a bottomless pit of pain. The head-butting she gave Arrik had been effective, but it had resulted in a searing headache that had only worsened with the fatigue, thirst, and heat. The sun's constant rays were an ever-present torture, and every sliver of light stabbed her retinas, furrowing through the folds of her brain to bring about new heights of pain and misery. Still, she kept up with Karian's pace, even though her legs burned.

There was no place for the weak in this survival game.

After another few hours, Karian wasn't three steps ahead of her anymore. He was a good ten paces in front, and constantly stopping to allow her to make up the distance. Rose was fading, and fast.

She had stopped looking ahead a while ago. Her head hung limp on her shoulder, pulled by its own weight. The only thing breaking the monotony of the sand was the constant trickle of blood oozing from

Karian's wound. Rose followed its trace in the sand, one grim drop at a time. It had abated in the first hours of their walk, reducing and even at some point stopping, but the wound had re-opened some time ago and blood stained the dirt ever since. It was a miracle Karian was still on his feet, a tribute to his incredible strength and stamina. He truly was a force of nature, but even a creature as formidable as him was going to fade at some point. In all likelihood, Rose was going to be the first to go down, and she knew it.

A few more steps, and the world started to spin. She stopped, bracing her weight with her hands on her knees, but to no avail. The ground met her butt with an ungraceful thump. The world was a spiral of dry, sterile sand and frozen blue, as the sky and the ground mixed in front of her eyes. She wasn't going to get up, not this time.

"We can't stop." Karian came to her side, and helped her sit up straight. After a while, the world stopped spinning and she latched onto his blue gaze. He was still the warrior, his face set in determination, but there was no harshness in his voice. "We need to cover more ground before we're safe."

"I'm done," Rose said, shaking her head slowly. She spoke the truth, and saying the words made it final. "I can't walk anymore. I need a break, and water, if we can dig out some roots. You need it too."

"It's not safe." Karian talked softly, but there was no mistaking him. He meant it. "Just a bit more, to those hovering rocks over there. They're large enough to make a shelter."

Karian pointed to a forest-like growth of tall rocks. It seemed impossibly far, but she knew he was right. After a few moments, she nodded, and he helped her to her feet. They walked slowly, but kept going.

Up close, she saw the pain painted across Karian's features at every step. His wound was oozing, inflamed and angry looking. It was infected. Pretty soon, he was going to need the kind of help she couldn't provide.

Her respect for him grew with every step he took on his bad leg, never complaining, never fading in his support for her. He was a rock, and all she wanted to do was to lean on him, on his strength. She had never wanted to rely on anybody more than him, and it scared her out of her skin. There was no time to dwell on her feelings, though.

Time blurred into an endless tapestry of misery while Karian and Rose walked to what appeared to be the beginning of a dense cluster of fallen rocks, where the mouth of a dark cave gave the promise of shelter.

Up in front, there was a tangle of the tall, dry shoots, and the promise of roots filled with sweet sap. When they reached it, Rose collapsed to the ground and immediately started to dig. Karian did the same beside her, although with considerably more dignity. Her fingers hurt and her skin was raw, but soon a large root found its way into her hands. Not losing a second, Rose bit in and sucked on the nutritive sap, her greedy lips latching on desperately.

Karian kept digging at her side, piling up fat roots, not pausing to drink.

"We have enough." He turned to Rose. "Let's get closer to the cave."

She followed him, sucking on roots as they went. The sun's relentless heat was somehow dimmed by the shadow of the rocks, and the shade was a welcome relief. She didn't have the courage to look down at her arms to see the damage. She would feel it soon enough.

Karian finally stopped in front of the mouth of the cave. It wasn't much, but it would have to do. "Sit and drink. I'll inspect the place." He dropped the pile of roots at her feet and started to inspect the cave. "It looks good enough for now. I'll have to pile more on the entrance to hide our heat signature. The entry to the shelter will be small, but we have no choice."

"I'll help you," Rose said quickly.

"No," he answered with a sharp gesture. "You're too weak already."

He started to pile huge rocks on each side of the cave's entrance. The rocks Karian moved would have taken two or three young, strong human men to move, and Rose was left awed at his superior strength. She wanted to protest, wanted to shoulder her share of the burden, but she was dry to the bone. Even at her peak, this was not something she could even have dreamed of doing.

She sat down on a rounded boulder and sucked on a fat root while she watched Karian, feeling guilty to the brim. It was hard work and after a few dozen rocks, it was clear that he was exhausted. His chest was heaving and he took more and more time between each rock.

"That's enough." Rose got to her feet. To hell with male pride, he was done. "Now, sit and drink with me."

"No, it isn't enough." Karian turned to Rose. His eyes were sunken and vague. "It won't keep us hidden from a heat signature scan if they fly over us tonight."

She walked to him, the largest root they had dug up in her hands.

"I'm fine," Karian protested, but he didn't move. "I'll drink when I'm done."

"You're done now." Rose planted her feet and faced him squarely. She gave him her best I'm-going-to-make-you-rest-myself look. "Drink. Now."

"I'm stronger than you think." He smirked, but it lacked its usual arrogance. "Besides, a Pretty Thing like you needs a bed to rest in tonight."

Exasperated, Rose shoved the root against his chest. Her heart constricted when Karian wavered on his feet and the root fell down. His weakness lasted only a second, but it was enough to convince her.

"You're about to collapse," she said, bringing her hands up and placing them on his chest. His skin was an inferno, but his face froze like stone at her words. Rose smiled at him, trying to appease his pride. "Besides, who's going to protect me if you fall? I'm defenseless, remember?"

Worry blazed in her gut as her hands ran up his chest to cup his cheek. The fever was too high, and she had nothing to bring it down.

Karian's eyes blazed with humor, and the corners of his mouth lifted in the beginning of a smirk. He followed her movements as she picked up the root and slammed it softly against his chest again, her brows lifted in a gently mocking way. He brought his hand over hers, the touch of his sharp talons sending electric waves across her skin. His feverish eyes softened and he lowered his head.

Rose lifted herself on the tips of her toes to meet him, and their lips connected. His heat burned her lips, and she fought the tears that came to her eyes. She couldn't let him see how scared she was for him, as she was sure his male pride would rebel at the idea of appearing weak in her eyes. Not that she ever would see him that way, but Karian was the kind of male who despised admitting to a weakness, even when it was obvious he was exhausted.

He leaned forward and his other hand slipped onto the small of her back, pulling her into the volcano of his body. His kiss was hungry and generous at the same time, his touch telling her what his words couldn't.

She lowered her feet and broke the kiss. Karian's blazing eyes met hers and he opened his mouth.

Something snapped to their left, and his face lost all its softness. He sniffed the air, and a cloud panned across his eyes.

"Don't move." He pushed her away, not rudely, but with enough decisiveness that she didn't resist. "It's not after you."

Rose opened her mouth to talk, but no sound came out. A sense of dread blanketed the dusk. She stood, clutching the root to her chest as Karian stalked in front of her. His hands were extended at his sides, talons at the ready, his legs widely spaced.

"What is it?" A slow shiver slithered across her nerves. She knew what it was, and it wasn't good. "Is it that big lizard-cat thing?"

The predator's eyes, cold and calculating, came back to the front of her mind. It was a nightmarish creature, lethal in all aspects, even for one as strong as Karian. Especially now that he was injured.

"An aakvan, yes. It smelled my blood. It knows I'm weak and it came for a quick kill."

Rose wanted to answer with something, anything, but her mind was a blank. A quick kill, yes. Predators targeted the weak, the sick, the old, and very young. The injured. Prey that was easy to kill. Like Karian.

She was still holding the root to her heart, like it could somehow shield them from the claws and fangs that ripped flesh to shreds, when a long shadow emerged from between the rocks to make way to another living nightmare.

This creature was much larger than the one she had encountered in the plain near the pod. It was so tall its head stood at Karian's shoulders, and it was twice as large as he was. Its snout was crisscrossed with long, ugly scars from previous battles, and its yellow eyes met Karian's stance with a cold intelligence that chilled the blood in her veins. It was a monster, purely and simply, and it was the master of this territory.

The aakvan stepped into the clearing, its claws digging into the sand and its fangs dripping with venom.

Karian's shoulders slumped. His talons fidgeted, and Rose could almost feel the waves of exhaustion emanating from his skin. Uninjured, the beast would have been a challenge to defeat, but in his state, Karian was no match, and he knew it.

They were going to die.

Chapter Twelve

Karian

The alien feeling filled his mind, penetrating each of his cells with a numbing cold, erasing years of painful training. It took a long time for Karian to understand what it was. It was fear.

He wasn't afraid for himself. His Eok warrior training erased the fear of death, and even pain, to a mere dust in the back of his mind. No, he was afraid for *her*. Even though he hadn't mated Rose, she was coursing through his veins as though they'd spent a lifetime together.

He would lose his life before allowing anything to happen to her.

Karian focused his attention on the eyes of the aakvan. It was a spectacular animal, well equipped for the rough, adverse living conditions it survived in. It was a formidable adversary when he was in his best condition. As injured and weak as he was, it was deadly.

Karian flexed his muscles, spreading his talons wide. His muscles twitched and a cramp took hold of his injured leg. He had lost too much blood, and now his muscles were weak with dehydration. The fever didn't help, blanketing his mind with fog and slowing his thoughts.

Yes, the predator had chosen weak prey in him.

The thought made him clench his jaw. He was Commander in Chief of the Eok armies. He wasn't going to be killed by an animal. He slowly shook his head, his senses returning to their old acuity by pure force of willpower. He wasn't defeated yet.

"Rose, run." He tilted his chin to the side, but his eyes stayed on the monstrous creature. "I'll hold it off for as long as I can."

"No way. I'm staying with you. With the two of us, we can scare it off."

Of course, he should have known the stubborn, infuriating female would choose this moment to defy his authority. He usually appreciated her spunky spirit, but this wasn't the time to juggle with death. This was a time where life could end at the tips of sharp claws and merciless fangs.

Karian was acutely aware of Rose's body, standing just a few paces behind him. He didn't need to look at her to know she was mesmerized by the predator in a way he knew very well. It was a deadly hypnosis, the same hypnosis prey experienced a few seconds before the death blow.

In front of him, the monster licked the air, flicking its forked tongue in his direction. He knew what the creature tasted.

Blood. Fever. Weakness.

Digging its claws deeper in the dirt, the aakvan waited for an opportunity to make its move.

Behind him, Rose moved and lost her footing. The predator's eyes flicked and its pupils retracted until only two faint lines remained in the yellow of its irises. It was going to pounce.

"GO!" Karian yelled, angling his body between the animal and Rose.

The monster followed Karian's movement, then a decisive flash crossed its eyes. Its gaze flickered between Karian and Rose, clearly assessing which one of them was the bigger threat.

After only a second, its gaze steadied on Karian. Its instincts told it to kill the bigger, stronger male before attacking the female. In the next heartbeat, the aakvan hunched on its hind legs, then jumped, claws at the ready. It had the speed of a reptile, moving in a blur of fangs and claws. A fraction of a second before the long, curved claws connected with his flesh, Karian dodged, dropping to the ground. As he dropped, he turned and slashed at the creature's underbelly with his talons. He managed to cut the unprotected skin, but his strike wasn't as deep as he wanted. The predator twisted midway in the air and returned the slashing motion with its own claws as its snout snapped shut an inch from Karian's arms.

Karian crouched on his legs, the pain from his injury nearly blinding him.

The aakvan fell on the dirt and rolled away before regaining its footing. The creature licked its underbelly where Karian's talons had slashed the skin open, then brought its head back, staring at Karian with a new glint in its eyes.

It was personal now.

Karian and the monster circled each other, while the aakvan flapped its tail on the ground in anger. The creature bled on the sand, limping slightly. Satisfaction welled in Karian as he recognized the signs of weariness in the animal's eyes. It was surprised to have misjudged its prey, and was now careful about how it was going to take him down.

Karian had hoped if he could injure the animal, it would realize he was no easy kill and walk away. It wasn't going to happen that way, though. Being injured only infuriated the animal, and now it was as much about retribution as it was about hunger.

One of them was going to die here, and it was up to Karian to make sure it wasn't Rose and himself.

A furious hiss escaped the animal's open mouth, exposing its fangs. Its spine rippled with wrath and it snapped the air, the sound both dry and chilling.

After another minute, the monster pounced again. The animal aimed its claws straight at Karian's chest, its mouth open and ready to snap at his neck. Just in time, Karian dropped, turning his back to the ground and his talons at the creature. As the monster's lower body was above his head, Karian slashed his talons, as far and as hard as his fading strength allowed.

He felt his face split in a wild grin as his talons embedded in the monster's thigh. A rage-filled roar filled the air, and the aakvan twisted in midair, its snout clasping on Karian's thigh, digging its fangs gums-deep into his flesh.

Karian screamed, pain and understanding mixing together as the sharp burn of venom spread in his muscle.

The monster let go of him and backed away a few steps, flipping its tail and hissing, but without the fury of before. It was limping badly and blood was gushing out of its wound in a steady flow, but it had won. Karian held his previously intact leg where the aakvan had bitten him.

A burn spread from the bite site, accompanied with a burrowing feeling, like ants on fire under his skin, alongside his veins. The venom was acting, leaving a numbed emptiness behind the pain of the inferno. The emptiness traveled up his leg, taking over his limb at a frightful pace. The ground raced to meet him, and Karian realized he had fallen down.

He tried to get back on his feet, but they seemed to be melting under his weight.

The monster took a step back, its cold stare assessing the effect of the venom. It was waiting for the poison to render its prey defenseless before starting to feast.

Karian blinked back the sudden sleep that threatened to take hold of his mind. He was losing his grip on consciousness. With a surge of willpower, he shook his head to fight off whatever terrible effect the venom had on him. Comprehension dawned on him, terrible and without mercy. He was going to die, and soon.

And after him, Rose was going to be killed.

Karian watched as the predator moved and hissed, thumping its tail on the ground impatiently. The world was starting to move in a slow, muddy fashion.

Rose's face came in front of him, her large gray eyes full of unshed tears. Karian held her gaze, knowing that if he let go, he would not come back. Darkness was going to swallow him, and death was going to follow.

The predator's tongue flicked and it tilted its head, its stare turning hungry.

Time was up.

His mouth formed the words, and he heard them in his mind.

Rose, go. Save yourself.

Karian turned his eyes to the monster, staring at the beast. He knew death was coming, and so did the monster. The beast slapped its tail on the sand a few more times, saturating the air with dust. An abrasive cloud spread, surrounding the world with an angry red glow, as if the air was preparing for the bloody scene that was to come.

Emptiness invaded his body, and his fingertips vanished into oblivion. The world spun in an endless spiral of darkness.

Rose

Something broke inside her at the sight of Karian lying on the sand, his head lolling on his shoulder, blind to the horrible death that was coming for him. A deep shudder raced down her spine at the idea of the aakvan's merciless fangs tearing through that magnificent body. His last words came to her mind. Even about to die, he thought more about her safety than his own.

Rose, go. Save yourself.

That was what Karian had said. Not *help me*. No, he'd said *save yourself*. Perhaps that was what gave Rose the motivation she needed to stay and fight. Perhaps it was only that Karian owned a part of her, and she couldn't bear the thought of being parted from him.

Rose leapt, covering the few feet separating her from Karian. She landed across his chest, and turned to face the creature as fast as she could. She was shielding him with her own body, her torso spread over the unconscious figure as best as she could. He was so much bigger than she, it was hard for her to protect him entirely.

Her eyes met the monster's stare, and she almost melted under its cold, calculating assessment. Its pupils reduced, then returned to normal, and its tongue flicked out, tasting the air. It lowered its head, and Rose was sure that if it could have, it would have snickered at her.

She should have felt anger. She would have welcomed the heat and bravery that fury usually gave her, but that didn't come. What she felt was pitch black despair, running along her nerves, shutting down every bit of hope she had.

The monster took a few steps, pacing in front of her with a heavy limp, then it stopped. Its flickering tongue poked through its snout again and she got a perfect, blood curdling view of the long, venom-dripping fangs inside its mouth. It was going to attack at any second, as its curiosity faded and its instincts took over, driving it to kill.

She was nowhere near as stoic as Karian had been in the face of her own death. Fear crept inside every pore of her body, its insidious cold furrowing through her last seconds. Answering a primal need for comfort, her free hand rose along her side with all the intention of clasping at her heart.

Midway, her fingers ran along a cold metallic object.

The ionic blade!

Without pausing, she wrapped her fingers around the hilt of the short sword, then brought it back in front of her. Its long, shiny metal was bare of the glow of power it was supposed to have. Rose's mind raced and she flipped it over between trembling fingers. It took a few seconds for her to understand she had to push on a small, oval indentation to engage the incredible power of the blade.

As soon as she pressed the switch, she felt the rumble of power run along the metal, sizzling through the dust as tiny particles of sand were obliterated into nothingness. Her arm shook, but she held the blade in front of her with both hands as the monster flicked its gaze to the pointy object.

It tilted its head, sensing the pulsation of electrical power coming from the weapon. It was an animal, and it had no idea that the blade could slice through its skin and bones as easily as through water.

Dismissing the small blade, the beast brought its stare back to her.

She sensed the impending attack before her eyes registered the massive mouth opening, intent on inflicting a killing strike. It didn't need to weaken her with poison. She wasn't threat enough. It would simply tear and eat her while she screamed. The image came to her mind: blood and gore spilling out of her torn abdomen while she stared helplessly at the sky, not even having the strength to scream.

The aakvan struck. There was a tiny fraction of a second when the beast's mouth opened and its neck extended to snap at her upper body. For this instant only, the animal was vulnerable. Rose ducked under the massive jaws, rolling on her shoulder like her father had instructed her. She flipped back under the creature, holding the blade clear of her body, and sliced at the soft skin at the junction of its neck and body.

Blood gushed out of the wound, drenching her in a metallic stench. It invaded everything. Her vision was a pool of red, her mouth filled with the coppery taste, and her skin was covered in the hot, sticky fluid. She was entombed in blood. A second later, the monster fell on its side, its tail flipping a few times, its jaws snapping, then it stilled. It was dead.

She stood over the body of the beast, the ionic blade between her fingers, watching as the pool of blood grew at her feet.

A sound coming from behind her tore Rose away from her contemplation, and she stared at Karian. He wasn't unconscious, but the paralysis had crept to his arms. He lay, propped up against the rocks, his arms limp at his sides and his eyes shining in his midnight blue face like beacons.

Rose rushed to him and her lips met his, not caring for the blood covering her face. Karian returned the kiss, but his lips felt limp. He was losing his battle. She pulled away and looked as his head lolled on his shoulders like a doll's.

He was gone.

She ran her fingers along Karian's burning skin, flattening her palm on his chest. Her mind was blank until a feeble heartbeat registered under her hand. He was still alive.

The wave of relief that hit her was enough to bring tears to her eyes.

The relief shrank and melted away. Karian was still alive, but not for long. Not unless she found help, and fast. The problem was that the only help available anywhere close was the same threat they were running from in the first place. Even if it meant a lifetime of slavery, she didn't have a choice.

Karian wasn't dying on her watch.

Her first task was to get out in the open and find the pod. Her eyes landed on the beast's carcass and the ever-growing pool of blood, which had started to disappear into the sand. The threat from the monster was gone, but the smell of blood and fast-decaying flesh could be a new threat of its own. It might attract more aakvans. She was lucky to have been able to strike this one, but luck had a bitchy way of running out when its patience was tempted too much.

There was nothing to do about it, though.

Rose looked down at the still-powered ionic blade. She picked it up between slick fingers. The blood on its surface had long disintegrated, and it shone, perfect, clean, and deadly. She took a few minutes, trying to remember where they had come from, then picked a direction.

Squaring her shoulders, she pushed her pace. She was making good ground, and soon, sooner than she expected, she found herself at the edge of the plain. One last boulder to climb before she landed on the dry, bare sand.

And found herself facing a hissing, terrifying, sapphire blue giant.

Chapter Thirteen

Karian

Karian slowly became aware of the cold of the steel table against his back. His brain twisted and kicked against the darkness veiling the world, but his eyelids still refused to obey his orders. Memories rushed through the fog, and he held on to them like a lifeline. The first one was the pain. From the minute the beast bit into his flesh, pain had taken hold of him like a jealous mistress, the venom spreading through his veins, setting his muscles in stone-clad agony.

Death had wrapped its long fingers around his throat and squeezed the life out of him. That was how he was supposed to end.

Then the most annoying, disobedient female in the universe threw herself between him and his fate. From the moment her frail, tiny body stood in the shadow of that monstrous beast, he knew. He had been wrong to fight it. There was no other female for him, on any world. Damn the consequences and all that came with it. She had the courage of a dozen warriors in her small, defenseless body, and the heart to match. In fact, if he was honest with himself, he had known all along—ever since she had first burst into that escape pod—he had simply refused to see it for what it was, even throughout the agony of the mating urges.

That last memory of Rose was enough to pull him through the remainder of the fog and back to consciousness.

Karian's eyes flew open and then shut again under the harsh, white light. A moment later, his eyelids opened a sliver to allow his hyper-sensitive pupils time to adjust to the change in luminosity. Finally, he blinked one last time and turned to meet familiar light blue eyes in the middle of a sapphire blue frown.

Arlen.

He should have known his younger brother would be the one to save him. A surge of emotions whirled in him, but Karian kept them under control. He scanned the medical room, its whiteness leaving no place for doubt. Rose wasn't with him.

"Where is she?" Karian's voice was hoarse, and far less powerful than he would have liked. "Where's Rose?"

"You mean the female we found on Saarmak?" The sapphire face crinkled in disapproval. "That's the first thing that comes to your mind? A female? After everything?"

A soft shake of his head, a stiffening of his lower lip. Arlen was getting angry. Karian couldn't blame him.

"Arlen." Karian stared at the male who stood by his bed, trying his best not to lose patience. "Where is she?"

He tried to move, but a white flash of pain shot through his leg, blinding him.

He was vaguely aware of medical equipment beeping and a commotion of people coming into the room, poking him with sharp things and talking in worried, hushed tones.

Time passed like a slow river, carrying pain and worries as he fought to swim back to the surface.

"Where is Rose?" Karian asked again as soon as he came back to consciousness.

"Karian, you need to calm down." Arlen's face contorted in a concerned grimace. "We nearly lost you to the Midnight God, twice. The aakvan's isn't a venom that easily forgives."

"I need to know." Karian reached for the hand that rested on his side, near but not touching his. He squeezed it and instantly saw Arlen's icy features melt. "I owe her my life as much as I owe you."

"The female is safe," Arlen said with a softer tone. "She had some minor cuts and bruises, and needed treatment for her sunburn, as well as dehydration and general malnutrition, but she recovered fast with our medical care. She's in holding now."

As his worries for Rose's welfare subsided, Karian became aware of his surroundings. He looked at his brother, truly seeing his face for the first time in ten years.

The long years since their separation had etched hard lines along Arlen's once juvenile, carefree features. As Karian studied the familiar face, he recognized some of the old softness, a smile around the eyes, a fullness in the cheeks. Yes, Arlen was still there under the veneer of harsh military discipline, but he was no longer the careless youth Karian had known ten years ago. All the lightness had been leeched from him. Karian wondered how life must have treated his good-natured brother to turn him into the cold, controlled male he sensed in front of him.

"It is good to see you." Karian spoke softly, the words not coming easily. He wasn't used to speaking of his emotions, but he knew he owed it to his brother. "You look grown."

"Your place was not an easy one to fill. I would be lying if I said I will miss being the Commander in Chief." Arlen smiled strenuously, obviously as ill at ease as Karian with the conversation.

"How is your mate? You must have younglings by now. Is your family house close to Mother and Father's?" Karian immediately regretted his words as Arlen's face closed up.

Images of his brother's mating, of the painful fight he had had with Arlen just moments before he'd mated the beautiful female he had chosen came to his mind, but Karian pushed them down. He wanted to forget the words spoken in anger, the hurt and betrayal on Arlen's face.

"Maral is well, thank you, brother." Arlen looked away. "We have not been blessed with younglings as yet, but there is still hope."

A heavy silence descended on them. Seconds piled on each other until the weight of the unsaid words between them began to asphyxiate Karian. He had to say something, anything. "Rose was a handful, I guess." Karian chuckled, and immediately regretted it as pain ricocheted along his bones.

"She's a hell-cat, that's for sure."

Arlen's face split in a large smirk, lighting his eyes with true amusement. The tension lifted, and Karian felt the old link between him and his brother spring back, solid as ever. The years might have passed, and an old wound might still ooze blood, but Arlen was his brother and nothing could shake what tied them together.

"She bit Khal. The poor fool had to go to medical. That will teach him to be cocky around females."

"Khal is with you?" Karian blinked, frustrated at the confusion he found himself in. "He must have passed his Rite now."

"It's been two years last month," Arlen answered soberly. "He's a good warrior, but he needs to learn discipline."

Karian nodded, and silence fell between them again. Khal: his youngest brother. When Karian had left, Khal had been but a youngling, still playing with wooden swords and chasing small animals around inside the walls that protected his family's house. The weight of those ten years settled on Karian's shoulders like a stone blanket.

"Mother and Father?" Karian's eyes latched on to Arlen's. "Do they know?"

"I informed them as soon as we came back on the ship. They're waiting for you back home."

Back on Eokim. He had held on to the thought of home for so long, it seemed impossible that it was within his reach now. His old life, his impressive rise to the highest rank in the Eokian military, all this seemed far and unreal. Like it had never happened.

Karian looked around the medical room and noticed the talons and fangs banner hanging over the door. The familiar emblem resonated in his mind. He was aboard *Honor*, the jewel of the Eokian fleet, and his old commanding warship. There was so much he had to do to go back to the male he was before. He wasn't sure he ever could be that male again. Not now that he had Rose in his life.

Nevertheless, he was determined to hunt down the Cattelans responsible for the slave trade on the Eokian moon where he'd been captured.

"You left the mating without telling anyone where you were going." Arlen cut Karian's thoughts short. "We didn't even know where to start the search."

There was old pain in those words. The weight of an unhealed wound separated them, and as Karian held his brother's gaze, he realized there may not be a way to erase the cruelty of the last words they had said to each other. Or the cause for those words. No, there was no going back.

"It was a Cattelans' illegal slave market," Karian said, knowing very well Arlen probably knew by then who had taken him. "They set it on Ajnyan. It was a trap. I should have waited for reinforcements."

"Yes, you should have." Arlen looked away and his mouth stiffened. "It doesn't matter now. You're back."

Arlen stretched out those last words, and Karian knew his brother had spent every waking minute of those ten years looking, searching for him. What his family had been through would have been nothing short of a total halt in their lives. All because of him and his recklessness in front of the slave market. Guilt and shame washed over him. He would have to make it right somehow with his family—he just had no idea how.

"I never doubted you." Karian said the words with calm and warmth, knowing what it would mean for Arlen. "I knew you'd find me someday."

Karian tried to sit up, but his arms gave way and he fell back on the table. Pain shot through his leg, and the world was swallowed in a colorless misery. This time, it didn't take long for him to fight through it and swim back to the surface. When he did, two blue eyes looked right through him. It hadn't taken long, but it was too much.

Arlen thought him weak. Weakness wasn't something an Eok warrior displayed, even less so the Commander in Chief. Clenching his fists hard enough to hurt, Karian summoned his training and pushed the pain down to the bottom of his mind as a remote, unimportant fact.

"Rose. She must be kept safe at all costs." Karian growled to show his seriousness. "She's mine."

"There was no scent on her." Arlen lifted his eyebrows in surprise. "When did you mate her?"

Karian hesitated long enough for Arlen to start looking confused.

"I haven't sealed the mating," Karian had to explain. "There wasn't an appropriate time."

"Then she's not yours." Arlen tilted his head and crossed his arms over his chest. "You need to mate her, or leave her to another who will. There are a lot of interested parties already."

"No one touches her!" Karian's voice boomed and filled the room, making Arlen pale. Satisfaction rose at the sight. He was still the superior warrior, and nobody was challenging him. "Rose is mine, and you need to make it known. Anybody who doesn't respect that will answer to me."

Arlen stared at Karian, his eyes wide and his jaw clenched. He wasn't used to being talked to like that, Karian could see. Karian now needed to take back control, or he risked losing it for good.

Attempting once more to sit up, Karian pushed on his arms until he was sitting on the steel bed. This time, he sat up straight, and glared at his brother until Arlen nodded his understanding.

"Nobody on board even knows what she is, except maybe Kamal, but he hasn't said a word." Arlen's voice fell and silence wrapped around the room.

Kamal. Karian couldn't go there, not now. Maybe never. His older brother was as raw a wound as he had been fifteen years ago, when they had last spoken.

"Where is he now?" Karian kept his tone carefully neutral but a storm boiled inside him, just under the surface.

"Back to his ship. He stayed until you were out of danger, then he left," Arlen answered, his tone matching Karian's. "He's gone now."

"Of course he is."

Silence came back, the kind that was heavy with unsaid words and un-kept promises. Karian made a small dismissive gesture, signaling to Arlen to let the matter drop, and pretended not to see his brother's slight grimace. Kamal was an eternal subject of disagreement between them, and he didn't expect Arlen to rally to his side anytime soon.

Karian forced himself to focus on what mattered most. They couldn't figure out Rose was human, not before she had his protection.

"It doesn't matter *what* Rose is. Only that she's mine, and not to be bothered."

"Fine." Arlen's eyes slid to Karian's leg, still wrapped in the heavy healing cloths, and then back to his face. "I'll have her brought to the females' quarters."

"No. Bring her to my personal quarters. And make sure only Khal or yourself escort her at all times."

"Your quarters?" Arlen frowned and opened his mouth to argue, but thought better of it and shut it. "Fine. I'll relocate her in your quarters, then. I'll tell Khal to babysit her. He's going to be delighted to have her as a sister-in-law."

Karian lay back on the pillow. Arlen spoke into the transmitter on his wrist, then nodded to him. Relief washed through his wrecked body. Rose was safe with his brothers, almost as much as if she was with him. Safer, even, considering the state of his health.

"How long was I in here?" Karian looked down at the tube that fed his veins with the healing and nutritious solution.

"Three full days," Arlen answered. "Still, your recovery is impressive. I don't know how many could have survived a bite like that."

"That's because they didn't have a little brother like you." Karian couldn't fight the smile that came. "You've been poisoning my life for a lot longer than that aakvan."

"Good to see you're still the same." But Arlen smiled, a true one this time, one which reached his eyes and illuminated his entire face.

Fatigue spread its long fingers around Karian's mind again. Now that it was safe and nourished, his body wanted to replenish itself. He welcomed the sleep, feeling his eyelids becoming heavier.

"I'm only alive because the Midnight God willed it. It was incredible luck that you found us that fast."

"Not luck, brother." Arlen looked at him, his face shedding his mockery. "Rose led us to you. She killed the aakvan with an ionic blade and was on her way back to the pod for the medical kit when we found her."

Karian's head lowered on the pillow.

"Of course she did."

Sleep enclosed him, and he drifted off. His last thought before being swallowed by the dreamless darkness of the healing sleep was that he had done it. He had claimed Rose. Now, all he needed was to tell her.

Chapter Fourteen

Rose

Her legs hurt from the pacing, but she didn't care.

Rose looked at the hideous expanse of white on the back wall, where only the faintest trace of the door was visible. Karian's private quarters were luxurious by spaceship standards, but they made her feel queasy. It was too white, too clean, and too cold.

It was a stupid, bare room. No frills to be found here. Only a mammoth-sized bed in the center, flanked by a series of drawers embedded in the walls and a circular table with two chairs, all in a sterile white polymeric surface. Not a dash of color to break the damned whiteness. She was so bored she could feel her brain turning into jelly. Everything in this room screamed of a rational, military mind.

Still, it was better than the holding cell.

Those Eoks didn't lose any time. As soon as she was cleared by medical, they locked her up like a common criminal. Rose shuddered with anger at the memory of the last time she saw Karian's two brothers. Who did they think they were, anyway? Sharp words and curses were all she exchanged with Arlen. That one was as cold as a fish, and had even fewer feelings. As for Khal, he hadn't been much fun since she'd bitten him.

Neither Khal nor Arlen had deigned to talk to her since. They wouldn't even let her know how Karian was doing. She had to scream and fuss and make a general scene just to know if he was still alive, and all the information she was given was a grim nod from Arlen.

Things had changed when they'd taken her from the cell to lock her up in the white room.

Then seven more days had passed. Ten days since they'd left the Saarmak moon. Ten days since those blue hunks had found her on her way to get help, taken Karian away from her in some sort of medical bubble, and locked her up.

The sound of heavy footsteps resonated from the hallway, coming in her direction. Rose froze, then turned to face the barely visible door, crossing her arms over her chest. She stuck her chin out, squaring her shoulders in the most intimidating stance she could think of. She was ready to pummel Arlen with questions until he told her more about Karian's situation. This time, he wouldn't get out the door without giving her some worthy information.

The door slid up, revealing two tall, blue males. The first one was Arlen, cold and sapphire blue, looking at her with an ever-disapproving expression on his face, and the second… the second made her heart stop beating.

"Karian!"

Rose jumped forward, her heart following a beat behind her. Her open arms closed around a firm, warm chest, and her cheek rested on his heart, eager to hear it beating. Emotions raged inside her, emotions she had kept on a tight leash up until just now, and tears began filling her eyes. Rose let them come, and soon, she was crying against Karian's chest, not caring about anything else but the fact that he was alive and well. That he was there with her.

My Karian.

A few moments later, she realized she was holding Karian, but he wasn't holding her back. Slowly, she peeled her face from his chest to look up at two blazing blue eyes in the middle of an expressionless, midnight blue face. His features were neutral, but his eyes blazed in a way she didn't understand. Why wasn't he returning her embrace?

"Rose. I see you were well cared for." Karian tilted his head to Arlen. "Thank you, brother."

"She was not an easy female to care for." Arlen frowned at Karian. "She will have to understand the proper way to act as your mate before we get to Eokim. She is not living in a savage land anymore."

Her arms fell from Karian's sides and she silently took a step back. After a second, she added a few more steps until she stood in the middle of the room, her empty arms hanging at her sides. Words came to her mouth, words she had spat at Arlen a dozen times before, but they caught on her tongue at the sight of Karian's nod of approval. Her legs turned into rods of steel as she watched Karian thank his brother for his service to *his female*, and dismiss him. As Arlen took his leave, not sparing a single glance for her, the steel melted from her legs and turned into hot, scorching lava. The door closed, and she was alone with Karian.

Lava poured down her spine, coursing through her veins, hot as fury.

Karian stared at Rose, his unreadable face closed off. It reminded her of that first time they'd stood facing each other, in the pod. Only then, he had been in a cage. Only then, he had been at her mercy. Now, it was her turn to be caged.

"You're healed," she said in a shaky voice, full to the brim with fury. She wanted to say so, so much more. She wanted to scratch his eyes out with her nails and kiss the life out of him at the same time.

"Yes, I am now at my fullest." Karian brought his hand up and passed it over his skull, breaking the stare to look down at his feet.

Rose squinted her eyes, glaring at him until he sighed and nodded.

"I am sorry I could not come sooner to talk to you. There were duties I needed to attend to."

Oh no, you'll have to do much, much better than that.

"Duties? Duties are important. I understand duties." Rose lifted a challenging eyebrow, crossing her arms in front of her chest. "Why would you forget your duties to come see me for five minutes? Please don't let me take time away from your important *duties*!"

The last words exploded, carried away on a wave of anger. Karian didn't flinch, didn't move, but his lower lip stiffened and his eyes flashed.

He was angry at her? No, this wasn't going to go down that way. She wasn't going to let Karian control this conversation.

"So, for how long have you been healed?" She flipped her hair out of her face with a jerky, angry movement.

"I woke up seven days ago." Karian straightened. "I have been working since, although gradually at first."

Lava turned to ice at the thought that he had left her in here, alone and forgotten. Rose struggled to control herself not to scream mindlessly at him.

"Nobody told me anything. They wouldn't even let me see you when you were in medical."

"Of course not. It is not Eok custom to allow outsiders in the medical wards."

"Oh," Rose breathed. *Outsiders*, he'd said. Her mouth dried up, and her throat constricted. Did he really think about her that way? "Well, you could have at least sent word."

Silence fell between them. She knew he was an important person for his people, and after all, she had no claim to his time, or to him. A cold furrowed inside her heart, and she forced saliva down her clenched throat. What did she expect anyway? They weren't lovers, they were allies only because of a strange twist of fate. Nothing more.

"What now?" She controlled her voice to keep it flat and toneless. "What's going to happen to me?"

This was the real question, wasn't it? She was at his mercy. He could do whatever he wanted with her, no one would interfere. Would he keep his word, or take advantage of her?

"We are headed toward Eokim." Karian looked at her with a calm resolve in his shining blue eyes. "In the meantime, you are to be confined to my personal quarters for your own protection."

"And does *your female* have a say in this?" Rose put as much scorn into the words as she could, which was a lot. "Or maybe I should forget I can speak and think for myself?"

"Don't take what Arlen said to heart." Karian winced. "He's just embarrassed you kicked his ass and lived to tell the tale."

"Damned right I kicked his sorry ass." She crossed her arms on her chest. There was so much she had planned to say when she finally saw

Karian again, and now that he was there, she didn't know where to begin. "When are you going to bring me back to Earth?"

Karian flipped his head up to her, his eyes like slits. His features were twisted in a pained-angry expression. For a heartbeat, she was scared, then it was gone. He hesitated, then shook his head.

"I'm not sending you back."

Karian's voice fell with a following of heavy silence. Rose almost collapsed under the weight of what lay behind the words.

"You can't do this. My family needs me." She fought to control the trembling in her hands. She took a step closer. He had to understand, had to know how desperate she was to get back to the people she loved. "You know this."

He stared down at her, his lips pursed and his eyes unreadable.

"I can't let you go." Karian inhaled, then held his breath before continuing. "I have claimed you as my mate."

"You have what?" This, she had not seen coming. Rose was stunned and confused, but she could feel the raging inferno of anger burning down in her mind, slowly picking up speed. "So now I'm what, your property?"

"No, of course not." His eyes flashed. He was getting angry. "Eoks mate for life. The females we take are kept safe and well-cared for all their lives." Karian straightened. "I am the Commander in Chief of the armies, and heir to the chief of the Erynian tribe. As my mate, you will be the second most powerful female in the tribe, after my mother. Many would wish to be in your position."

"Okay, then why don't you go and mate someone who wants it?"

Karian's already pinched lips thinned to a slim white line. His shoulders tensed and his brows furrowed into a fearsome frown. She didn't give a shit. She wasn't property, and this mating was nothing but disguised slavery.

"If I hadn't claimed you, you would be free to be taken by any other male on board this ship. Believe me, there are lots of males who would stake their claims on you, and not in the gentlest way. Even Khal would be tempted."

Rose shut up and let that sit for a while. What Karian said dissipated some of her anger. He was right. It was easy to forget how the world saw humans when she was with him. When he was there, she felt normal, strong. She felt free. It was an illusion, of course. Rose was not free, and she certainly wasn't safe. She was a human female, and she belonged to the strongest, or the highest bidder. She belonged to anyone who was powerful enough to stake a claim on her.

Still, she rebelled against the idea of being a mere possession. Maybe even because it was Karian staking a claim on her. She couldn't accept being owned, not by him. Not after everything they went through.

"I should be your mate just so another male doesn't grab me?" Rose shook her head and lifted her eyebrows. She wasn't convinced by his explanation. "I don't buy it. You're the Commander in Chief, all you have to do is give an order, and I'm back home."

"Yes, but it will not be enough to protect your village. What I'm proposing will give the Eoks' protection to your entire family."

"How?" Rose stiffened. Hope flared, but it was tempered by confusion and a healthy dose of skepticism.

"By our laws, the entire family of any female mated to an Eok warrior is considered to be Eokian. This means your family will be protected under Eok law. An attack on any of them will be considered an act of war against the entire Eok nation."

She hadn't expected that. Surprise and hope merged together in her mind and she found herself stunned. All she'd ever cared about was going back to her family, to keep them safe, but Karian's offer was a thousand times better.

Still, it meant she was losing her freedom forever. But what choice did she have? Even if she managed to convince Karian to send her back, what real protection could she offer her family? Nothing, that was what. In becoming Karian's mate, she was giving her family safety and freedom for as long as they lived.

"What about the rest?" She knew this wasn't part of their deal, but she couldn't help it. She had to try to save everyone. "My family can't survive on their own. We need the entire village."

"I will put a motion to the Ring Council to expose the existence of free-born humans," Karian said with calm, measured words. Like this was just a conversation. Like this wasn't going to end slavery for an entire people. "It is illegal to hunt and enslave free people, has been for a century. Anyone who is born free shall remain free. Humans will even regain their rights to the Earth's natural resources."

Rose looked straight at Karian. He returned her stare, locking gazes with her. His face was a stone mask, void of any hint of emotion. On her side, emotions raged a mighty storm.

"What's in it for you?" She was breathless, and her words went out on raspy whiffs of air. "Why would you do this for me?"

"You saved my life," Karian answered, his eyes shining with an intensity she didn't recognize. "I am repaying my debt. A life for a life."

He stood straight, his hands clasped together behind his back and his legs spaced wide in a military stance. His eyes shone with a cold calm, waiting for her to say more. Rose watched him, a stone settling down in the pit of her stomach. There was no trace of the wry, darkly humorous male she had befriended on Saarmak.

You did more than just befriend him, and you know it.

The male who stood before her was the Commander in Chief of the army of the most powerful warrior race in the Ring. He had no place in his life for softness.

Still, better to be Karian's mate than any other.

"So you said to Arlen that I'm your mate, and that's it? We're mated, just like that?"

"Of course not." His gaze pierced right through her. "There's more to it than that."

"So what you're saying it's that it's a fake mating?" She did her best to keep her voice low and steady. It wasn't easy. "We're pretending?"

"No." Karian shook his head slightly, staring at her with intent. "There is no pretending an Eok mating. For my tribe to recognize you as my mate, it has to be real. Once you are my mate, there is no turning back."

His calm words settled between them. Her ears rang as if Karian had screamed. No turning back, he'd said. This was a lifelong decision, and it wasn't even one she had made. Karian had made it for her. That it was for the best was beside the point.

"As soon as we complete the Mating Ceremony, I'll send a fleet of Eok warriors to Earth to protect your village. But you can never go back. You'll live on Eokim with me for the rest of our lives."

"What if I refuse?"

Karian inhaled deeply, then exhaled. "I'll still send a fleet of Eok warriors back to Earth with you, but there will be no way for me to ask them to stay and protect your village. You will be on your own. I won't have the legal standing to make a motion before The Ring."

Rose nodded. She knew what would happen, then. They would be found, sooner or later. Now that the Cattelans knew there was a human village still out there, they would be relentless. It was only a question of time.

Only now, it didn't have to be. All she had to do was accept Karian's offer.

"Okay, then." She swallowed and wiped her sweaty palms on her pants. "I accept."

Karian stared at her for a long time, then nodded. After another pause, he turned and walked to the door. Before going out, he turned his head halfway.

"We are going to seal the mating when we arrive on Eokim."

Rose watched the door for a long time after Karian was gone.

Chapter Fifteen

Rose

A few days later, Rose was in the midst of another pacing contest when there was a loud, single knock on the door. It slid up to reveal a now familiar sapphire blue face, grim as usual. He stayed at the doorstep, unmoving.

"Arlen." She stopped in front of him, crossing her arms over her chest. "Please, come in."

"Nice to hear you with better manners. How refreshing."

Arlen stepped in, and she looked around, bewildered by his empty hands.

"I don't have your dinner, if that's what you're thinking. Not that it's my job to serve food anyway."

"Of course not." She lifted her chin. "Someone might think you're at my service. That wouldn't do."

"No, it wouldn't. You might not care, but I have been acting as Commander in Chief for the past ten years." His mouth tightened. "I am now the Second in Command of the Eok fleet, not a female's servant. I am here to tell you we arrive on Eokim in an hour."

"So soon? Why didn't Karian come to tell me?" She couldn't care less about Arlen's ego, or that he didn't like being her little errand boy.

"He didn't have time." Arlen opened his mouth to add something, then closed it.

"Don't lie to me." Rose narrowed her eyes at him, trying to read what he was hiding. "I can see straight through you. What happened?"

"It's not for me to say why." Arlen stiffened, anger flashing in his eyes. It was always so easy to get at him. "Something came up, but Karian's taking care of it."

If anything, she had learned that about Eok culture: they were loyal to the bitter end. Arlen wouldn't tell her anything if Karian told him not to. With what she hoped was an intimidating frown, Rose chose not to press him. It was like trying to squeeze juice from a rock, anyway. Arlen wouldn't talk.

"Am I coming with you to meet him?"

"Yes." Arlen turned to go, but stopped and turned his chin toward her. "He cares about you. More than you seem to know, and certainly more than he should. Don't ever betray him."

With that, he walked away, and she had to skitter across the floor not to lose sight of him. The ship was still an odd sight, one she hadn't become accustomed to. It was a complete battle station, one of the pride of the Eok nation. It was Karian's old commanding ship, and the one Arlen had claimed for his search for his brother.

The hallways and floors of the Eok ship were nothing like the Cattelans'. Where the slavers' ship had been white and cozy, the Eok warship was a model of military efficiency. The walls and ceiling were metal panels, without paint and unpolished. Instead of a string of soft yellow lights to make the way clear, there was a pathway of harsh white flood lights, stripping every corner of the least bit of shadow, making people appear sick and flat.

She hugged herself as she followed in Arlen's long footsteps. Her heart fluttered and her knees were weak. Nervousness was eating at her. Rose hadn't seen or talked to Karian since agreeing to mate him, and she wasn't sure how he expected her to act in his presence now that they were virtually engaged.

As they walked, every warrior they passed eyed her with inquisitive, searching expressions. They knew who she was, but not necessarily *what* she was. If they knew she was human, they would have been far more stricken. As she went, all sorts of nefarious scenarios traveled through her mind.

Maybe Karian had changed his mind. Maybe he was sending her back to Earth after all?

Arlen finally stopped in front of a large four-panel door, which slid up without so much as a squeak.

There, in a full half circle of glory, was the dizzying vision of a glowing green orb. This was planet Eokim, home to the Eok warriors. This was to be her new home as well. The sight filled her with a strange mixture of fear and elation, making her heart flutter and her stomach constrict. Their journey was over. A new life was waiting, one she knew nothing about.

The reality of that life slapped her across the face and she found herself breathless. She had accepted the mating with Karian without hesitation when she knew she would be saving her family, and possibly the entire village by doing so. She didn't doubt he would treat her well, and she would spend a lifetime in comfort, but she hadn't allowed herself to picture that life. Now it was in front of her, so close, yet so far. Somewhere on that green globe was Karian's house, Karian's family and friends. Karian's entire world was waiting.

In front of the glass wall, his broad back to her, stood a tall, midnight blue male. Karian was fine looking in his Eok uniform: tight-fitting synthetic leather black pants and vest. The fabric of the pants hugged his muscled ass and thighs, and the vest outlined the perfect triangle of his shoulders. He exuded power and masculinity. Every time she saw him, her insides churned with desire.

"Rose!" Karian turned from the view and smiled at her. "I wanted to talk to you before we land on Eokim." Karian walked up to her and took her hand in his, then looked up at Arlen. "Thank you, brother. You can leave us now."

"Remember what we talked about, that's all I'm asking." Arlen exchanged a look with Karian, and something passed between them.

Karian's smile stiffened, and the corner of his eye twitched, but he stayed silent as Arlen took his leave. After the door sealed behind Arlen, Karian's hands closed on her shoulders.

"We're going to land on Eokim in a little less than an hour." Karian's smile melted down imperceptibly. "There's a change of plan from what I wanted to do originally. We're going to have to get to the Tribe Hall immediately."

"Okay." She nodded, suddenly suspicious. "Why?"

"The Mating Ceremony will take place as soon as we land." His face was all serious, and his voice was authoritative. "A mating doesn't need a ceremony to be official, but in our case, having witnesses is essential."

"So soon?" Rose swallowed through a closed throat.

Karian straightened and his face set in stone. "The Mating Ceremony is to proclaim our union publicly to the tribe, and to the rest of the Ring."

A chill traveled down her spine. She had given Karian power over her destiny, at the cost of her freedom in order to ensure her people's safety. This was what she was afraid of, having Karian take her ability to make decisions away. Already, she could feel her relation to him shift from what it had been on Saarmak. She wasn't his partner anymore. She was his mate, his subordinate.

"You're doing this to facilitate the motion to the Ring." Even though it wasn't a question, his slight nod answered her. "Why didn't you talk about this with me?"

"All you have to do now is be my mate." Karian's face remained expressionless, but she knew him enough to understand he was deadly serious. "You can trust me."

"I guess it's a relief."

But it wasn't.

Rose shifted to the side and took a few steps toward the window that panned to give a complete one hundred-and-eighty degrees view of the planet.

"So this is Eokim?"

"Yes, this is home." There was so much longing in those words, Rose felt guilty about shedding a shadow on his return. "There is little time. You need to prepare for the descent."

"I own nothing but the clothes on my back. There's nothing to prepare."

Karian came to stand behind Rose and two hands settled on her shoulders. Her heart surged at the contact, delighting in the comfort and safety it procured. She noticed another ship approaching the surface, not too far behind the Eokian warship.

"That doesn't look like an Eok ship." She pointed to the ship, and Karian's hands clenched.

"That's because it's not." His hands retreated. "This is a Ring diplomatic ship."

"What's it doing here?" Her words lacked oxygen and her voice died before finishing her question. Because she knew. "They heard about me?"

Rose turned to face Karian. His mouth was thin and his eyes shone like stone, betraying nothing.

"Yes," Karian said. "I had hoped not to frighten you with this. There is no danger. I have claimed you as my mate. By Eok law, you are Eokian, as well as your family. The Mating Ceremony will simply give it more political power. Many people will attest to having seen a free human mate an Eok warrior."

Rose stayed silent a few more seconds. Were things ever going to be easy? She had already given away her freedom, she had nothing more to give.

"Okay, so let's do it." She lifted her eyebrows. It was a no-brainer. "What's that Mating Ceremony anyway?"

"The mating is a public bite, so everyone sees the bond." He looked at her with what seemed like an apology in his eyes.

This won't be good.

"A bite? Like an actual bite?" Rose's hands closed around her arms in an involuntary self-hugging gesture. She remembered the feeling of Karian's fangs on her skin the last time they had kissed, but had never thought he would actually bite her. Had she? "You've got to be kidding me."

Karian inhaled deeply, like he had already prepared his answers for her questions.

"The first bite between a couple releases a complex venom that enters the female and male's bloodstream and activates the link between mates. The effect on the couple is only a by-product of the venom."

Rose lifted her brows, urging him to continue. He couldn't stop there.

"The Mating Venom is highly aphrodisiacal. It'll make us, well, crave each other until we seal the union."

Rose pondered this for a few seconds.

"So we'll be horny for a while." This wasn't exactly a surprise. She remembered the feeling that had made her skin crawl with erotic pleasure each time Karian kissed her. This Mating Venom was probably to blame. "That's all?"

He stared at her for long seconds before turning around to contemplate his homeworld.

"That's all you need to know."

An hour later, Rose was sitting in the two-person transport flying across the Eokian landscape toward the Tribe Hall. Eokim was a green planet, nothing like the arid desert of Saarmak. There were no forests, but a lush cover of shoulder-length grass blanketed a land made of rolling hills, with the barren teeth of a jagged cliff here and there.

In the distance, a lonely river marred the monotony of the grassland like a blue snake.

"Your world is beautiful," she said truthfully. "I'm happy it's so green. I don't think I would have loved a desert world like Saarmak."

As the transport floated over the grass, she noticed something.

"Do you have towns here?"

"We live in family units, with a house for each couple, surrounded by a stone wall." Karian pointed to the round rooftop of a structure in the distance. "Eokim is a wild planet, with many predators lurking in the grass, looking for easy prey. Inside the walls, females and younglings are safe, but you must never wander outside alone."

"I'm used to predators lurking around!" Rose chuckled, but when Karian turned to her with a serious expression, she relented. "Very well, but I don't think you have anything worse than our bears and mountain lions!"

"Eokim is a rich planet, with plenty of large and small beasts. We have prides of killkons on this side of the Long Lake. They're not to be underestimated, especially in this season when the herds of meerits have migrated for their youngling season."

"I do hope I see some of them one day."

"You have your whole life to see killkons, and as for a meerit, my mother always keeps one as a pet."

Rose remained silent at this. Her whole life, he had said. She let her mind go blank, staring at the green beauty of the wilderness. It was soothing to allow her worries to seep through, unattended. The last few weeks had been a raging hurricane of dangers, and these brief moments of safety were a balm on her strained nerves.

"There!" Karian pointed in front of the transport. "The Erynian Tribe Hall."

She followed Karian's finger and lost her breath. There, amongst the tall grass of the plains, stood a round enclosure, large enough to fit a hundred of her villages back on Earth. The ground was made of polished white stone, and in the center towered a castle-like building that appeared to be carved out of pure night. As they approached fast, she realized the castle was made of dark blue stones, with speckles of white and purple. It had a tower with a rounded roof, and a series of arched windows ran from the ground to the top floor on all sides. It was a stunning building, and in the dimming of the setting sun's light, it seemed to sparkle.

Karian's transport hovered over the wall and stopped in the middle of a large lot. Rose waited as he jumped out, then walked around to help her down. As she landed beside him on the stone ground, four figures stalked toward them.

"Father!" Karian opened his arms and bear hugged the tall male in the center of the group. "Uncles! Cousin!"

While the males hugged and greeted each other, Rose stood behind, flapping her hands at her sides self-consciously.

"There's someone I want you to meet." Karian turned and grabbed her by the shoulders, pulling her alongside him. "This is my mate, Rose. Rose, this is my father, Enlon. These are my uncles, Argen and Wyrl. And this is my cousin, Erlock, Argen's youngest son."

The four males looked down at her, curiosity and amazement clear on their weathered faces. Enlon was easily identifiable by the markings on his skin. He had the most of the three older males, marking him as a superior warrior, a force second only to his formidable son, Karian.

Argen and Wyrl looked strikingly similar to Enlon, but when her gaze slid to Erlock, Rose paused. He was different from the others, and when she looked more closely, she understood why. His face was deprived of the scar pattern the other warriors displayed with pride. After a while, Erlock's eyes narrowed and he straightened, understanding she had noted the absence of warrior's patterns on his body. Rose quickly looked away and smiled, but she got the impression her slight wasn't going to be forgiven by the male. This one had a resentful streak in his eyes, and the way his gaze grazed her body made her want to cover up more than the synthetic cotton clothing did.

"Nice to meet you," she managed to mutter without melting down and disappearing between the cracks of the stone ground.

"Welcome to the Erynian tribe." Enlon gave her a large smile, so like Karian's that her guts twisted in warmth. "From the bottom of my heart, dear."

"Welcome," Argen and Wyrl said in concert.

"Thank you."

Karian gave his family another shoulder slap before turning to Rose.

"Now, let's get you to my mother."

The inside of the Erynian tribe ceremony hall was as splendid as the outside, with floors of pure white stone, polished and reflecting the light on those walls made of night. Rose's small steps sent muffled sounds in between the clacking of Karian's boots as they walked in the long hallway.

"Here. I have to leave you before this door." Karian turned her so she was facing him. "Don't worry. Mother will take great care of you."

"Okay." Rose swallowed nonexistent saliva as her throat and mouth suddenly dried up. "I trust you."

Karian locked gazes with her, then his fingers closed around her chin and he gently lifted it. Not breaking the stare, he planted a kiss on her closed lips, then withdrew. His eyes flashed wildly for a second before he turned and walked away.

As Karian disappeared behind a corner, the heavy door creaked and Rose turned to stare at the radiant smile of a strange creature.

"You must be Rose!" the creature said in a soft musical voice that sounded more like a song than speech. "I'm Arlia, Karian's mother. We are all so excited to meet you."

Arlia was only slightly smaller than Enlon, and her heavily muscled frame was made even more impressive by the lacy dress draped over her shoulders and tied with a delicate bow on one side. Her physical strength contrasted strongly with the softness of her voice, and Rose couldn't help but stare at her with wide eyes. Her face was round and her nose large and flattened, with high cheekbones. The overall effect gave her a graceful, feline appearance. Her skin was a soft muted yellow, as were her eyes and hair, which was long and wavy, brushing her waist in a heavy cascade. Arlia was a golden beauty.

Compared to her, Rose felt like an insect on the wall.

"It's very nice to meet you, too."

Arlia smiled and took Rose's hands in her much larger ones. Her skin was soft and warm, and it calmed Rose's worries.

"Come now, my dear, let me present you to the others."

Arlia stepped sideways and motioned for Rose to enter a large room. There, she waved her arm to include about three dozen females, all standing around and peering down at Rose with various emotions ranging from degrees of curiosity to open hostility. All of them wore gowns and various other exotic clothing, clearly designed to be elegant. They were from a great number of species, and it made Rose's head swim to stare at the different eyes, skin, and features on all of them. Some had scales and long, lizard-like arms and legs, some had a covering of fur on every inch of their bodies, and at least one had an extra pair of limbs, which she folded under the first set as she stared at Rose with pitch black eyes.

Rose couldn't help but wonder if they saw her being as strange as she perceived them.

Arlia pulled her along and presented her to each female, stating the name of the male she was mated to and his station in the tribe. Soon, the names and faces blurred until the string of strangers became a faceless mixture. Finally, only one group of females remained, and as Rose stepped forward, the fog lifted from her brain. These females were tall and slim creatures, and they walked toward Rose with a deliberate grace.

"Avonies," Arlia whispered in Rose's ear. "This is Elvira." Arlia pointed to a small creature to the right. She was the color of morning dew, a liquid white with a sheen of pure silver. Elvira was a stunning creature, and although she met Rose's eyes with a scowl on her face, her vivid dark violet eyes didn't hold the hostility of the others. "Willa, Illya."

Arlia paused then gestured to the female in the center of the group of Avonies. "And of course, who could forget Maral."

In the center of the group of Avonies was the most beautiful creature Rose had ever seen. Her skin was a silvery white, shining and luminous like the inside of a large sea shell. She was smaller than Arlia, and her frame was delicate and elegant. She wore a dark silver gown that hugged her slim body closely, and her thick black hair hung heavy on her shoulder in an intricate braid, showing two pointed ears. Her large purple eyes had vertical pupils that shrank when she stepped closer, and she stared down a straight nose at Rose, her nostrils flaring in distaste.

She looked like a butterfly, and had the predatory stare of an eagle.

"Maral is Arlen's mate. Now that Karian has returned, she is mate to the Second in Command of the Eok fleet." Arlia talked with measured words, and Rose had an inkling those two weren't exactly on good terms. "They have been mated for ten years now."

"I met Arlen on the warship." Rose forced a smile on her face even though what she really wanted was to hide behind Arlia's skirts like a child. "He's very lucky to have a mate as beautiful as you."

Maral's lips lifted in condescension, and she tilted her head at the compliment.

"So, this is what a human looks like." Maral's fluted voice stabbed through the air like a crystal arrow. "I don't see what all the fuss is about. There's not much to it, really."

Maral shot a disdainful look at Rose, taking in the plain synthetic cotton pants and shirt, wrinkled from the trip and hanging shapelessly around her body. Anger flared inside Rose, red hot and burning. So she wasn't wearing a sparkling gown, and her hair was a rat's nest on her head. After the last few weeks she'd had, Rose bet Maral wouldn't look her best, either.

Rose opened her mouth to answer a few chosen words to this alien bitch, but Arlia squeezed her upper arm, cutting the flow. Maral was provoking her, the least she could do was to return the favor.

"Thank you." Rose gave her a brilliant smile, and was rewarded by a constricting of Maral's vertical pupils. "And don't worry, I'm sure the novelty will pass. They will go back to admiring you in no time."

Maral's eyes flashed a dangerous glint of pure, undiluted hatred, but she kept silent. Beside her, Willa and Illya squinted their eyes, looking like they wanted nothing more than to wrap their long, fine fingers around Rose's throat and squeeze the life out of her. Rose shot a fleeting glance at Elvira and the Avonie flashed her a wry smile, but it was gone before she could be sure of what it meant. For all she knew, Elvira was looking forward to a bloodbath as a distraction from her pampered life.

"Follow me." Arlia brought her hand to Rose's shoulders, smoothing the goosebumps under her warm palm. "It's time."

Then Arlia turned and walked to the door that Rose knew lead to the stage where the mating ceremony was going to take place. Suddenly, her throat closed and her heart beat stronger and faster. Beyond those doors, her life would be forever changed.

As Rose passed by her, Maral gripped her wrist. Her long fingers were cold and her grip surprisingly strong.

"Don't think you won, human," Maral hissed, her tiny fangs inches from Rose's face. "Savor being the mate of the Commander in Chief while you can."

"Let go of me before I rip your eyes out of your face," Rose whispered softly enough that only Maral and the other Avonies could hear. She was surprised at the savage possessiveness she felt. "Karian is mine."

"Be careful what you wish for, then." Maral glared at Rose, her poisonous stare like invisible acid.

She whirled around, then stalked gracefully away, disappearing before Rose came to the realization that she might have escaped the dangers of Saarmak and the Cattelans, but she was nowhere near safe.

And she had just made a new enemy.

Chapter Sixteen

Rose

The stage was a semi-circle of stone so black it seemed like it absorbed the glow from the large orbs of golden light hovering ten feet above the floor. The orbs cast a golden shine across the faces of the audience, revealing eyes alight with curiosity and excitement. The air was heavy with the taste of arousal coming from so many bodies pressed together to witness her joining to Karian.

They weren't here for just a regular mating. They were here to witness the exotic mating of a creature thought to be extinct and the most powerful warrior in the tribe.

This was the most exciting spectacle of their lives.

Rose stepped to the stage, conscious of the flowing of her new gown around her body. Although she was incredibly grateful to Arlia for the opportunity to change, she felt awkward in the strange clothing. Rose wore a long, flowing gown made of layers of sheer fabric in progressive shades of yellow and pink, tied in a knot on both shoulders. She fussed with a stray curl that had escaped the fancy headdress Arlia had made her wear. It was an intricate gold piece, covered with gemstones and silver ornaments, trailing through her hair like a river, making the curls appear tamed and purposeful instead of unruly. The rest of her clothing was as magnificent and foreign as the headpiece.

Rose took her first step onto the platform and shivered at the cold of the stone on her bare foot. The stone wasn't just absorbing the light, it was gorging on the heat from her body as well. Another step brought her into the golden light from the orbs, and a wind of excitement traveled across the audience. Looking down at herself, she stifled a smile.

The light was dancing on the fabric of her gown, making the yellow and pink shimmer, so that she appeared soaked in pure sunshine. She smiled inwardly at the thought of Maral, sitting there, watching her coated in the color of sunset, being admired by everyone.

She must be gritting those tiny, sparkling teeth to the bone.

Finally, Rose walked to the middle of the stage, alone, as instructed. She turned her head, scanning the audience for familiar faces. Males outnumbered females by a ratio of at least five to one. The females were scattered across the place, watching with eyes ravenous with curiosity, but also edged with a hint of tension.

A door opened at the far end, and a tall, midnight blue figure walked on the stage with the grace of a mountain lion. Rose's breath caught and her heart lurched at the sight of him. Karian was male power made flesh, dressed in loose black pants and a sweater made from a shimmering fabric that glimmered gently under the golden orbs. She admired the magnetic pull of him, from his square shoulders down to the muscles of his chest and the roll of his thighs. His face was set with strong lines, too strong and masculine to be pretty, but calling to her in the most primal way. Her belly quivered and heat spread between her legs.

It's the Mating Venom, nothing more. My body craves it, but I'm still in control.

Rose stared at Karian as he walked toward her, his movements fluid, too agile for any human, and yet full of power. The tug in her belly grew and grew until she had to fight an urge to run to him and wrap her legs around his waist. He stopped inches from her, towering over her, his eyes shining in his unreadable face.

A rumble went around the audience, excitement and anticipation filling the air, covering her tongue with an aftertaste of lust. Her nipples were hard and erect, protruding from the wispy fabric like beacons. Her body was responding to him and he hadn't even touched her.

Then he moved.

Karian's right hand cupped her cheek as his left arm wrapped around her waist, pulling her closer. She was trembling, her every sense on high alert. He lifted her chin, and she blinked at what she saw. His eyes were a blue more intense than she remembered, almost shining with a light from within. As they rested on her lips, a shiver ran along her body, like thousands of fingers running over her skin with exquisite erotic tenderness.

The audience was transfixed, exchanging whispers and gasps. Comments in low, husky voices traveled from person to person. Rose turned to watch an endless succession of strange faces, flushed with anticipation, eyes shining and mouths halfway open. They were there to see. They wanted to witness.

Rose risked a glance at the first row of spectators. Maral was there, at Arlen's side. Rose's gaze locked with a purple glare, angry and flashing a row of small, wicked fangs in a hateful grin. Next to them were Arlia and Enlon, looking like they had swallowed a swarm of hornets.

They shouldn't be surprised. Something isn't right.

Rose's throat clenched and panic took hold of her bones, making her feel as though they were made of water. Her vision blurred, invaded by tiny specks of darkness, threatening to wash reality away.

"Focus on me." Karian brought her eyes back to him, and the twirling blue in his irises grew enough to cast shadows on his cheekbones. "There is only the two of us here. Nobody else."

"That's not true." Her words were scattered with shivers. "I'm scared, Karian."

His lips landed on Rose's. The contact flashed, intense and entrancing. Karian's tongue pushed through, probing the entrance to her mouth, and she immediately opened it to allow him in. Her tongue slid over his teeth, stopping on his fangs. A tiny bit of pressure, and the Mating Venom tickled her taste buds with its tart and spicy cinnamon taste. In the next instant, the Mating Venom rushed into her bloodstream, making her damp with want. The faces of the crowd faded to a hidden corner of her mind, shrinking in the face of her mounting need for Karian's body.

Karian broke the kiss and locked gazes with Rose again. His eyes were two slices of heaven.

"My mate." His voice was layered with a deep, primal possessiveness. There were worlds of promises in those words. Her heart pinched at the thought of the life that would never be. Karian didn't love her.

He was mating her because he owed her, to repay her for the life she had saved.

Stupid, stupid girl. Don't dream. He owns you, he doesn't love you.

The thought made her strong enough to pull her heart out of the way, allowing only the erotic, inescapable pull of his body on hers. If she allowed her mind and heart to be fooled, she was going to be lost in the sensation of him. Already, she was his all the way to the core of her bones, to every cell in her body.

"Be mine." Karian brought his eyes closer to hers. They were shining, casting a blue light filled with a want so deep, it made her head swirl and her heart race. "Rose. *My* Rose."

"Yes." Rose gave her answer, unable to resist. If she were damned for it, she couldn't resist. Everything in him made her crumble and fade to dust with desire. "You're mine. My mate."

Then his mouth was on her again, and there was no place for words. The crowd faded, then disappeared, hidden behind a veil of passion like no other. Her freedom was slipping out a little more every time he kissed her. The worst part was that she didn't care at all.

Karian broke the kiss and went to stand behind Rose, his chest molded to her back. Muscular arms enveloped her. As she was surrounded by his body, her breathing became fast and shallow, her skin prickling, hyper-sensitive as she was aware of every inch of it touching his.

Karian's mouth closed on her neck and soon his tongue caressed the skin, taunting it. Heat spread where the Mating Venom covered her skin, generating an influx of sensual sensations along her body, spreading a trickle of pleasure deep down in her belly. His hands closed on her stomach, pulling her into his warmth. His arousal was hot and hard on her back, filling her with a hollow ache for his flesh that made her core clench and scream for him. Rose wanted him, all of him.

The crowd was heavy with silence.

Rose closed her eyes to them, not wanting to allow anyone in to the center of sensation that was her physical connection to Karian.

His fangs slid down from her throat to her shoulder, grasping the fragile curve between his powerful jaws. The tickling of his fangs became more intense and she knew he was getting ready to bite. A flutter of fear arose at the idea, but it was quelled under the intensity of the pleasure brought by the venom. This was going to seal the mating and render public what was a lifelong commitment.

Karian's fangs sank into her flesh, triggering a flood of Mating Venom to rush through her bloodstream. Instantly, Rose's pleasure exploded, unruly and savage, making her scream, thrust her head back and arch her upper body. The sensation spiraled, multiplied, sending wave after wave of complete ecstasy through her, one after the other.

Rose was still panting when Karian pulled his fangs off her.

Slowly, her mind shed the fog of pleasure. It was like she had been in a tunnel, with only Karian at the other side. Nothing else had mattered. Nothing else had existed.

The first thing to come into focus was the sounds. Shouts and comments, hundreds of voices, talking all at once. Excitement and disbelief transpired through the sound of the crowd, but she didn't dare look, not yet.

Disbelief and confusion jostled side by side in her mind.

When she opened her eyes again, it was to stare into the bottomless pit of a blue so intense, it burned her thoughts before they had a chance to form.

Something had happened between them, something she couldn't define. She could see it in the way Karian held her tightly to his chest, facing the crowd over her shoulders. He was panting, too, and she could feel the muscles in his perfect chest moving under his sweaty skin, rippling with tension.

The crowd went silent, and a palpable wind of tension filled the air. Rose's eyes caught on a pair of purple irises, shining in hatred and surprise, and something akin to hurt.

Behind her, Karian was panting. No, Rose realized, he wasn't panting. He was filling his lungs in a succession of deep breaths like he was going to swim underwater for a long time. He stopped and his hands grabbed hers, then he extended her arms fully, presenting her to the crowd. His throat started to shake, the vibration coming from low in his chest, so strong her entire body vibrated in tandem with him.

Then a sound like no other filled the air.

It was somewhere in between a roar and a lullaby, possessive and masculine, yet strangely poetic. Rose didn't need to ask what he was doing. Karian was stating his claim for all to hear.

The sound went on and on, impossibly long, inflating to a level so loud she tried to put her hands over her ears, but Karian's grip on her wrists was of concrete.

The crowd was a landscape of silent statues, their faces a mesmerized blank. Rose's gaze locked with Arlia's, and the other female clutched the star-shaped pendant on her chest, her face a mix of violent emotions.

Then the mating song stopped.

Karian panted behind Rose. Slowly, strong fingers liberated her wrists.

As soon as she was free, Rose flipped around to face him. His eyes were shining, casting a blue glow around his face, and he seemed flustered, and a bit stunned, too. Their gazes locked, and it was like she was punched in the guts. There was something in those blue eyes, a depth of emotion she didn't understand. Then it was gone.

Karian straightened, then faced the crowd.

"So be it known that I, Karian, son of Enlon of the Erynian Tribe, take this human female as my bloodmate, from this day until my last."

Karian turned to Rose, locking their gazes together again. His jaw was tight and his lips pressed together in a cruel, hard line. Gone was the illusion of warmth and affection. His entire body radiated power and male strength. The intensity of his stare burned through her, slipping through her bones and settling in the pit of her stomach. Without a word, he turned and walked away, his back straight and his biceps bulging as he stalked out of the ceremony hall in a handful of long strides.

Rose was left blinking, alone on the stage, watching the closed door.

What just happened?

The crowd erupted. Everyone was talking at the same time, shouting, and causing such chaos that Rose didn't even notice Arlen until he jumped on the stage and stalked up to her. His face was a mask of anger so violent, she was tempted to turn around and run away. Before she could give in to the impulse to flee, Arlen grabbed her upper arm in a steel grip, forcing her to face him.

"Do you have any idea what he did?" Arlen's eyes threw knives. "You'd better not betray him, Rose, or you'll have me to answer to."

Without giving her time to respond, Arlen stormed out after Karian.

She was left alone for the second time on the stage, with a few hundred pairs of eyes on her, ranging from curious to outwardly hostile. Most of them were stunned, and a few even had the wimpy, teary look of someone who had just witnessed the most romantic thing in their lives.

A movement attracted her attention back to the edge of the stage. Arlia and Enlon were standing there, a few paces away from her. They, too, had climbed on the stage after Arlen. Enlon's face was unreadable, but Arlia wore her emotions as clear as daylight.

She was as angry as she was scared.

In a cutting fashion, Arlia motioned for Rose to come to her. Rose hesitated only an instant, then walked to the couple, wary of their new attitude toward her. Clearly, things hadn't gone the way they were supposed to go. Both of them had been happy about the ceremony, Arlia especially. Now they looked like they wished she had never been born.

Rose passed in front of Enlon, who watched her with calm, calculating eyes before walking after his two sons. Arlia motioned for Rose to follow with a sharp jerk of her chin, then started to walk without talking.

"Wait!"

Rose caught up with Arlia as she reached the door at the back of the stage. Arlia grabbed her arm as she walked out, too fast for Rose's shorter legs, so Rose was forced to jog behind her.

Anger flared inside her, muffling the confusion and fear to a hollow sound in the back of her head. Whatever their reason for being angry at her, they weren't being fair.

"I said, wait!"

Rose stomped her feet solidly into the ground, forcing Arlia to either stop or drag her like a ragdoll. Arlia swirled, baring her fangs in a blood-curdling hiss. Rose took a step back but didn't cower away. She was too angry, and too confused, to have the good sense to be scared.

"Why are you doing this?" Rose controlled her voice to a normal level, but she was dangerously close to losing her temper. "What the hell happened out there?"

"You don't know." It wasn't a question. Arlia said this to herself, almost like she was reminding herself why she wasn't ripping Rose's throat out. "Of course you don't know."

A long shiver ran along Arlia's body, as if she was shedding her desire to shred Rose to pieces. She blinked a few times, her beautiful golden eyes losing the dangerous glint coating them.

"Tell me," Rose pushed her again, reassured they weren't going to resort to violence. "Why do I feel like Karian did something he shouldn't?"

Arlia stared at Rose, her golden eyes filling with a glow of tears that threatened to spill at any moment. Pressing her lips together, she took a deep breath, then nodded to herself.

"It's not for me to tell. Wait there, Karian is going to come to you."

When Arlia turned around and walked away, her steps weren't as fast. Rose watched her leave, a growing unease in her chest.

Chapter Seventeen

Karian

Karian stormed down the long hallway, ignoring Arlen's shouts at his back. His blood was boiling with a lust so violent it was a miracle he wasn't insane by now. The struggle to keep control of the emotions that filled him to the brim with an impulse to run after Rose was a losing battle.

The cravings were only going to get more intense, and the only way to subdue them was to give in and join with her. The physical union would have to wait. He didn't trust himself in Rose's presence yet. Karian needed to calm the storm of primal urges that had taken hold of him the moment the mating bite was given. In his current state, he might hurt and scare her, and he would never allow that.

A bloodmating. How can it be?

He should have been more aware of his extreme reaction to Rose, he should have been more careful. But even then, how could he have predicted it? It didn't matter. Prediction or not, there was nothing he could have done to avoid taking her as a mate. He knew that now. The attraction leading to a bloodmating was not meant to be ignored. He would have scourged the entire Ring to find her if she had gone away after they met.

He wouldn't tell her, either. Not when she thought he'd taken her only because of duty.

A hand closed on his shoulder and Karian turned, fangs hissing with fury.

"Calm down, brother." Arlen removed his hand and took a step back.

"I'm calm," Karian growled, low in his throat. "I'm going to the meeting room, that's all."

Arlen didn't answer, but by the way he raised his brows, it was clear he wasn't fooled by his brother's attempt at denying the truth. With a loud sigh, Karian shook his shoulders, unknotting his muscles.

Without talking, he walked again, but at a more measured pace. Arlen followed, his silence a comment in itself. Karian was already deep in his own thoughts, sharpening his focus with all the discipline of a lifetime of rigorous training.

Karian and Arlen entered the meeting room, where Enlon and Khal were already waiting for them. Also present were his uncles, Argen and Wyrl. Together, they represented the higher council of the Erynian tribe. Their faces were serious and the large screen that panned the back of the room showed a sleek ship adorned with the Ring's emblem on its hull.

The Ring's diplomatic ship was a bad omen, one that gave clues that Rose's presence on Eokim was already known.

"What news of the Ring's ship?" Karian's voice had his usual steel-cutting edge, and it satisfied him to know that even if his mind was a swamping madness, his exterior didn't betray him. "They didn't have authorization before entering our airspace."

Arlen's face was set in stone, no emotion visible on his once carefree features. His younger brother was at his side, and for once Khal kept silent. His father's face was serious, but Enlon stared at his newly mated son with unusually soft eyes. Of all of them, he was the only one who understood what having a bloodmate meant.

"Obviously, they were warned of your mating," Arlen said. "People are going to start asking questions, and we'd better have answers—and soon. This isn't just any other female. She's human, Karian. *Human*."

"I know she's human, but she's also my mate." Karian's voice was a low growl. "*Bloodmate*."

"The entire Ring thinks humans are extinct except for the few that are kept in the breeding facilities for genetic preservation purposes. Only a few specimens are approved by the Genetic Preservation Board to be sold, and we all know the prices they sell for." Arlen spoke calmly, his hands flat on the dark stone of the table. "She's a novelty. She's the biggest scandal since the wiping out of the last Algoic specimen two centuries ago. We can't pretend as though she's just like any other."

"Her status is protected, no matter what." Karian set his eyes on Arlen. His brother's was the finest strategic mind of the tribe, and Karian often wished he understood all the gearing and workings of his brain. However, he didn't need to, as he trusted Arlen as much as he trusted himself. Eok loyalty ran deep, even more so between brothers. "Whoever is on that ship knows they can't take her away."

"Perhaps," Arlen conceded. "How did you came by this human? She had to have a buyer, somewhere. The Cattelans don't meddle with fruitless trade."

"Rose was born free. She was never a slave." Karian talked softly, but there was no mistaking the deadly edge in his voice. "Her parents were from a group of humans who escaped the breeding facility twenty-three years ago. They have been living free on their homeland for over two decades."

A stunned silence followed Karian's explosive declaration. Enlon's eyes widened and he brought one hand over his mouth. They all understood the implications of this.

"I will put a motion to the Ring for Rose and her village to be recognized as free humans," Karian said in a decisive tone.

"If you succeed, the humans will fall under the homeland law, and they will gain a protected status inside the Ring," Arlen said with a dead tone. "Their trade will become illegal."

"Someone will lose a fortune," Enlon said. "We need to know who we're going up against."

"Who is aboard the ship?" Karian turned to his uncle Wyrl, the commanding officer of the tribe's communications.

"Trade Minister Knut made a formal request for an audience with Enlon an hour ago." Wyrl patted the long scar traveling down his face, his eyes lost in thought. "He's the director of the Genetic Preservation Board, and his family is the one controlling the natural resources extraction on Earth."

"Of course. It all makes sense now." Enlon nodded. "The Knut is the most powerful Avonie clan after the royal family. If the humans gain a status in the Ring, they'll lose everything."

A thick dread settled over the assembly. The Avonie civilization wasn't a warrior one, but their connection by commerce made them powerful. They had numerous allies, both inside the Council of the Ring and around many other nations. They were officially allied with the Eok nations, but merchants didn't share the warriors' sense of honor.

"But what do they expect to gain by coming here?" Khal spoke for the first time. "The mating has already taken place. There's nothing they can do about it."

"They didn't plan on Karian making a public mating so soon, and certainly not on him taking a bloodmate." Arlen took a deep breath. "They were probably going to claim the human escaped, or was stolen from the facility. If she's a slave, then it changes her status. There are precedents for this. You would have to pay her price or give her back."

"She is bloodmate to the Commander in Chief, my son." Enlon spoke with an even voice, but Karian sensed the undertone of steel. "They know we'll never give her back. It would mean war."

"War, yes." Arlen nodded, his face as still as stone. "Or simply a debt the nation could never repay."

Silence fell over the males sitting at the table. Karian felt a surge of anger roiling inside his mind, filling him with a cold, calculated hatred.

"Khal." Karian turned to his youngest brother. "I am tasking you to go to Earth with a detachment of warriors to find and protect Rose's family. I trust you will take care of them as if they were your own."

"Of course." Khal's face glowed with fierce joy. "Thank you, brother, for giving me a chance to prove myself."

"Kamal is already on his way," Arlen said, as low as a whisper, but it was enough to cast a deafening silence around the table. "I have received word he will be arriving on Earth in two weeks at the most."

Karian paused, not wanting to ask more about his older brother. Finally, he nodded to Arlen. "I'll meet with Minister Knut." Karian flattened his palm on the table. "He doesn't get to talk to the Erynian tribe Chief without the proper diplomatic dispensation. The Eok nation isn't a weakling under the Ring's thumb."

After a few more minutes, Enlon left with Argen and Wyrl.

As soon as the door closed and his father had left, Karian felt the wave of feelings overcome him in a way that was completely contrary to all his training. He got up and walked back to the sitting room where Rose was sure to be waiting. He shouldn't have left her alone, especially if their enemy was as powerful as the Trade Minister.

There's nowhere safe now. She's in constant danger.

Arlen walked beside Karian in the long hallway.

"You know he will do everything in his power to stop you from even putting that motion in front of the Ring Council?" Arlen spoke first. "Minister Knut is a wealthy, cunning male. He's not going to let you rob him of the trade that made his family rich beyond all others so easily."

"He hasn't won yet," Karian reminded his brother. "He's not the only cunning male in the Ring."

Arlen gave Karian a rueful smile. "You know I'm with you. Always."

"I know."

They finally arrived in front of the door. The brothers faced each other, their gazes expressing what words couldn't. How Karian had missed his family: their constant support and the trust he could not give anywhere else. So much had happened since he left, so much time he would never get back. Karian would have to make amends to his brother somehow, but it would have to wait until Rose was out of danger. She was the absolute priority.

"Are we going to talk about it, or are you going to pretend it didn't happen?" Arlen leaned on the door, blocking Karian's way.

"You're talking about the bloodmating." Not a question.

"Obviously." Arlen scowled. "Does Rose know what it means?"

"No, she doesn't." Karian glared hard at his brother. "And she won't until I tell her."

Arlen answered Karian's warning glare, his lips pinched in a tight, angry line. He disapproved, that much was clear. "She needs to know," Arlen insisted, not willing to let go that easily. "She can't think this is a normal mating. Karian, there hasn't been a bloodmating in the Erynian tribe since Mother and Father."

Karian nodded. He knew. Bloodmating was a once in a generation occurrence, something that happened only when an Eok warrior found a female so perfect for him that he made her a part of himself. It wasn't something an Eok planned, it was something that just happened.

Something he had never thought would happen to him. Something that changed everything.

"Saving Rose is the only thing that counts."

"Yes, it is." Arlen inhaled deeply. "Now, I'm going to go make sure my own mate is well. I haven't seen Maral in four weeks."

Arlen stood aside and Karian pushed open the door.

Inside was a tall, slimly built male. Trade Minister Knut was waiting for him.

"Minister Knut." Karian stood in the doorway, leashed violence traveling down his body in successive waves of frustration, coating his tongue with a veneer of bitterness.

Karian's gaze went to the back of the room, where two tall figures stood at attention, their faces carefully devoid of emotions. Ilarian guards, the best warrior species there was—after the Eok. Trade Minister Knut had chosen his bodyguards well.

Minister Knut was sitting at a small round table, a glass of everfresh juice in his long, elegant fingers. The shining liquid shone softly like a precious stone. Drinking such a liquid was an ostentatious display of wealth and power, with a single glass costing more than the annual salary of most high-ranking officers in the Eok army. It was a message, sent directly to intimidate Karian with his wealth and power.

Dark purple, almost black eyes locked onto Karian, ruthless and cunning. The Avonie male had pale, almost white skin, and his slim body was clad in a traditional diplomatic Ring outfit, with white synthetic silk pants and a coat buttoned to the neck with the Ring emblem embroidered on his chest: a string of planets linked by a chain.

Yes, this was the Ring. As much a protector as an oppressor.

"Commander Karian." Minister Knut tilted his head and his thin lips stretched in a glacial smile, exposing small, wicked teeth. "It is nice to see you have recovered from your unfortunate encounter with the Cattelan outlaws."

"An *unfortunate* encounter?" Karian felt his blood boil and curdle in his veins. "I was kept in a cage for ten years. It seems a little more than unfortunate to me."

Minister Knut nodded in apparent contrition, which made Karian's anger all the more burning. A dreadful suspicion insinuated itself in his mind, making him want to close his fingers around the sleek white neck of the Minister and squeeze until his life ran out.

He knew all along. He's the one behind the slave market. He knew I was in that cage, and didn't lift a finger to stop it.

The thought made Karian dizzy with a hatred that ran deeper than anything he felt for the Cattelans. Minister Knut wasn't some low-life, amoral slaver. No, he was a rich diplomat, with enough power and wealth to keep an entire medium-sized city comfortably for a decade. He had no need to amass more riches, no need to betray an old ally other than to feed a perverse greed.

Traitor. You sold me for a sack of gold.

"Why have you come?" Karian's voice was calm and flat, betraying nothing of his feelings. "I have a hard time thinking you came all the way to Eokim simply to make sure I'm well."

"As relieved as I am to learn of your safe return to your homeland, it is not." Minister Knut took a careful sip of the precious juice and smacked his lips in apparent delight. "I am here on a purely business matter, I am afraid."

Yes, that's what I'm afraid of, too.

Karian nodded, then made a small gesture for him to continue. He wasn't going to sit in the company of that treacherous male.

Just as the Minister was about to talk, there was a commotion on the other side of the door. Feminine voices rose and the door opened to reveal a stunned, angry looking Arlen and a flushed Rose.

"What's happening here?" Rose stalked into the room, her flowing gown moving around her body. "I've been waiting for over an hour. Nobody told me anything."

The fluid, revealing fabric glided over the curves of her body, hinting at the treasures Karian knew were hiding underneath. Minister Knut's dark stare fixed on Rose's moving body, sliding over her with an owner's appreciation.

A growl grew in Karian's throat, an instinctive reaction to another male looking with envy upon his mate.

"There she is," Minister Knut said, his lips pursing in delight. "Commander Karian, you have my eternal gratitude for taking such good care of my property."

Rose stopped dead and stared, wide-eyed, at the Trade Minister. He answered the stare with an opening of his arms, as though he expected Rose to come and take refuge in his embrace.

That was more than what Karian was able to endure.

Karian growled viciously and came between Rose and the Trade Minister, shielding her with his body. A male hand closed on his arm, and he was secretly grateful for Arlen's presence. Attacking the Trade Minister while he wore the Ring's diplomatic colors was a sure way to lose his life. Of course Minister Knut knew exactly what he was doing in provoking Karian.

A quick glance at the two Ilarian guards in the back revealed that they hadn't moved, but their hands were on the hilts of their ionic swords, ready for any signs of impending violence. Yes, Trade Minister Knut knew exactly what he was doing.

"Who are you?" Rose's voice was strained, and Karian knew she was fighting not to let it break. She stepped aside and faced the Trade

Minister. Her eyes were dark and brewed with a storm from within. She knew already. He saw it in the way her fragile limbs were stiff and her jaw was clenched, making the jugular vein in her neck pulse with anger.

"Do not worry yourself, dear." Minister Knut stood up, his fine suit falling in clean lines over his slim body. "Tension is not good for your fragile human body. I do not want to have to put you in medical isolation when I bring you back where you belong."

"Nobody is bringing my mate anywhere!" Karian's growl turned into a roar at the last word. "You have no authority here."

"On the contrary." Minister Knut turned glittering eyes to Karian. "This female is a prime specimen, one that is worth a lot of money to me. I am merely claiming back what is mine."

"I'm not your property," Rose exclaimed, her tone turning from uncertainty to anger. "I'm nobody's property."

Karian closed his eyes at this, then, when he opened them again, he set them on the smug smile of Minister Knut. This was exactly what the male wanted to hear. That she wasn't his.

"Rose, keep quiet." Karian glared at her with as much authority as he could. She flinched, and hurt spread over her face like she'd received a blow. His heart constricted at the sight but he had no choice. "The human is mine under our law. I have mated her in front of witnesses. She cannot be taken from me."

"But she was not free to be claimed." Minister Knut's smile vanished and a frown formed on his brow. There was nothing left of the sophisticated, mild-mannered diplomat. He waved to the two Ilarian guards waiting in the back. The two males took wary steps toward their master, their silver eyes steady on Karian and Arlen. "She is a slave, and unless you can pay her price, I am afraid she will have to be repossessed."

"I'm not a slave. I never was." Rose's voice came again, and even after Karian growled at her, she kept talking. "I am a free human. I have been all my life."

Minister Knut pursed his lips and reached for the rest of his ever-fresh juice, emptying the cup before speaking. He kept his gaze fixed on Karian.

"There are no free humans." He lifted his pointy chin. "That one is the property of the Human Breeding Initiative, unless we can come to an arrangement. A good businessman is always ready to compromise." Perverse enjoyment leaked from every pore of the Minister's body. "Information can be extremely valuable. Enough to free you from the debt you will contract if you refuse to hand her over."

"I know what you're going to say, Trade Minister," Karian said. "And my answer is no. I won't give you the location of the human village."

"Well then," the Minister said, the faint black lines of his pupils reducing to hairline fractures in the dark purple irises. "I will be expecting full payment, or the return of my merchandise by the end of the cycle." An evil pursing of his thin lips exposed white fangs over skin of alabaster. "As a token of good will, I won't even charge you for the enjoyment you had of her body so far."

The words hung in the air for a second, then a furious female cry ripped through the air. Rose rushed to the Minister, her hands in front of her, her fingers curved to scratch eyes and skin. It was only the reflexes born of a life of rigorous training that made it possible for Karian to grab her before she laid a hand on the Trade Minister. That she was ignorant of the Ring's laws wasn't going to be an excuse if she faced a capital sentence. There was no mercy to be expected from the Ring.

"Leave while you still can, Minister," Karian growled. "You have overstayed your welcome on Eokian soil."

With one last assessing look at Rose, the Minister calmly walked out of the room.

Chapter Eighteen

Rose

The door closed on Minister Knut's back with a clean, muffled sound, and Rose turned to Karian, fury coursing down her nerves like sparks of electric fire.

Mad wasn't even close to describing how she felt.

"You should have stayed silent!" Karian's face contorted in anger when he turned to face her. "You have no idea what you could have done."

"Are you for real?" Rose glared at Karian, transposing all her pent-up anger to him. "You're saying this is my fault? That I should have been a good little *slave* and shut my mouth?"

"You're not a slave." Karian's eyes shone with fury and his mouth had a cruel edge. "You're my mate. You should trust me to do what's best for you."

"How could I trust you when you tell another male that I'm your property?" Her voice rose, and by the end of the sentence, she was screaming. "That male told you I was a slave and all you could say was that I was yours, not his? This isn't what I signed up for. I'm nobody's property."

"You're mine by law," Karian raged. "You have to obey when I give orders."

"Are you listening to yourself?" Rose felt hot, angry tears burn her eyes and it took all her willpower not to let them fall. "I should never have trusted you."

Karian's mouth closed to a painfully tight line, tendons ran lines of tensions in his neck. He took a step toward her, and she stifled her impulse to step back. She wasn't backing down, not this time, not ever. Not when he betrayed everything she fought for.

"By saying you're not mine, you're only complicating things." Karian spoke with barely held control. "Minister Knut is searching for any way to invalidate our mating. He claimed you were an escaped slave, and that I had no right to claim you as mate. All he cares about now is to recover you and to find out where the rest of the free humans are."

Rose sustained Karian's glare, her chest heaving up and down in fast, jagged succession. Forcing her breathing to return to normal, she let the meaning of his words enter her mind. She realized she wasn't angry with him. She was scared and confused, and more than a little hurt at the idea of being a mere possession, but she wasn't angry with him. Not when he had sacrificed his own chance at happiness to repay the life debt he had toward her.

"So, he is the one?" Rose asked softly.

"That was Trade Minister Knut," Karian answered. When he looked upon her again, all traces of anger had left his face. Instead, he looked worried and tired. "He's the Ring's Trade Minister, as well as the director of the Human Breeding Initiative. He owns the human breeding facility, and he's the one who approves all sales of human specimens. His family owns all the rights to the Earth's natural resources."

"That's why he says he owns me." Rose felt a terrible calm settle on her mind. The person who possessed control over the fate of those trapped inside the breeding facility was always so clouded in shadows that she had begun to envision him as a bogeyman, a creature larger than life, and more terrifying. Now that she knew the face of her enemy, it left her cold. "He's the one who's trying to find my family and enslave them."

"He's incredibly powerful, and he's richer than you can possibly imagine. He's going to try everything he can to prevent me from putting that motion through the Ring, and believe me, he can do a lot, even here on Eok soil."

The strange cold lifted and Rose felt a new savagery fill her mind. "We should kill him." The words were soft, but what she felt was anything but. She could almost feel her satisfaction at ending the smug Minister's life. "Before he leaves Eokim."

"That's what he hoped I would try today." Karian shook his head. "He was wearing the colors of the Ring—as a diplomat. Prime Councilor Aarv's punishment would have been fast and merciless. Hundreds of thousands of Eok lives would have been lost. Females and younglings, the elderly, it wouldn't have mattered. There is no pity for those who defy the Ring."

"How could the Prime Councilor of the Ring do something so hideous?" Rose stared with horror at Karian. "How could he hurt helpless children?"

"Prime Councilor Aarv isn't a he. She is the matriarch of the Mantrilla." Karian's gaze turned serious, and Rose had the distinct feeling she should be afraid. "The Mantrilla have little in common with species like ours, who nurture their young and live in mated pairs. Every decade, each female lays a hundred eggs, and their young prey on each other until only the strongest remain. Their males are few and weak, and generally do not survive the sexual encounter with the females. They revere power and strength. Prime Councilor Aarv will have no qualms about killing Eok younglings."

Silence fell between them, and Rose contemplated the horror of what Minister Knut was willing to do to protect his wealth.

"He's a monster." She talked with a closed throat, her voice a barely audible whisper.

Karian nodded. "This is who we are dealing with. He might not be a warrior, but he's ruthless, and will stop at nothing to keep what he believes is his."

"What happens if he wins?" Rose hugged herself. "What of the people in my village, my family?"

Karian stayed silent, but the hard line of his mouth softened. Pity and sadness showed in his eyes.

She didn't need Karian's answer. She knew. If there was no motion in front of the Ring's Council, there was no protection for the humans living free back on Earth. For a motion to even be considered, proof was needed. The only proof was Rose. If anything were to happen to her, the humans would be lost.

The weight of the responsibility that lay on her shoulders felt like a blanket of lead, making it hard to breathe. The immensity of the task Karian had committed to for her sake made her head dizzy. She didn't understand why he had decided to help her so. By rescuing her from Saarmak, he had already repaid his debt. By tying his life to hers in a mating, he was now as much a target as she was.

The Trade Minister wouldn't abandon the search, not now. It was only a matter of time before the village was found. Her only hope was that Karian's people found it before the Minister. Even then, they would protect only her close family: her mother, her brothers. She wasn't even sure Eokian law would protect Aliena, as she wasn't a blood relation, but she had been a part of Rose's family since her own mother died, leaving her an orphan.

"Don't worry, Pretty Thing."

Karian's tone was calm, but there was a fire burning underneath his words. Now that his anger had subsided, Rose recognized the telltale signs of arousal in his fiery blue eyes, in the way his gaze lingered on her face, her lips, her throat. He was the warm, stunningly attractive Karian from the pod again. The one who had made her feel safe and protected. The one who had regarded her with respect and admiration. Rose felt the tingling of desire wake in her body.

"I won't let anything happen to you, or your family. Soon my brothers will find your village."

Karian reached for her, and she gratefully nestled her head in the hollow of his neck. Rose closed her eyes and allowed herself to rest in the scent of him. It soothed her, allowed her gnawing fear to subside to a manageable level.

"I trust you." She twisted in his arms, and wasn't surprised to feel the hard push of his arousal.

Heat spread in her body, concentrating between her legs, making her burn with a craving that had nothing to do with the dangers ahead.

Karian's hand slid to the small of her back and his fingers spread, pushing softly on her body to press her against him. His warm mouth closed on the tender flesh of her neck, and an inferno of desire coursed along her nerves, making her skin prickle with heat and raw, untamed lust.

Chapter Nineteen

Karian

*M**idnight God, she feels good.*
Her smell was in his nostrils, her soft body molded to his like perfection. His instincts rose unbidden, and Karian felt the urge of possession rise up, wild and violent.

He reigned in his most primal instinct, knowing the savagery of his desire would hurt his new mate, make her fear him. He would not suffer the fear of him in her eyes, would not allow it. He would never hurt her, was unable to. Rose was the oxygen in the air, the color in the sky and the fabric of life itself.

He wanted to take her, make her body bend to his will, and feel her quiver with rapture. He wanted to hear her scream his name in ecstasy.

As Rose's hot breath caressed his body, Karian raged against his desires. The savagery of the Mating Venom was filling his veins, and even though he had planned on returning home before he sealed the union, he knew he couldn't wait. Not now that she was hot and melting in his arms.

"Rose, slow down." He lifted his arms from the small of her back, allowing her to step away. "We should wait until we're safely home."

"You've already mated me." She lifted her head to him, and those storm-gray eyes raged thunder straight to his soul. "I'm already yours."

Her breath brushed his lips, and Karian's seed stem twitched painfully, his seed sacks tightening. He had to explain it to her. He wanted to tell her about the bloodmating, the wonderful, terrible truth of it. She deserved it. She was so hot, so pliable and full of passion. He had to tell her, give her the chance to push him away.

Karian opened his mouth to talk.

And closed it on her lips.

Rose answered his kiss, pushing her soft, pliable mouth against his. Her lips parted, and the invitation sent a shock of lust into his brain. Karian took possession of her mouth, his demands aggressive, masculine in their absolute quest for surrender. Her taste invaded him, driving him to the edge of his wild desire. She tasted so good. Spicy and sweet, fresh and rich. Rose was layers upon layers of heaven.

Karian pushed his stiff stem against the supple skin of her stomach.

Rose moaned in his mouth, and her small hands ran over the muscles of his back, leaving flashes of heat in their wake. It was becoming harder and harder to breathe normally. He was drowning in his lust.

"Rose, if you want me to stop, you have to say so now." The words came out, and as he said them, he wasn't sure he could stop even if he tried. "I won't be able to later."

"I don't want you to stop." She whispered the words, her small hands running along his biceps. "I won't be able to bear it if you stop touching me."

"You're so soft." He closed his eyes. "I want you so bad it hurts."

"I want you too. Take me, Karian, take me now."

"No," he said, smiling at her willingness. "I will not take you so easily. I have pictured taking you since the moment I saw you enter the escape pod. I will make you scream my name, then, when you think you can't take any more pleasure, I'll make you forget who you are."

Rose began to talk, but he silenced her by taking her mouth again. There was no more room for words. Karian invaded her mouth with his tongue, a precursor of the possession to come. Rose moaned again and pressed her stomach on his stiff stem while her hands closed on his buttock.

He brought his hands up, his talons fully extended, then ripped the sheer fabric of her gown. She gasped when he looked down at her round breasts, where the dark, pink nipples stood, erect and hard. He dove in, closing his lips around the tiny nubs, then sucked greedily while his other hand closed around the second breast. Karian kneaded the soft flesh, at the same time sucking and flicking his tongue on the other breast. Rose was breathing hard, her chest arched for him.

When her moans became pained, he took pity on her and switched, attacking her other breast with his hungry mouth. She felt so good, was so aroused. The smell coming from her drove him wild, made his stiff stem pulse and ache with anticipation. He wasn't going to give in just yet, though. He wanted her completely satisfied before he entered her body.

Her smell grew and grew, invading his nostrils. He couldn't resist anymore, he wanted to taste her.

Karian lifted her in his arms, and she wrapped her legs around his waist, grinding her sex on his stem. He laid her gently on the stone

VENOMOUS CRAVING

floor under him. She stared at him with her large, stormy eyes darkened by desire.

"I want to look at you." His voice was a growl. "I'm going to see all of you, then I'm going to lick your sweet essence until you come for me."

She didn't answer, but her chest heaved faster. That was all right, she didn't need to talk. She watched as he parted the fabric, revealing the ivory skin of her stomach. His eyes locked onto the dark, soft cover of hair hiding her moist, warm heat. This was the origin of that wonderful, intoxicating smell. His fingers sought the feeling of her sheath, and his stem ached to feel her tighten and squeeze around it.

He licked his lips in anticipation, then lowered himself over her body until his face was over her sex. His fingers ran up along the silken length of her thighs until they reached her sensitive lips. She gasped when he parted them, exposing her inner folds. She was glistening with her juices.

Karian flicked his tongue on her nub. Her taste was stronger down there, wild and spicy, driving him mad. He dove in again, closing his lips on her, sliding his tongue up and down, from her sheath up to the bundle of nerves giving her pleasure. Rose jerked her hips upward, whining softly under the sensation.

Midnight God, she was so sensitive, so responsive. No wonder males had waged wars to obtain one of these females.

Rose's pleasure was building up, intensified by the mating compound responding to him, heightening her pleasure. He reached with his finger and inserted it into her soft depths. She gasped and her walls clenched his digit, sucking it in with convulsive motions. She was ready to shatter for him, release all that sweet essence he had dreamed of since that first time he had touched her.

"That's it, Pretty Thing, come for me."

"Don't stop!" she urged him on, moving her hips around him. "Please, don't stop."

Karian dove back in, sucking and flicking his tongue on her nerve knot. On instinct, he reached with a second finger, stretching those soft walls, then rubbed the inside of the nerve knot, attacking it from both sides. Rose screamed, the sound filled with ecstasy as she released her pleasure, again and again, until she finally collapsed.

"You're mine. My mate."

Karian climbed on top of her, then grabbed her knees and brought them up, opening her channel to him. Rose stared, her eyes cloudy with her recent pleasure.

He lowered his face to gaze at her. She stared back, silent and unmoving.

Lowering his hips to position the tip of his stem at her entrance, he allowed his instincts to take over, lowering his mouth to her neck, flicking his tongue along the soft, sensitive skin. He could feel her heartbeat under his tongue, the vein pulsing, her arousal making it beat faster.

He ran his tongue lower, following the bloodstream to the round of her perfectly white shoulder, to the exact spot where he had bitten her a few hours ago. There, his tongue lapped at his mark on her skin.

"I can't wait anymore," she moaned in his ear. "Please, don't make me wait."

Her words broke the strange fascination the pulsing blood vessel had for him. Karian's hands clenched on Rose's hips, steadying her under him. He controlled his breathing, opening his mouth to encase the tender flesh between his teeth.

He let gravity push him down, the tip of his stem stretching the entrance of her female sheath. She was so hot, so wet and inviting, but he wanted to be careful, not hurt her in his haste. Slowly, he moved further inside her, and her slick walls enclosed his engorged flesh until he had impaled her to the hilt. His seed sack was tight against her skin, pulsing with a need to mount her with a savagery he could barely contain. Soon, he wouldn't be able to control it.

Rose moaned again, pushing her hips up against his shaft as her walls quivered around him. Her pleasure was already building up again, with the Mating Venom raging through her.

Karian pulled back until his stem was nearly out, then pushed in again in one slow motion. Rose responded by pushing back, increasing the contact. Mating Venom rushed through his body, making his mind whirl with the desire to bring about his own release. He wouldn't, though. He wanted her to have another release before he had his own.

Judging by the way her walls quivered around his stem, it wasn't going to be long now. He gripped her hips tighter, and dug his fangs into her flesh without breaking the skin.

Just then, she exploded. Rose arched her back and screamed her pleasure, grinding her hips against his pounding stem. She screamed and squealed until she finally settled, her pleasure spent.

His seed sack was painful and full and, at last, Karian gave way to his desire.

Karian pounded harder, faster, deeper, allowing his instinct to drive him. One final push, and he embedded himself deep inside her body, releasing his seed with a powerful roar.

Rose yelled in rapture as the Mating Venom in his seed forced her into yet another orgasm. They rode the ecstasy together, sealing the mating that tied their lives together.

When his seed sack was empty and their pleasure was spent, Karian pulled up and stared into the striking gray eyes of his mate.

My bloodmate.

The word felt like it was always meant to be.

"What was that?" Rose spoke with a shaky voice. "This was incredible."

"We are mated." Guilt washed over him, tempering the elation of the pleasure they had just shared. He should have told her about the bloodmating. "Your body and my body will always crave each other, and no other."

She swallowed, her eyes wide and dark.

"How?" Rose licked her lips and moved, so he lifted himself up from her and settled at her side. The physical loss sent a stab of pain through his chest, and he appeased it by holding her close to his body.

"We are now tied together, you and I. The Mating Venom that links us makes it impossible for me to desire another female, and you shall never have pleasure with another male, for as long as we both live."

"So it's always going to be like that?" Rose brought up her hand and cupped his cheek. The contact jolted him with a rush of desire. "What about if we're apart?"

He controlled a wild impulse to hiss in fury at the notion of having her far from him. The chemicals that linked them would only make this worse over time. He needed to let her know, warn her before she made a mistake that made her frightened of him.

"Now that the mating is done, every time we kiss, or even touch, the compound will activate our lust... until we consume it." Karian made a point of speaking slowly, to control his mounting desire to take her again. "If we spend too much time apart, the call for one another will make us weak with it. I can never be too long away from you, or you from me."

"I don't understand." Her eyelids became heavy as lust grew inside her, too. "Arlen spent weeks away from Maral, and he didn't seem weakened by it."

"Some matings are stronger than others," Karian said, knowing he should explain the bloodmating, but not wanting to break the wonderful intimacy of the moment with his revelation. "Young mated pairs tend to have a stronger link."

She nodded, then her face lit up in a teasing smile. "How do any of you have time to be fearful warriors, then?"

Her leg ran up his side, making his stem hard again.

"Do not worry yourself," he growled down her mouth, taking it with a hungry kiss. "The mating lust subsides, little by little. In a week or so, we'll be able to go about ten minutes between matings."

"A week?" Rose looked at him with wide, scared eyes, breaking the kiss. "I can't have sex that long! I'll be sore before this day is over."

Karian laughed, and she punched him playfully on the shoulder.

"You idiot! I believed you!"

"A male can only hope." He took her mouth again, flipping her underneath him in the same motion. His hard stem pushed at her entrance, already craving another union. "But no. We will live a perfectly normal life after this day."

After that, there was no need for talking.

Chapter Twenty

Rose

Three hours later, Karian and Rose were flying over the Eokian grassland in the direction of Karian's family house.

"Your family will wonder where my gown went." Rose flattened her palms on the pants of her old synthetic cotton clothes.

"We'll just tell them the truth." Karian turned to face her, a mischievous grin on his lips. "You couldn't get enough of me."

Rose laughed and punched him playfully in the shoulder. It felt so good to be relaxed and close to him again. To gain back the Karian she had met on Saarmak, not the Commander in Chief. It gave her hope for a future together.

"There!" He pointed in front of the transport. His face was split in a large grin, and he looked like a giddy child. "It hasn't changed a bit."

Rose followed Karian's finger. There, amongst the tall grass of the plains, stood a round enclosure, large enough to fit all of her village back on Earth. The ground was covered in small stones and clumps of vegetation. In the center was a formidable dome slashed with openings, which she immediately understood was the house. The dome was made of a white material that looked like clay. There was no door, only an oversized entrance flanked by an ornate arch. On the sides were oblong slashes, clearly intended to be windows, and through which Rose could see a cozy interior. From the central and larger dome departed long hallways leading to other, smaller domes, fashioned in the same manner.

It was an impressive way of building a house, and spoke of the depth of the relations between the members of a family, as they all lived under the same roof.

Karian finally flew over the wall and inside the enclosure, into a large open area where another transport was waiting. Rose paused while Karian jumped out to help her on her feet. As she landed beside him on the ground, Arlia and Enlon came out of the house and walked toward them, strained smiles on their faces. Following Arlia, with constant exuberant jumps, was a strange creature resembling a small horse, with long, flowing white fur.

"Father!" Karian opened his arms and bear hugged him, then almost submerged Arlia in his embrace. "Mother!"

Arlia closed her eyes and hugged Karian for a long time, her face torn in a storm of strong emotions. Finally, they broke away from each other and she cupped Karian's cheek in her hand, caressing the skin with her thumb in a loving gesture that was all too familiar. Karian had done the same to Rose at times. Seeing so much love churned emotions inside Rose that threatened to overflow, and she had a hard time suppressing the trembling of her lips.

"You've got a new meerit!" Karian bent down and allowed the creature to sniff his hands, then rubbed its head with apparent affection. "What's this one's name?"

"That's Maak," Arlia answered with a laugh. "He'll be one year this month. He's quite the little rascal."

The meerit left Karian and lifted its head to stare at Rose. It had large, deep blue eyes and long lashes over a snout resembling the beak of a duck, giving it a mellow, sweetly comical appearance.

Rose smiled at the creature and extended her hand to it. The meerit bounced forward and lapped at her hand, its entire body shivering with excitement. Rose laughed, unable to restrain herself in front of the creature's obvious good nature.

"He likes you," Arlia said with a smile. "He doesn't always take to strangers."

"Well," Rose straightened up and watched Maak bounce to Arlia's side, "I like him too."

"Welcome to your house." Karian grabbed Rose by the shoulders, pulling her alongside him. "This is the house where I was born, and where our own first youngling will be born."

Karian's parents looked down at Rose with warm, generous eyes. She was reassured that their attitude was no longer the same as it had been after the mating, as she didn't think she could have stood to live in a house where everyone hated her.

"Welcome to our home." Arlia smiled and reached for Rose's hands in her much larger ones. Her skin was soft and warm, and it felt good to touch her.

"Thank you."

Rose watched with a pinch in her heart as Karian's parents turned and walked toward their house. Enlon's arm circled his mate's shoulder with a tenderness born of long held affection.

As Rose followed them inside the house, Karian's arm around her body, she wondered if she would ever share that kind of easy, warm love with her new mate.

An hour later, as the second sun was fading over the grassland, the family was sitting at the table for their first meal together.

On the long table was an impressive display of food. It was more than Rose had ever seen, even in her village's Fall Harvest's feast on a good year, where the does were fat and the garden had yielded loads of produce. On the table were roasted meats, steamy grains, and heaping plates of vegetables dripping with tasty sauces. It was dizzying to see, and her stomach contorted painfully at the sight.

The only one who seemed be immune to the contagious atmosphere was Maral. She sat with her back straight and her eyes darting heinous looks around, eating tiny morsels fit for a songbird. She turned the food on her fork a long time, eyeing it suspiciously before bringing it to her mouth, a perpetual air of distaste on her lips.

Rose had never disliked a person more in her life than she loathed Maral at that table. How dare she turn up her tiny, beak-like nose at the feast Arlia had worked so hard on? Was she always like that? How terrible it must be for them all to live with a creature like her.

"Is it good enough for a human palate?" Maral spoke for the first time since she'd sat at the table. "This is a feast worthy of a bloodmating."

"Hold your tongue," Arlen cut her off. "It's none of your business."

Maral fell silent and looked at Arlen with narrowed, resentful eyes.

The clacking of forks on the plates was the only sound filling the sudden, heavy silence. Rose's gaze went from Enlon to Arlia, but they kept their eyes stubbornly on the food, chewing each morsel scrupulously before swallowing. They didn't want to answer her stare.

For once, she was eager to hear what Maral had to say.

"A bloodmating. What is that?" Rose asked, measuring her words. Karian dropped the piece of meat that hung from his fork with a wet splash. All eyes went to Rose, wide and uneasy. Maral's glimmered with unveiled satisfaction, and she shoveled a blood-red piece of meat between her tiny, pointy teeth.

"Don't concern yourself about that." Karian tried to smile, but it came out as a sneer.

"I'd like to know."

All eyes skittered away from Rose.

"It means you're special," Maral spat out the words. "And that Karian had better do his best to keep you safe."

Karian dropped his fork on his plate, splattering sauce on his clothing.

"I thought that was always the case." Rose frowned, then turned to Karian.

"Of course it is." Karian lifted his eyes to Arlia, who smiled tightly and nodded.

"Now, dear," Arlia chipped in. "You should eat more. You're way too thin."

A light chuckle of approval ran across the table. Rose stared at them, refusing to be led away from what was obviously an important piece of information.

"You don't know about the bloodmating, do you?" Maral's amused voice cut through the air, light as a diamond blade. "Well, let's just say that more than just *your* life hangs in the balance now."

"What are you talking about" Rose snapped her head to Maral. "Who else is in danger?"

"Maybe all of us are!" Maral hissed, the sound furious between her wicked, small teeth. "We were all perfectly safe and free before you brought your problems here."

"Humans weren't." Rose bit out her answers, swallowing what she really wanted to say. "My family wasn't. They're scared, and cold, and hungry. They're hunted, hunted every day!"

"With your presence here, you've made us all a target," Maral spat, her crystal voice as cold as her eyes. "Now all they need to do is get rid of you to cripple the whole tribe."

Karian turned and hissed at Maral, all fangs out. Both Enlon and Arlia blanched. Maral recoiled, gliding her chair away from the table, as if she were preparing to run for her life at any moment. It wouldn't surprise Rose at all if she had to.

"You'd better stop talking about things that don't concern you," Karian hissed at Maral.

"I don't want her inside our house." Maral stood, her face full of anger, twisting her delicate features into an ugly mask. "She's a liability."

"Shut up, Maral," Arlia spoke from where she sat, her face neutral but her singsong voice shaking with repressed anger. "This is not your home, it's mine."

Maral didn't answer, but pinched her lips and shot Rose a poisonous glare, then fled down the long hallway to her private quarters.

"I apologize for Maral." Arlen stood as well. "She must be tired."

Arlen turned away, not waiting for an answer from the people at the table. He walked to his private quarters, his broad shoulders slumped and his head hanging down like under a heavy weight. The silence that followed was loud with unspoken words. Everyone continued to eat, but the cheerful feeling was gone.

"When are you going to put the motion to the Ring?" Rose turned to Karian.

"Soon." Karian sighed when Rose frowned. "The next Council isn't for another two weeks. We have to wait until then."

"What are you we going to do until then?" Rose hugged herself, unable to push the fear away. Two weeks was a long time, anything could happen to her until then.

"Khal and Kamal are doing everything they can to locate the village." Karian picked up another bite of meat. "In the meantime, all that matters is that you're safe."

"No! That isn't what matters to *me*," Rose said, a bit more forcefully than she had wanted. "What matters to me is the village full of people who could end up in chains any day. What matters to me is my *family*."

"There's nothing I can do for those people." Cracks were beginning to appear in Karian's cool veneer. His eyes were shining with anger and a vein pulsed at his temple in a steady staccato, ready to explode at any moment. "Ensuring your safety *is* within my power, however, and I fully intend to do it."

"Even if it means keeping me here against my will?"

"Yes!" It was Karian's turn to snap. "Even if I have to lock you up in our bedroom and tie you to the bed."

"I'd like to see you try."

Rose stood straight, the chair clattering on the floor behind her, her shoulders quivering under the intensity of her emotions.

Karian looked at her, his face an unreadable mask. Rose slid a glance at Enlon and Arlia, who both looked purposefully at the food in their plates. Shame burned her cheeks at the scene she'd made in the presence of Karian's family, and she immediately regretted her words.

The clean sound of wood sliding on stone broke the silence as Karian stood up, wiping his mouth neatly before laying the napkin beside his half-empty plate.

"I think we will retire to our private quarters now." He shot a strained smile at his parents. "Thank you, Mother, for the wonderful feast."

"Yes, thank you very much." Rose forced the words through clenched teeth, shame and guilt making it hard to speak. "It was delicious."

Karian extended his open hand to Rose, and his piercing gaze trapped her soul. After a few moments, she placed her palm in his bigger one. His fingers closed around hers and a visible tension leached from the air.

She followed Karian down the long corridor leading to their private part of the house.

They finally arrived at the end of the hallway and in the first room of their private quarters. It was a large living room, with a small dining table and a few chairs and sofas in front of a large ground to ceiling window. Wind blew softly inside, making the aerial curtains flutter like long fingers waving tentatively.

This central room led to a number of other rooms. Rose could see the foot of a large bed in the closest one, and her guts twisted with a sudden fire. She snapped her hand away from Karian's and stomped her feet. "That's enough," she said. "We're alone now, no need for that nonsense."

"No." Karian turned to her, his eyes reduced to slits. He was as angry as she was, if not more. "No need for nonsense."

Chapter Twenty-One

Rose

"When were you planning to tell me I was a prisoner?"

"You're not a prisoner, you're my mate." Karian took a deep breath and when he looked at Rose again, he wasn't as angry anymore. "You are the only proof of the free humans' existence. You are the only one standing in the way of Trade Minister Knut's continuing prosperity. Don't think he won't have eyes on you at all times, ready to take advantage of any opportunity to take you away—or worse."

"I know." Rose heard her own voice, deflated and void. She had known all along, she had just needed to hear it aloud. She was the only one who could either damn or save her people. If she was captured, they would find ways to extract the information from her, one way or the other. If she died, the proof died with her and they would relentlessly search every square foot of the entire planet until the humans were found. Rose's personal happiness wasn't important anymore, not in the face of all the others'.

The thought should have taken her anger away, but it didn't. It only made her burn more.

"You only have to stay inside the family walls for a short while. It's not going to take forever."

Karian ran a hand over his skull, looking straight at Rose with his jaws clenched and his eyes burning with a fiery desire. Now that they were alone, the Mating Venom was running its wicked course, and the attraction was palpable in the air around them. Karian's chest heaved and he watched her with dark eyes filled with carnal need. Rose felt her body respond despite herself, the Mating Venom in her blood answering the call of Karian's desires.

She began pacing the room, not caring about the exquisite furniture and the ostentatious luxury of everything. Fury was running through her veins, hot and acidic, making her itch with the urge to scream and hit.

"You lied to me," Rose accused him, pointing her finger in his direction. "You said you would help my people, but all you care about is owning me. You're no better than Trade Minister Knut."

"That's unfair and you know it." Karian stared at her with more hurt than she wanted to see in those beautiful eyes. "You're safe here, and as my mate, you have to be my priority. You may not like it, but it's for your own good."

"Who are you to decide what's best for me? And don't even try to say my mate, 'cause that's not going to cut it." Rose took a step closer, anger and attraction battling in equal measures. "You didn't even discuss this with me. You can't make decisions for me like you own me."

Karian stared at her, his mouth a thin, pale blue line. There was something he didn't dare tell her. Something she needed to know.

"Whatever it is, you can tell me." Rose took a step closer. Her hands were burning with the need to touch him, and it took all her willpower to stop herself from reaching out and laying them flat against his hard chest.

"I am doing everything I can, not only to save you, but to save all the humans." Karian's eyes shone with an emotion she was afraid to understand. "Please trust me."

"Why? Why are you taking so many risks for me? You didn't have to take me as a mate, not if this was so dangerous."

He covered the remaining distance between them, standing over her. He was so close, his smell entered her nostrils, making her heart race and her blood run faster. He cupped her cheek in his palm, then rubbed her skin with his thumb in that heart-wrenching way he had.

"It doesn't matter why." Karian's voice was husky, and when his hand slid to the nape of her neck, she shivered with pleasure at the contact. "All that matters is that you're mine."

He lowered his head and his lips covered hers. His strong hands grabbed her waist, pulling her close enough to feel his already hardened flesh. Lust flowed through her veins, reaching every treacherous cell in her body, filling her with the need for him, the craving for his touch. Karian deepened the kiss. Everything else blurred as her flesh quivered under his touch, his tongue invading her mouth.

Her body surrendered to him, to his desires. She was obliterated by the pleasure of his touch, leaving nothing behind but the lust for more.

He broke the kiss and Rose breathed in as his fingers dug into the hair at her neck, forcing her head back, exposing her throat. Sharp fangs slid over her skin, sending lightning bolts of arousal straight between her legs, where her flesh already screamed for his possession. His tongue glided between the fangs, lapping and twisting, spreading the Mating Venom on her skin, making them both mad with the mating heat. His fingers dug into her flesh, and his erection pressed against the softness of her stomach until she was nothing more than a beast made of lust and surrender. She was panting, and the warm wetness spread between her thighs, where she was aching for his touch to fill her. Aching for his possession and the rapture that came with it.

This was different from all the times he had touched her before. He wasn't making love to her. He was possessing her, bending her to his will and desires—and what was worse was that Rose desired it as much as she feared it. Karian had lost the control he always took so much care to display, letting his passion come to the surface as his fangs and tongue ran the length of her throat to the top of her breast.

Yanking the fabric away with one hand, he denuded Rose of her clothing in one violent motion, leaving her panting, naked, in front of him.

He gazed down at her body, his eyes shining with possessive passion, his mouth hanging slightly open, revealing the tips of his fangs. His Eok-fashioned pants were hugging his legs closely, revealing the hard bulge of his erection.

Rose's hands ran over his arms, feeling the strong muscles quiver under her touch as her fingers covered them. She grabbed the top of his sleeveless vest and slid it from his shoulders, letting it fall behind him on the floor. She breathed hard as she ran her hands over the intricate pattern of the scars on his chest, running her fingertips on the tiny bumps witness to so much repeated suffering.

Her fingers ran lower, over his stomach and down to the waist of his pants. Karian kept silent, watching her every move as her fingers freed his seed stem, which bounced forward and straight to attention. He hissed when she grabbed the length between her fingers, reaching all the way to the tight skin of his seed sack.

"Mine." Karian's speech was more a growl than words. "You're mine, Rose."

"If I'm yours, then you're mine, too."

The statement made a glimmer pass over Karian's irises and he pushed his pants down, kicking his boots away in the same motion. They stood in front of each other, naked, their chests heaving in the same fast, furious rhythm.

Then Karian pounced. Fast, too fast for her naked eyes to see, his arms encircled her waist and he lifted her, sliding his hands to her thighs, parting them as he lowered her until his seed stem was poised at her entrance.

Their gazes collided, prisoners of one another.

Karian lowered her until she was impaled on his hardness, her legs wrapped around his waist, her drenched walls stretching to accommodate his length.

"Mine," he growled again and he lifted her, only to lower her again, sending flashes of pleasure right through her brain. "Mine."

In so many ways, Rose wanted to protest, but there was so much pleasure. Karian lifted and lowered her again, pounding with his hips at the same time, his strength and hardness reaching every one of her nerve endings. The Mating Venom rushed through both their bodies, enhancing the pleasure tenfold. Within minutes, Rose was at the edge of rapture.

"Yes." The words left her lips without her approval. "I'm yours."

Her words made Karian pound harder, burying into her deeper, with more force, as pleasure built inside him. He wasn't controlling himself, he allowed his passion to take control, thrusting inside her with abandon. Without warning, ecstasy broke out, tearing through her in a tidal wave of pleasure, wiping out everything she was to leave only an empty shell behind.

A second later, Karian's fingers dug into the flesh of her thighs and he pushed one final time, burying himself inside her with a deafening roar. His cry of pleasure lasted while hot semen spilled inside her womb and she screamed again, another climax ravaging her body, brought on by the Mating Venom in his seed.

They rode the final climax together until they were panting, void of energy.

Each time she thought having sex with Karian couldn't be better, he brought her to new heights, showed her a depth of rapture she didn't think even existed. It was as if her body ceased to be her own, and all she could do was watch as her power slid through her fingers with every kiss he gave her, every touch that made her quiver, every time he pushed her over the edge of ecstasy. Rose was going to be lost before long.

Karian lowered her to the ground, his blue gaze never leaving hers. Outside, the dimming light licked the skin of his face, making the sharp relief of his scars more pronounced. He was more alien than she had ever seen him, here in this home that was his, in possession of everything he deemed was his possession—Rose included.

As her feet touched the floor, he lifted his hand to cup her cheek, rubbing his thumb over her skin. The affectionate gesture was so overwhelming, she felt tears tickle her eyelids.

"My Pretty Thing." He said the words with an underlying tenderness that left her heart torn. "My mate."

Karian bent and lifted her in his arms, then walked to the bedroom she had noticed when entering the private quarters. He lowered her softly onto the bed, then came to lie down by her side, pulling a soft blanket over their naked bodies. She snuggled into his arms, allowing his warmth to penetrate her flesh, melting her reticence into an enticing cocoon of safety.

"What now?" She closed her eyes, allowing sleep to overcome her senses.

"The real fight begins."

Rose drifted off to sleep with Karian's dire words etched in her dreams.

Rose woke up in the morning to find Karian gone and the three Eokian suns high in the sky. Karian's side of the bed and his pillow were cold to the touch, attesting that he had left some time before. She hadn't even noticed him leaving.

As she got up from the bed, dragging the sheet around her naked body, she really noticed the interior for the first time. The bedroom was large and circular, much like all Eok construction, with a polished stone floor. In each room were floor to ceiling windows, allowing the breeze to flow freely inside.

The clay house was perfect to shield its inhabitants from the heat of the day and maintain a comfortable warmth during the cold nights. As efficient as the structure was, it was also surprisingly beautiful.

The furniture in the room was sparse, but of exquisite quality. The large bed in the middle of the room was flanked by four massive posts, the precious wood carved and polished smooth as she ran her finger on the intricate carvings. Wood was an expensive commodity on Eokim and had to be imported from other worlds, as the wilderness was covered with grassland. The bed, large chest of drawers, and four chairs were true testaments to the wealth of Karian's family. Treasures demonstrating the importance of their owners.

Looking around the comfortable room filled with the rest of Karian's wealth, she felt more alone and alien in this house than she ever had on Saarmak. There, Karian and Rose had been on the same level, fighting together for their survival. On Saarmak, they'd been partners and friends. On Eokim, she was a pampered female to be kept in a secure enclosure. Only a step above a slave, when all was said and done.

A cool breeze caressed her skin, and she shivered. Suddenly, she didn't care for the warm richness of the wood.

Rose quickly dressed and walked outside, intent on finding Arlia, who was no doubt already working hard on her extensive gardens. The enclosure was filled with patches of gardens where Arlia grew different kinds of vegetables. Around the perimeter were trees heavy with strange fruits and berries.

Rose's gaze ran around the enclosure separating the house from the Eokian wilderness, up to the clay wall setting its limits.

In the distance, a flurry of white fur attracted her attention. Maak was there, following his mistress in her daily tasks, bouncing around excitedly after small animals scurrying in the garden. Rose approached, and as she neared, Maak saw her and ran in her direction.

"Nice to see you, too." Rose rubbed the meerit's head, then smiled at Arlia. "What are you working on?"

"Just tending the mushberrie bushes." Arlia extended her open hand, in which some pale green orbs were glowing. "Once harvest season has started, I can't stop, or I'll lose them."

Rose picked up the green berries and popped one in her mouth, crunching the juicy fruit between her teeth. A sweet, intoxicating taste with undertones of cinnamon invaded her mouth.

"They're delicious!" She put the rest of the berries in her mouth and ate with gusto.

"I agree." Arlia returned to her task of picking the mushberries and continued to fill her large basket. "It's a pity they don't keep. I have to turn them into jelly, jams or pie every day, but it's worth it."

Rose agreed and silently went to work beside Arlia, filling the basket. The other female turned her face to Rose, surprise brushing her features, then smiled and returned to her work.

Rose spent the rest of the day following Arlia and helping her with her daily tasks. Arlia had an extensive garden, and Rose was amazed at how much food she produced in such arid conditions. She was a good farmer, and Rose had lots to learn from her.

"This is enough for today," Arlia said as she stuffed the last long purple vegetable from the vines growing on the trunk of a fruit tree into her woven basket. "Vegetables like ivak taste better fresh, and we have enough for tonight's dinner. Let's get back inside."

"You're a wonderful gardener," Rose said, grabbing her end of the heavy basket and walking alongside her to the house. "Are all Eoks' mates this skilled at farming the land?"

"Hardly!" Arlia scoffed. "I'm Relany. Our females are as strong as our males, and we all work the land. It's in our blood to provide food for our families using the resources of the planet. Most females wait for their mates to bring back a kill from their hunt, and buy the rest from traveling merchants coming from the town."

"Where is this town? I didn't see any sign of it when we came here."

"It's mostly underground." Arlia smiled at Rose. "Soon, we'll go there to buy fabric. Those clothes aren't fit for a beauty such as you!"

Arlia and Rose gathered the basket and brought it into the kitchen. Rose followed Arlia's lead in preparing the meal. After a while, Arlia put her knife down and stared at Rose.

"Thank you for helping me."

"It's only normal," Rose answered truthfully. "You can't be the only one preparing meals for five people every day."

"That's what I usually do," Arlia answered, going back to cutting her vegetables. As she leaned on the counter, a sparkle attracted Rose's attention.

"That's a nice necklace."

Rose looked as Arlia picked up the crystal, star-shaped pendant and flicked it between her fingers.

"Enlon gave it to me on the day of our mating." Arlia smiled, her eyes lost in a faraway memory. "Nobody could have predicted ours would be the only bloodmating of our generation. Still, we were so perfect for each other, I wasn't even surprised when it happened. Of course, everybody else freaked out, especially Enlon's family."

"Why is that?" Rose reached and grabbed Arlia's hand. "What's so special about the bloodmating? Karian hasn't said anything."

"Yes. It doesn't surprise me." Arlia pursed her lips, like she was trying to prevent the words from coming out. "Don't worry. Karian will tell you in his own time."

Rose didn't answer, but got back to work. In a little over an hour, the kitchen was clean again, and a delicious meal was cooking in the large ovens.

"Well, I'm going to freshen up before Enlon arrives."

Arlia hugged Rose before going away. Rose watched as she left, her powerful body moving in long strides. She was a good person, a person Rose was fast learning to love. There was a lot of her in Karian, in his calm strength and his generosity. Her throat tightened and she turned her gaze away.

She didn't belong in this place, in this family. She was an outsider, she always would be. She was only there by an incredible error of fate, not because of true love. She was nothing like Arlia.

Chapter Twenty-Two

Karian

I knew it would happen, sooner or later. It's only a matter of luck they haven't located the house yet.

Karian stared at the three Cattelans lined up against the wall of the Erynian tribe Hall. Blood was still seeping out of their ears due to the shock of the ionic grenades that had been used on them. Their black clothes were standard military issue, without emblems or any other identifiable signs as to their employer. Their yellow eyes stared steadily at the setting suns, unblinking.

Rage coursed through Karian's veins in a steady flow, making his thoughts as clear as ice.

"Why haven't they been kept alive for questioning?"

"They fired on my team with ionic charges," Erlock answered, his eyes cast down, his mouth closed in a tight line. "There was no choice but to use lethal force. I will not have my men put their lives at risk just to capture those criminals alive."

"An Eok warrior always puts the good of his mission before his own life," Karian answered, not caring to spare the other male's feelings. His disgust for his cousin Erlock had always been hard to disguise, but never so much as it was now. Erlock was a coward, one of the few who were unable to complete the Eok warriors' training and who lived a life of safety and comfort on Eokim without ever risking their lives for their fellow Eoks. Karian knew Erlock had ordered the security forces of the Tribe Hall to use deadly force as soon as the first ionic charge had zipped by.

"I apologize for my error in judgement," Erlock answered, his brows creased with resentment. "There was no identification on the bodies. There was no way of knowing where they came from, or why."

"We know why they came," Karian said sharply, unable to contain his contempt for Erlock. "Trade Minister Knut sent them to abduct or kill my bloodmate. Because of your incompetence, we can't prove it, but it doesn't change the fact."

Erlock bent his head, silent. Karian knew his cousin would not forget this insult. Whatever he lacked in moral and physical strength, Erlock made up for in his capacity to scheme. And he never forgot a slight, holding a grudge for years until he found the perfect opportunity to lash back at his opponent.

Karian was about to ask more about the details of the Cattelans' attack when a transport hovered over the wall and a familiar figure jumped out, then walked hurriedly toward him.

"There is news from Earth." Arlen didn't bother with niceties. "Kamal has found a human female."

"The village was located?" Karian nodded his approval. Eok efficiency was legendary, but the mission wasn't an easy one. "Rose will be relieved. She's been so worried about them."

"I'm afraid it's more complicated than that." Arlen frowned and shook his head. "The human is a female named Aliena. She was gravely ill, but even so, she's refusing to provide any information regarding the village. She insists she will only speak to Rose."

Karian took a few seconds to digest the information. Aliena was a familiar name, and in a flash, he remembered.

"She is Rose's cousin." Karian cursed under his breath. Would those human females' stubbornness know no bounds? "They grew up together. If she's half as stubborn as Rose, she won't talk to any of us, no matter what we say."

"Then you'll need to bring Rose to the Erynian Township." Arlen didn't look pleased, and for good reason. He glanced at the Cattelan corpses with disgust. "It's going to be practically impossible to ensure her safety. Not with only one week remaining before the Council. Those three are not the last ones who are going to try to take Rose away—or worse."

Karian nodded grimly. The Erynian Township had the only receptor strong enough to receive a transmission from Earth. But the town was a constant bustle of activity, with strangers and Eoks alike mixing and engaging in various trades. It was an almost impossible location to secure. It was the perfect place for an ambush.

He couldn't let Rose expose herself by going there. He had to find a way to convince Aliena to reveal the location of the village without endangering Rose.

"Go back to the township," Karian ordered Arlen. "I'll talk with Rose and find a way to convince her cousin to talk to us."

"Those humans are impossible, you know that?" Arlen shook his head in disbelief.

"Yes, I know." Karian couldn't help the smirk that pulled on his lips.

Arlen nodded, then walked briskly away and jumped back in his transport. Karian turned toward his cousin, who had stayed silent during the conversation.

"Call me immediately if there is anything else," Karian addressed Erlock. "Raise the threat level to red and triple the patrols. No one lands on this side of the Long Lake without my knowledge. And no more errors."

Erlock didn't answer, and Karian didn't wait for him to. He jumped into his transport and sped away.

His rage had turned into a burning need to hold Rose close to his body, to feel her safe and unharmed in his arms.

Rose

"I forbid it!" Karian paced up and down the bedroom in the dimming light of the second sun's fast demise. "I can't guarantee the town's safety. Just today, there were three Cattelan assassins at the Tribe Hall."

He turned to face Rose, then resumed his pacing. It was obvious he was furious with the outcome of his brother's mission on Earth. He was so focused on his anger that he wasn't hearing one word she was saying. Rose was beginning to have enough of his high-handed attitude. She wasn't some delicate flower. She had no desire to be put in a vase and left on a windowsill to look pretty until she faded. She wasn't going to let him push her away when she was the obvious solution to a problem, even if it meant putting her at risk.

"I'm the only one who can help," she answered, angered by the stubborn frown on his brow. "Your trackers aren't going to find my people, they're way too clever to leave a trail. Your blue hunks won't find them."

"Kamal found one pretty easily," Karian snapped, the words going out with a bite hard enough to break skin. He stopped his pacing and turned to face Rose. His skin was shimmering under the fading light and his shirtless torso looked like a sculpture. He looked good enough to lick. Rose stifled her desire to get up from the bed and trace the lines of his hard chest with her fingertips. "She's recovered from her injuries and she'll talk soon."

"You're putting your fingers in your eyes up to your elbows if you think Aliena will give you anything," Rose scoffed. "And don't fool yourself into thinking that your brother found her, either."

"What do you mean?" Karian blinked, clearly confused.

Rose inhaled sharply. She couldn't believe his male arrogance.

"She was already sick when I left." Tears welled up in her eyes at the memory of Aliena's body, skin and bones under a cover of cold sweat, fever eating away at her, one minute at a time. "I was so afraid she was going to die—had died. Someone must have decided your people were her only chance."

"And it wasn't a moment too soon." Karian shook his head in consternation. "Kamal said she spent the last three days in the medical pod, hanging between life and death. He's never seen a female so mistreated before. He wants to choke the life out of whoever did this to her."

"Well, then he can close his big, chunky hands around Minister Knut's throat, and when he's finished with him, he can do Arrik." Rose lifted her hands in irritation. "Pushing Aliena won't help. Whatever her condition, she won't talk. She's never going to give up the location of the village. You have to let me talk to her."

"Humans!" Karian made a pinched face. "No, not humans. Females! So stubborn."

"Yes, we're stubborn." She crossed her arms and lifted her chin in challenge. "You'd better spend your energy on what matters instead of things you can't change."

He cast her an irritated look. Rose narrowed her eyes, meeting his glare without flinching. From the way his jaw was clenched, she could tell he knew she was right. The only way to get Aliena to reveal the location of the human village—and Rose's family—was to let Rose talk to her cousin. For that, they needed a receptor strong enough to receive and send communication from Earth, and the only receptor powerful enough for a live transmission was in the Erynian Township, in the communication room of the Tribe's Council Hall.

Karian cast her another smoldering look, then resumed his pacing.

"You have no choice. You need to bring me with you to the town tomorrow." Rose stood. She knew her next argument was going to destabilize him. "Plus, Arlia wants to buy fabric for some clothes. I can't stay in Khal's old youngling tunics, and my synthetic cotton clothes are already worn out."

Karian's head snapped back to her and he pressed his lips together in an upside-down smirk. It obviously took him by surprise to hear her talk about female concerns. He gave her body a slow assessing look, his eyelids heavy with desire.

"You look good in any clothes." His face changed and his irises darkened to the color of the sky after midnight. "But Mother is right. You should buy whatever clothes you want. *As soon as it's safe.*"

"I'm going to come to town with you, talk with Aliena, and then I'll go shopping with Arlia." Rose clacked her tongue against her teeth and made a small exasperated noise. "I can't stay hidden in this house forever. Whatever measures you decide to ensure my safety, I'll follow them. You can even lumber me with bodyguards to follow me around."

Karian's lips reduced to a thin line and he shook his head, but she saw in his eyes that she had won.

"Your feet won't even touch the ground if I see so much as a smirk that I don't like in the crowd," he said.

"Understood."

"Good."

Karian growled, the sound so frustrated and so male it made Rose break out in a laugh. That had the effect to shake some sense into Karian, who smirked at her with humor.

"I'll need something nice to impress people at the Ring's motion." She smiled slowly, feeling her attraction to Karian work itself into her body. She extended her legs on the bed and leaned back on her elbows, allowing her mane of curls to fall behind her shoulders, spreading over the covers. "I'd also like some more practical clothes, like Arlia's."

Karian took a step closer, his face dark and stormy, his lips hard and kissable at the same time. "You'll have to promise me to follow security protocol at all times."

"I promise I'll do everything you say." Rose pursed her lips invitingly and laid her hand on her hips. His eyes followed her every movement, his Adam's apple bumping up and down as he swallowed. "So tell me, what do you want me to do?"

"You're only trying to prevent me from thinking straight." But he took a step closer and his gaze traveled down her body, tightly clad in the black fabric, hugging her curves in a lover's embrace. "I'm assigning four elite guards to you at all times. You're not to leave their sides, and you're to obey them if they see any threat."

"That's acceptable," Rose said, rolling on her stomach, tilting her head up tentatively. "I'll even hold their hands if you want me to."

Karian growled, the sound rolling out of his throat in a husky warning. "Don't." He reached for her hair, softly grasping a fistful of curls between his long fingers. "I can't think straight with you looking at me like that, and I can't think straight with the thought of you putting your hands on any other male."

"Better lay *your* hands on me, then."

Karian's lips lifted in his sexy, gruff smile. His hand on Rose's hair lowered to her neck in a gesture that might be considered threatening coming from any other male. It sent electric shocks of arousal down her body, sparking a more carnal craving.

"You're the only thing I've been able to think about all day," he said in a husky voice. Slowly, with his shining blue eyes fixed on her, he lowered his head and closed his mouth on hers. The kiss had a hunger in it that spoke of long held passion, and as he massaged her lips with his, her own hunger rose. She was surprised how much she wanted him, how much she craved his touch, his body. His contact was like a drug.

"Those Cattelans you found at the Tribe Hall," she said, pulling away from the kiss. "How come they didn't come directly to the house?"

"The location of the family house is a well-kept secret." Karian slid his hand lower down her shoulder, then grasped one of her breasts. "Only Eoks know the location of the chief's house, and no warrior would ever betray the Erynian tribe. They were blind in the grassland, probably waiting to follow a transport to the house."

"More will come."

"Knut will try many things to get his way," Karian said, obviously absorbed by the sight of her breasts under the light fabric. "They will wait for any opportunity, but the Eok nation is not undefended. Only onc more week, and the Council will hear us."

Rose reached out, her hands closing on Karian's arms, feeling the firm, raw muscles underneath the skin. She pulled him in and he answered her call. As she turned around to face him, he lay on top of her as she welcomed him. Their kiss deepened as their bodies touched and merged.

His hands slid over her hips, and Karian pressed his erection between her legs. At the sensation of his hard, hot length against her belly, her walls clenched and squeezed, demanding, screaming for the thrust of his hard flesh inside hers. She reached up and cupped the throbbing bulge in his pants, making him draw a sharp breath at the touch.

All of a sudden, desire and passion broke loose. Karian's lips left her mouth to leave a trail of fire on her neck. Each time his lips closed on her skin, he opened them just enough that his fangs scraped her epidermis, spreading Mating Venom, making her skin burn and ache.

She rubbed his hard length, losing her control over what little sanity she had left. Her body had a will of its own, acting on a hunger it could never fulfill, trying to quench a thirst that would never be quenched.

"I'm going to make you forget everything that's not me." Karian's lips brushed her ears. "I want you to scream my name so loud it's going to be carved on your mind."

Rose melted into a warm puddle of want as he pulled away just long enough to peel her clothes off in fast, hungry movements. It was like the bed was a living being, embracing her back as Karian leaned over her, spreading her legs apart with his knees. His hand slid from the insides of her thighs, climbing up to the hot dampness between. His large thumb rubbed over her most sensitive place, making her spine crawl with fast, deep shivers of pleasure.

He was so male, so utterly and completely male. She hungered for more of him.

By then, his eyes were a midnight blue so dark it was almost black, the lines of his face stretched in a desire so powerful her whole body responded in a surge of heat. The Mating Venom was acting fast, making every cell in her body respond to his touch.

Each stroke of his body shot raging bolts of fire up every inch of her, erasing everything that wasn't raw pleasure.

"I can never let you go." Karian met her eyes. "You're mine forever."

"Yes," Rose answered, melting with desire. "I'm yours."

Then he took possession of her mouth again and her mind was a blank canvas of pure sensation. In one long motion, he slid inside her, joining their flesh as one. The sensations filled her, overwhelming her senses.

Her pleasure built up, unruly and savage, more intense every time his body stroked hers. Then, without warning, rapture exploded, making her scream, thrusting her head backward and arching her back. Karian's own climax came in hot jets inside her and he roared, his pleasure joining hers. Rose's orgasm spiraled, multiplied, sending wave after wave of complete ecstasy through her, one after the other.

At that moment, she knew.

Her life was never going to be the same. She had been kidding herself, thinking she had mated him only with her body. Her mind was as intimately enslaved to him as every inch of her skin. They were tied by more than just flesh. His soul was branded into her, his bones knitted into hers. They were two parts of the same soul.

When she opened her eyes again, it was to stare into the bottomless pit of a blue so intense, it burned her thoughts before they had a chance to form.

She was still panting when Karian pulled off her.

Slowly, her mind shed the fog of pleasure. It was like she had been in a tunnel, with only Karian at the other side. Nothing else had mattered. Nothing else had existed.

She was still shaking with pleasure when she fell asleep with Karian at her back.

Chapter Twenty-Three

Rose

The next morning, Rose woke up when Karian stirred and got out of bed. A slow smile spread over her lips at the sight of his naked body in the early morning light. The man was built, with lean muscles bulging on his thighs and a round, perfect ass.

"Stop staring at my butt." Karian turned his head to shoot her an amused glance. "If you don't stop, I'll have to get back in this bed, and we'll be late for your meeting with your cousin."

"We wouldn't want that," Rose said with a chuckle, and slapped his hand away as he reached up her calf. "Don't start something you can't finish."

"Oh, I can finish it."

"Sorry." She wriggled away. "I'm not letting you distract me."

Karian turned away with a rueful smirk and started to dress. In record time, both of them were ready and flying in the direction of the township. Arlia and Enlon were to meet them later, after Rose had talked with Aliena.

On the way, Rose stared at the expanse of the grassland, its soft, moving surface drifting under a caressing breeze. The landscape was a dizzying sea of green, and she looked around, wondering where the township was hidden. There was nothing in the distance that suggested a large city.

Then the transport hovered over a large, round-topped hill.

"We're here."

"That's the town?"

Karian chuckled and as Rose looked over the side of the transport, the hill broke open to reveal a sparkling underground landing strip.

"It's underground!"

"The best defense system there is." Karian watched her reaction. "This is the biggest town on the southern hemisphere of Eokim. You have to stay by my side at all times. No exceptions."

"No exceptions." She flashed him a brilliant smile as the transport lowered into a cylindrical enclosure made of shining metal and blinking lights.

"This is the High Council's special landing strip," he explained. "Only a handful of people know its location. It's the safest place in town apart from the Council Hall."

"It's incredible."

Two serious looking males walked in their direction, their blue eyes shining in the low light. Above, the hilltop closed with a clean hydraulic sound, sealing off the landing strip from the world above.

"Commander Karian." The first male spoke with clean military efficiency. "The way to the Council Hall has been cleared. It's safe for your bloodmate to travel."

"Frey, Dimyon." Karian tilted his head in greeting. "Has the communication link to Earth been established?"

"Yes, Commander Karian. You have about ten minutes. After that, Earth will be out of alignment."

Karian helped Rose down and put a protective arm around her shoulders. They immediately proceeded to walk at a brisk pace. Rose struggled but she kept up with them, not wanting to slow them down. The landing strip was incredible, dug out of the white Eokian stone and fitted with almost silent hydraulic gears, opening the hilltop wide enough to easily fit a transport carrying a hundred people.

Rose followed Karian down a long tunnel, at the end of which stood a familiar sapphire blue male displaying his usual grim attitude.

"Seems like your cousin is as stubborn as you are," Arlen said as Rose neared the door. "I'm starting to rethink the theory that humans were hunted to extinction. Your kind was probably just exasperated to death by its own female."

"It's nice to see you, too." Rose flashed Arlen her best smile. "You know, I think maybe this task is a little overwhelming for someone so sensitive to female stubbornness."

Arlen grunted, then spun around and walked away.

Karian's hand slid to Rose's elbow, squeezing it, then he bent down to her ear. "Quit playing with my brother." His voice barely concealed his amusement. "He's a well-respected warrior."

"He's a high-handed jerk, and he had it coming."

Karian chuckled and, in front of them, Arlen's back stiffened.

They finally arrived at a large room in the center of which was a huge oval table, flanked by a series of heavy chairs big enough to seat the big warriors comfortably. There was a control panel to one side, with a technician working on setting up the communication link with Earth. The entire back wall was a screen, filled with a buzzing static.

"Let's start." Arlen talked with his back turned to Rose, but he was no longer stiff and angry. He was as focused and efficient as always. An Eok trait, if there ever was one.

The static on the back wall fluttered and gave way to a familiar face. Rose forgot everything else as she gazed into the eyes of her oldest friend.

"Aliena." The words came out, breathless and heavy with relief. "It's so good to see you."

"It's good to see you, too." Aliena smiled, stretching pale skin over sharp features. She was painfully thin, but even so, she was still as pretty as ever. Her high cheekbones highlighted large, deep brown eyes so dark the irises were almost indistinguishable from the pupils. Flowing black hair, like liquid silk, spread on each side of her small face.

"I was so afraid we'd never meet again." Rose let out a rush of air. "How is everybody?"

"Hanging out fine," Aliena said. "Turns out Ferrin's brother is not half the asshole the rest of the family is. He's been taking care of us since you disappeared."

"Martin? I never thought about him that way." Rose remembered the young, slim man of barely twenty. He was always under his older brothers and father's ruling, never speaking up, never objecting to any of the nonsense. "He hunted for you?"

"Hunted for us, made sure we had enough wood for the fire, even went to get me some sapling for my tea. He tried his best to get me better." Aliena glanced over her shoulder at an unknown person in the room. Her face clouded over, then she turned back to Rose. "He's the one who left me for the Eoks to find. He said a slim chance was better than nothing. He saved me."

A low growl answered Aliena's last words. She looked back with a defiant glare and narrowed her eyes. "He did," she said forcefully. "He left me out in the open where he knew they'd find me."

A male voice answered something Rose couldn't make out and Aliena's face turned red. Whatever her cousin had heard, she didn't like it. Aliena snapped her head back to Rose.

"You'll find the village at the coordinates you see on the commu-link." Aliena flipped her hair. "The Eoks would never have found them. You did good to insist on speaking to me. I'd never have given their location otherwise."

"Thanks, Aliena." Rose felt hot tears fall down her cheeks. "We'll save them all, you'll see."

"Listen, while you're fighting the Ring, I'm going to go after your—"

A fizzy burst of static invaded the screen, cutting off the remainder of Aliena's sentence. Rose watched the flurry of white and black for what felt like an eternity.

"We have the village's location." Karian's voice came from behind, and a hand closed on her shoulder. "Khal is already on his way. I should have confirmation of their location before the day is over."

"What about Aliena?" Rose turned and locked gazes with him. "Is she going to join us here? She looked like she still needs medical treatment."

"Kamal is taking care of her for the time being." Karian made a face that told her things weren't going smoothly for his brother. "He doesn't want to let her out of his sight. After she's well, he's going to work on locating your father and the other missing men from your village."

"Father..."

The shock was enough to make her dizzy. Rose had been so focused on rescuing her mother, brothers and cousin that she had forgotten about him. She realized she had subconsciously assumed her father was dead, even though she had no proof or indication of it. She had just given up on him. Shame and guilt stung her in equal measure.

"I'll have more news as soon as Kamal gets a lead on their location." Karian's hand left her shoulder. "Earth will be within reach at the same time tomorrow."

"Why don't you attack the breeding facility?" Rose asked, but she knew the answer. "He could still be there with the others."

"It's under the Genetic Preservation Board's protection. Attacking it would not only be illegal, it would be a declaration of war on the Ring itself."

"And hundreds of thousands of innocent lives would be lost." Rose understood. Karian was Commander in Chief of the Eok armies. He was a loyal soldier, and a born leader. He would do everything he could to keep his promise, but even he couldn't provoke the full strength of the Ring's wrath.

"For now, the only thing you can do is wait. The Ring's next session is in just one week. Until then, you are the humans' only hope. You are the only proof. All that matters is to keep you safe."

"Thank you." Rose's throat closed under the strength of her emotions. "For everything you've done."

"Now, about your shopping..." Karian opened his mouth to add something, but closed it as a tall, golden-haired figure strolled into the room.

"I've been waiting for you forever!" Arlia walked up to Rose and hugged her closely, then withdrew. "Now, let's get some quality time together. You need the distraction, and I could use the amusement."

Arlia took Rose's hand in hers and began chatting about which color scheme would most complement her skin tones.

Rose turned to see Karian watching with a dark, conflicted expression on his face. Finally, he gave a jerk of his head and four synthetic-leather clad males entered the room and stood at attention. Their faces were closed and their eyes were on high alert, like danger was lurking in every corner. Seeing them flayed her already raw nerves.

"Bodyguards," Arlia said with a shocked smile. "We're only going to the fabric square. We're going to be finished in an hour, two at the most."

"Rose shouldn't even be in town." Karian answered politely, but there was steel in his voice. "I'm allowing this, but only if you both agree to obey the guards at all times. Okay?"

"All right." Arlia shrugged. "I'll keep Rose safe. You have nothing to fear."

"I know." Karian smiled, the warmth of it making Rose's belly clench with emotion. "I'll see you both at the house later."

Karian bent over and kissed his mother on both cheeks before turning to Rose and putting a burning kiss on her mouth. Then they left for the fabric square, the four guards following them like huge, muscled shadows.

As she sat comfortably in the transport with Arlia and Enlon, Rose patted the green sheer fabric she had chosen at the market. It felt awkward and wrong to be choosing fabric and thinking about how good it was going to look on her body, when she knew the people she loved still lived in great danger.

The wait was starting to eat away at her.

Rose and Arlia finally arrived home, then went their separate ways into their private quarters. At the end of the afternoon, Rose headed back through the long hallway leading to the kitchen.

Upon getting closer, she heard the hushed sounds of what seemed like a heated argument. The voices spoke fast, their words clashing into each other, but their tone was low, as if they didn't want to be overheard.

As she came to the doorway of the large common room, Rose saw Arlia and Maral behind the rounded counter that ran the length of the kitchen. Arlia's back was turned to Rose, but Maral's face was visible. As she saw Maral's angry expression, Rose immediately wished she had stayed away.

"Don't you dare tell me what I can and cannot do in my house," Arlia said. "You're my son's mate, don't ever forget that. This is my home, not yours."

"You heard what Erlock had to say about humans, especially females." Maral's eyes suddenly found Rose's, and even in the distance, Rose saw her pupils reduce to slits. "She's nothing but a slave. An animal."

The sharp sound of the slap reverberated against the rounded walls. Maral's cold eyes widened, her black pupils dilating until there was almost no more purple left. She raised a delicate hand to her cheek, touching the fast-reddening skin as though she couldn't believe what Arlia had done. Rose could barely believe it herself.

Maral hissed and showed her wicked little teeth, but recoiled as Arlia growled viciously. Between the two, Arlia had clearly won the physical contest, although Maral's deviousness was an advantage Rose wouldn't discount in a fight. That one was full of bile and as deadly as a snake.

"*You.*" Maral's gaze went from Arlia to Rose, making the stronger female turn around in shock. "It's all your fault."

Maral whirled around, her flowing gown following in a graceful flurry of sheer fabric, and stalked out of the room to her private quarters. Rose was left alone with Arlia, who looked like she had swallowed a cushion full of needles.

"Good afternoon," was all Rose thought to say. "I hope I'm not interrupting."

"Midnight God, no!" Arlia chuckled, allowing the humor to break the tension from her shoulders. "Maral is just being Maral. Don't pay any attention to her."

"Is Karian back?" Rose cast a look around the empty room

"He's with Enlon and Arlen at the township." Arlia stared down at her cup, but her lips lifted at the corners. "They should be back for last meal. You can holo-call him if you want. He'll pick up for you."

They heard a crash, then Maral's crystal voice could be heard. She was beside herself, shouting and talking too fast for them to understand. Rose didn't need to understand her words to know she was the cause of Maral's anger.

"She's too spoilt, and she can't bear not to be the prettiest female around anymore," Arlia said with such disapproval Rose had to smile. "She has a wicked heart, but she can't do anything against you."

"She's spoilt all right." Rose approached and thanked Arlia when she handed her a full cup of a warm liquid, white and opaque, smelling strongly of peppermint and sugar. "As far as the prettiest, I think she still has that one. I've never seen any creature as beautiful."

"Avonies are beautiful, and Maral is a great beauty, even for her species," Arlia conceded, taking a long sip of the liquid in her cup. "She's jealous of you."

"Jealous of me?" That was a surprising thought if there ever was one. Rose couldn't think of anything the beautiful Maral could want that she possessed. "I have nothing, not even clothes."

"You have the one thing she was ever refused," Arlia said, still gazing at her cup. "You're Karian's mate, and that's all there is to it."

"But she's Arlen's mate. Why should she be jealous of me?" Arlen was a handsome male: tall and strong. He was a bit brooding, but he was smart and loyal to a fault. Maral should count herself happy to be the mate of a male like him.

"That's a long story." Arlia smiled sadly. "And not a lovely one."

"She and Karian were lovers, then?" Bile churned in Rose's stomach at the thought, and she realized that for the first time in her life, she felt jealousy about any female who might touch Karian. He was hers, and nobody else's. "He never told me that."

"Not lovers, no." Arlia sighed, then seemed to decide she could go on. "Maral was sent to Eokim by her family to find a mate. She immediately set her sights on Karian. He was the strongest young warrior in generations, and was newly appointed Commander in Chief of the armies. No other warrior ever had that honor at such a young age. He was already a legend, and the chief's heir to boost. Whoever his mate was going to be, she was going to be the most powerful female of the tribe."

"So she wanted him for his position." Rose stared at Arlia, shocked and disgusted by the possibility. Eoks were completely devoted to their mates, and taking advantage of that was wrong and selfish. "How come she mated with Arlen, then?"

"When Karian scorned her, she seduced his little brother." Arlia's eyes darkened with anger at the faraway memory. "He had passed his Rite the summer before, and he was full of youth's rash passion. All he saw was the greatest beauty of them all, and she had chosen him. Karian tried to prevent him from mating her, but you know how Eoks are when they feel the mating urge. There was nothing anybody could have done to stop him. He was crazy about her. He cherished her, gave in to her every whim, but soon, he understood the cruel truth. She didn't care about him, she only cared about power, and he simply didn't have enough. He's been unhappy ever since."

Rose and Arlia fell silent. There was nothing Rose could say to alleviate Arlia's sadness at the fate of her son. Eoks mated for life, and Arlen was going to stand by Maral no matter what.

"I'm so sorry." Rose looked inside the cup and brought it to her lips, then took a small sip. The liquid was thick, sweet and strongly perfumed with a taste that mixed peppermint and oats. It was delicious, and another, longer sip filled her belly with a comforting warmth. "I don't want my presence here to cause any trouble."

"This is your home now," Arlia said, staring directly into her eyes. "Karian chose you. This makes you more precious to us than anything."

The words filled Rose with guilt. Arlia didn't deserve to be lied to.

"Karian didn't really choose me," Rose said carefully, considering each word. "He didn't have a choice."

"What do you mean?" Arlia lowered her cup to the countertop, her eyes wide as she stared at Rose with shock.

"I mean, Karian claimed me as his mate to save me, because I saved his life. It was because he owed me, not because of love." Arlia's face had frozen and was suddenly devoid of all expression, but Rose kept talking. "It's just an accident that he made me his bloodmate."

"Is that so?" Arlia's tone was neutral, but her golden eyes shone with something Rose didn't understand. "Karian told you that?"

"Not in those words."

Arlia didn't answer, but her eyes softened. She sipped from her cup, her long fingers wrapped around the clay surface, encircling it completely. After a few moments, she lowered it and extended her hand to touch Rose's arm.

"Whatever his reasons, Karian chose you of his own free will. You have his heart." Her voice was soft, but the seriousness of her words penetrated Rose's body and a cold shiver ran up her spine. "There is no turning back once a bloodmating has taken place. Not without a sacrifice I'm not willing to make."

There was a warning under those words, but Rose was too caught up in the rest of what Arlia had said to pay attention to it. Karian had chosen her. Hope surged, unabated, and Rose clung to it, unable to restrain herself.

Chapter Twenty-Four

Rose

The next morning, Karian was gone again and Rose shivered in the cold bed. She curved up in the fetal position, gathering the sheets around her body, allowing the memory of last night to come back. They had made love until the early hours of the morning, losing themselves in each other like nothing else existed. The Mating Venom was acting up, making them crave each other more each time, turning them into lust-driven fools.

I'm needing him more each time. I'm going to get lost if I allow this to get any worse.

As many times as Rose said this to herself, she knew there was nothing she could do to prevent it. She wanted to think her craving for Karian was only the result of the Mating Venom, but deep inside, she knew it wasn't. Her need for him ran bone deep, as intricate a part of her body as the ligaments and tendons holding her frame together.

She was simply afraid to name the feeling that tied her guts together every time she saw his eyes burning with desire, making her heart lurch to her throat each time he entered a room. She ran her hands over her arms, making the skin prickle with the memory of other, male hands. Rose closed her eyes, allowing the images to flow over until a rush of desire came up. She opened them again. There was no point in allowing her treacherous body to react to a promise that had no chance of being fulfilled.

Getting up, she dressed quickly in Khal's old youngling clothes, then headed to the kitchen. She liked the supple, well-worn synthetic leather tunic and leggings, which hugged her body closely without hindering her movements. She preferred it tenfold to Maral's long gown, which made practically any physical task impossible. Having finished, Rose wondered what she should do with her time. There was nothing to do but wait until the Ring Council meeting, and she was going to become mad with the tension if she didn't find herself a task to take her mind away from the worries and fears that came with it.

Heading for the kitchen, she reflected that Arlia liked to keep busy, and probably had a long list of tasks for the day ahead. A long day of work in the garden was exactly what she needed to tire her body and free her spirit.

Rose entered the empty kitchen, surprised not to see Arlia there.

"Arlia?" Her call echoed off the round ceiling, carrying like a song across the room. No one answered to her calls out in the gardens, either, not even Maak. Arlia wasn't home. Rose shrugged it off. After all, she hadn't been in Arlia's life for long. She knew nothing of the other female's habits. She could easily be visiting friends.

Rose picked one of Arlia's harvesting baskets, then went outside. The mushberries needed to be picked, or they would spoil under the heat. She looked forward to the simple task, and the fresh morning air was perfect for it, so she went out with eagerness and found the bushes with their green, round fruits. The branches were bent from the weight of the berries, and she stuffed her mouth with the sweet morsels as she went along.

A sudden thump made her jump and she swerved around, her heart beating faster. The wall's door, which sealed the house off from the Eokian wilderness and all the threats it contained, was banging against the heavy frame.

Walking slowly, Rose approached the door, intent on closing it, then her eyes picked up a familiar paw print.

"Maak!" she called, her voice dying quickly in the emptiness of the grassland.

Nothing but the perpetual soft wind answered her. Rose swallowed and looked at the sand over the two feet or so between the wall and the beginning of the grassland, not sure what to do. Arlia loved her pet, and Rose herself had gotten attached to the gentle creature in the two weeks since her arrival on Eokim. She would be sad if anything happened to it, but she knew the risk of venturing outside the walls. In only Khal's old warrior's clothes, with no weapons, she was no match for a predator armed with fangs and claws.

Just as she was about to turn away, a high-pitched, pathetic cry traveled over the grassland, and Rose felt her resolve break. She turned and rushed inside, then grabbed a long knife from the kitchen and ran back outside. At the threshold of the house's enclosure, she paused. Fear prickled on her skin like goosebumps. Maak, Arlia's pet, was a creature of softness and comfort, he was even less equipped to face the dangers of the wilderness than she was.

Straightening her shoulders, she stepped outside the family walls for the first time. A hot, dry wind licked her skin, making her heart flutter with fear. The air outside the walls was somehow different, harsher and less indolent than inside. It was a wild air, air meant to burn lungs in a desperate run from predators.

With trembling hands, Rose held the five-inch blade high in front of her and stepped onto the dry dirt outside the walls. The door closed behind her, and the lock clicked into place.

As she stood outside, she wondered just how big a mistake she had made.

She stood with her back flat against the door, feeling its smooth, cool surface through her clothes. In front of her, about two feet from the enclosure, was the grass that covered the entire Eokian landscape.

Karian's words came back to her.

Eokim is a wild planet, with many predators lurking in the grass for easy prey.

Yes, that was what she was. Easy prey, trembling and defenseless. The short blade she took from the kitchen wasn't going to protect her in a fight with anything bigger than a large dog, and she doubted the wild animals Karian talked about were as gentle. No, the Eokian predators were waiting for her with fangs and claws, and with hunger for her tender flesh.

Rose paused and scrutinized the landscape. The land was flat around the family enclosure, and she was able to look freely at the Eokian world.

It was a dizzying sight, all that grass, covering the earth as far as the eye could see on every side, blanketing everything in a treacherous green velvet. Panic prickled the back of her neck at the idea of the creatures hiding underneath the cover of that lush vegetation.

Looking into the distance, she noticed the faint gleaming of a number of roofs over the grass, in the distance. Those were other Eokian houses, surrounded by their own walls, securing the members of the family. They were too far away to give Rose any hope of help if she needed it.

Her eyes strayed to the beaten dust on the dry dirt around the walls. Paw prints of a large animal were still visible, spaced evenly and moving towards the tall grass only a few yards from the door. Beside the animal's paw prints were other prints, the sandal imprints clearly recognizable.

Rose's heart sank deep in her chest, like it was suddenly set loose in its prison of bones.

Arlia.

Maak had ventured outside, probably in search of scraps of food, and Arlia had gone after him.

"Arlia?" Rose called, but only the wind answered.

She steadied herself, hugging the blade to her chest so hard it hurt.

With a few steps, Rose entered into the grassland. It closed behind her, swallowing her. She could disappear and there would be no proof that she had ever existed. The stalks came to her shoulders, giving her the impression of swimming in a sea of green fingers. The tips of the taller shoots tickled her chin, like hidden hands reaching out from under the cover of grass to graze her face. It was a ghastly feeling, and it made her want to run back to the house and hide inside the walls, but she couldn't leave Arlia outside alone, not when she could be in need of help.

The prints were hard to find in the grass, but she made progress. Rose pushed aside the stalks to find the paw prints, traveling at a sluggish pace until the walls were about a hundred yards behind her. There, a patch of grass appeared disturbed, a large portion of it flattened, the plants broken.

A bright red scar marred the ground, making Rose stop in shock. She gathered a bit of the slime between her fingers, rubbing it between her thumb and index finger. Blood. This was blood. It was fresh, not coagulated yet. She looked down at the ground with new eyes, finding more blood and a few tufts of the silken white fur.

Whatever happened to Maak, it wasn't good.

She had to find Arlia, and fast. Even if there was no indication that she had been there when Maak was attacked, she could still be in danger. Rose took a step, then stopped.

A cold hand gripped at her insides. On the ground, between her feet, was a shiny object, almost buried between stalks of grass. Rose squatted and picked up the star-shaped necklace, its twirling crystal casting rainbows across the green of the grass. It was Arlia's necklace, the one Enlon had given her after their bloodmating.

Rose's breathing accelerated until it was fast and harsh, and fear invaded her senses, increasing them tenfold. She feverishly put the necklace around her neck and searched the ground for signs of Arlia, but found nothing else.

"Arlia!" she shouted, throwing caution to the wind. If any predator was in the area, it had probably spotted her anyway. "Arlia, can you hear me?"

She waited, scrutinizing her surroundings for signs that Arlia was there, but nothing moved. She picked up the pace, following the blood trail. It was easier than following the paw prints, but it filled her with dread.

Please, let it not be hers.

A good half hour later, the dome of Karian's house was shining in the distance. Rose tried to swallow but her throat was closed off. Telling herself she wasn't scared didn't change anything.

Nobody even knows I went out.

Rose had made a mistake by rushing out, but it was too late now to go back.

She went back to the blood trail. She was still able to follow it, but it was becoming fainter by the moment. Either the predator had picked up its pace, running away with its prey, or the meerit had stopped bleeding, a sure indication that it was dead.

Where is she? I've been walking for over an hour, I should have found her by now.

Taking a deep breath, Rose put her head down and walked, then stopped when she found herself at the beginning of a small clearing, where the grass had been beaten to the ground. There, a lump of soft white fur lay on the trampled grass, its silken length painted in bright red. She approached Maak's remains, squatting down at its side, then ran her hand over its head, pulling the long hair away from its eyes. The two large blue orbs fastened on her, and the meerit opened its flat mouth, letting a pathetic call out of its jaws. Rose's gaze ran over the plump body; its stomach was torn open and guts spilled on the ground. There was nothing she could do for Maak. The creature was dying in horrific pain.

Maak bleated again. Pain, so much pain in those blue, trusting eyes. Rose's heart lurched and tears ran down her cheeks.

"Hush." She ran her fingers along the softness of Maak's head. "It's going to be over soon."

Rose brought forward the sharp blade and set it on the animal's throat. Maak looked at her. Understanding and acceptance flashed in the animal's eyes, and something akin to gratitude.

She pushed on the blade, putting her full weight behind it.

Maak's bleating was choked off as the blade cut its throat, and a torrent of blood gushed out, covering her hands in red. In a second, the blue eyes lost their shine and she knew he was gone. Rose choked back a sob, then got to her feet.

Arlia was out there somewhere, and she wouldn't give up until she found her.

"Arlia, are you there?"

She had steadied herself to repeat her call when the grass on her left began to move.

Her first instinct was to think it was Arlia, unable to call out, but hearing her and trying to attract her attention. Then the grass moved again, but this time in a different spot, and Rose realized her mistake. This wasn't Arlia.

Her chest heaved faster as adrenaline rushed into her bloodstream, making her muscles ready to run. Rose knew what those new creatures were even before the first snout appeared between the grass stalks. Karian's words were etched in her mind and a slow, deep shiver ran down her spine.

We have a pride of killkons this side of the Long Lake.

The creature that stepped into the small clearing was about three feet tall, its head coming to the level of her elbows. It had short, black on green brindled fur, matching the grassland in a perfect camouflage. It was longer than it was tall, reaching a good seven feet in length, and six legs gave it agility and extreme speed. It was a surprisingly graceful animal, with a shapely body and a long tail, which flipped the air in rhythm with its steps, making it appear as if it was dancing and not stalking its victim with deadly intent.

The three shining copper eyes of a second killkon appeared from the darkness, settling on her, and a long, forked tongue tasted the air in a flicking motion. At a glance, Rose understood they were male and female, a mated pair of hunters.

Time was suspended as the killkons locked their gazes on her. She slowly stood up, her knees shaking with utter terror. She clutched the kitchen knife between her fingers so hard it hurt, its smooth wooden handle slick with the meerit's blood. The blade wouldn't help her fight off that nightmarish predator. If she was lucky, she might deliver a good blow and injure one of them, but not both.

They were frozen, beasts and woman alike, sizing each other up in an unmoving challenge. Rose was a novelty, an unknown quantity, and the predators were curious, flicking their tongues forward and staring at her with their terrible, intelligent stare.

Carefully, Rose inched backward, fighting against her instinct to turn around and flee. This would trigger the hunt and kill instinct of the predator in a sure way. Her only chance was to make herself appear as challenging an adversary as she could, so they lost their interest in her and returned to eat their freshly killed prey.

A few seconds later, the large male killkon walked over to the dead meerit, sniffing the body of the animal before tearing into its flesh, forgetting Rose's presence altogether. She had won her bet with him. She was large and standing her ground, and the animal preferred the safety of an already dead meal to the exhaustion of hunting down a second animal.

As Rose inched back a second step, the smaller female killkon twisted her head, her deadly gaze flickering with intelligence. She knew what Rose was doing, and she was deciding whether to allow her to leave with her life or not.

In slow motion, Rose lowered the blade, holding its handle with both hands for fear of letting it slip to the ground. The female killkon wasn't finished with her: either because she hadn't concluded her analysis of Rose's strength, or because she knew the male was going to eat the lion's share of the meerit and she wanted to have more prey to feast on.

Another step back made the female killkon snap her jaw, the sound of her teeth making a clean, dry crackling in the air, but she still didn't move from where she stood. Copper eyes locked on her with blazing intent. Rose's heart beat so fast it hurt and the rush of blood drowned all other sounds as it flooded into her body, saturating her muscles with oxygen and adrenaline, readying them for the fight or flight that was to follow.

Because she knew what that look meant. The female killkon was just like Rose; she wasn't about to pass a chance for a kill if she had one.

In the next heartbeat, Rose decided against running. Those six agile limbs gave the female killkon such a superior advantage that Rose wasn't going to be able to go more than a dozen steps before she was on her. It was better to face the killkon than to have her dig her claws into Rose's back.

Rose lifted the blade in front of her and lowered her stance as if she was throwing a spear.

The female killkon moved on her six legs, so smoothly it seemed like she was gliding above the ground. She took a few steps to Rose's side, moving in the opposite direction of her mate. Rose knew what she was doing. The female killkon wanted to push Rose to her mate, closing her escape route, because even if the male killkon was busy tearing and swallowing the meerit's flesh, he wouldn't be able to resist the call of the hunt and would be on Rose the second she attacked.

Rose backed away, keeping both killkons in front of her as much as possible while the female kept her slow stalk to her side. She could feel the female killkon's intent drifting off her in waves of calculated violence. She was a cold, bloodthirsty killer, and she knew exactly what she was doing.

I'm going to die.

Tears came to Rose's eyes as she finally backed to the edge of the small clearing. The female killkon wasn't going to allow her to leave. She could feel the remaining seconds in her life slipping away. Tears broke out of her burning eyes, but Rose didn't dare to even blink. She was sure the killkon would seize this opportunity to make her move, and that there would be no second chance to defend herself.

Rose's foot grazed the grass at the edge of the clearing, and the female killkon hissed. It was the only warning sign she gave before leaping to the side, her slender body twisting in mid-air, her jaw open, ready to snap at the back of Rose's neck. Under pure instinct, Rose fell to the ground, slashing upward with the short blade, hoping she would cut the animal deeply enough to injure it. The killkon was smart enough to recognize the threat and twisted her abdomen out of the way, but not fast enough for the blade to spare her entirely. The sharp blade slid over her ribs, and the killkon screeched in pain.

The female killkon landed on her side, crashing on the ground in a cloud of dust. Blood splattered the green and black fur with bright red, like the blossom of a vicious flower. The male killkon stopped tearing the meerit's flesh and looked up, surprise and understanding plain in his face. He took a step towards his mate, his tongue flicking, tasting the blood. A ripple traveled down his spine in a wave of hostility that made Rose's blood freeze in her veins.

The female killkon stumbled to her feet, then flicked her tongue at the blood on her ribs. She slowly turned her head back to Rose and hissed again, but this time the sound was different. It wasn't the sound of the first hiss, full of challenge and bravado. No, this sound had anger and blood sewn into each breath of air slipping through that mouthful of fangs.

She wasn't playing anymore. She was out for blood.

That was all it took to turn Rose's intention of fighting off the monsters into a primitive need for flight. She turned around, still gripping the hunting knife, and ran.

Chapter Twenty-Five

Rose

The tips of the grass flicked against Rose's jaw but she barely registered the burn of the tiny cuts.

All her energy was focused on the shining dome of the house, impossibly far away in the distance. Tears ran freely down the sides of her face and her legs pumped hard, beating the grass down, leaving a trail of broken stalks behind her. Her confused mind wondered how she was still alive, how the killkons hadn't dug their claws into her back already.

Then Rose was closer and closer, the door to the walls shining in front of her, taunting her with safety.

She was going to make it. The killkons had decided she wasn't worth the chase.

"Open the door!" she screamed at the top of her lungs.

The door was getting closer by the second. Elation made Rose double her efforts. Hope was a powerful drug, and only the smallest taste of it made her crave more until all of her was consumed by it. She had hope of survival, where only a few minutes before, she was sure death was coming for her.

A movement in the grass on her left made her look to the side, peeling her eyes off the house's roof for the first time since she began to run. There, the grass moved in time with her, keeping up pace behind her heels. Another rustling noise came from Rose's right, and she snapped her head around to see a similar pattern in the grass.

They hadn't abandoned the chase. They were hunting her in their highly efficient, vise grip fashion.

Hard dirt slammed underneath her feet. She was in the clearing around the house's walls. Rose's hands hammered on the door. She screamed and slammed her open palms against the wood, calling frantically. It stayed closed.

"Oh, God." She turned around, her back flat against the door, its scorching heat searing her flesh through her clothes. Reaching up reflexively, she realized Arlia's necklace was missing. She must have lost it during the chase.

The grass moved and a large snout emerged from between the stalks, gleaming copper eyes settling on Rose. The male killkon's eyes shone with resentment, and he dug at the ground around his paws with his long, wicked claws. He was furious Rose had injured his mate. This was personal, a one on one standoff with the beast. Rose had no doubt who was going to win it.

A few moments later, the grass parted and the female killkon appeared. She was visibly exhausted and panting heavily. When she took another step, placing her paws just outside the grass perimeter, Rose saw she was limping badly, the chase probably having exacerbated her injury. Her cold eyes shone with a blood curdling rage.

Silently, Rose raised the knife in front of her body, its tip trembling. The blade was streaked red with fresh blood and the sun danced on the metal, sending a rainbow of sunlight across the grass.

The male killkon stepped forward, his tongue flicking the air in Rose's direction once. Then he hissed, his impressive jaws open and the sound of his wrath rippling across her face, making it numb with terror. He hunched his front paws slightly, then sprang into the air, his paws extended and claws at the ready.

A screeching sound invaded the hot, dry air.

The door at Rose's back vanished and she fell onto the ground, the impact making her jaws snap shut. A sharp pain invaded her mouth, soon followed by the coppery taste of blood. Right in front of her, where she had stood a few seconds ago, a cloud of dust hid three looming shapes, and as she blinked the sand out of her eyes, she recognized a tall blue figure facing two low, green forms.

The green forms of the killkons moved in perfect harmony, circling the tall blue figure.

That slim waist, broad shoulders and strong, elegant movement: Rose knew who it was.

Karian.

She tried to call to him, but her throat constricted and she could barely let out a whisper. Her legs weighed a ton and her body refused to obey as she watched Karian battle the two deadly predators. He moved with the efficiency of a feline and the strength of a bear, slashing with his talons and twisting to meet both attackers at once. He was as deadly as he was savage, and her guts twisted in both worry and awe.

Time seemed to stop and the three figures stilled, giving the cloud of dust a chance to settle. Karian had his back to Rose but she could see both killkons, the male and female on each side of him, slightly closer to the grass. They had him in a vise grip.

The female killkon was the first to make a move. She lurched, targeting Karian's shins. Immediately afterward, the male killkon jumped, aiming his larger body at Karian's neck. It was a deadly attack, performed in perfect synchronicity.

Karian ducked just in time to miss the male killkon's attack on his neck. The male killkon went rolling in the dust two feet away, while his mate's jaws snapped the air an inch from Karian's leg. Karian twisted around and grabbed the female killkon's slim neck in his powerful grip. The female killkon screeched and writhed, her tail whipping the ground and her paws scratching the air.

A sickening snapping sound tore through the air and the female killkon's body went limp. Karian opened his hands, allowing the body to fall into the dust. Looking down at the dead animal, Karian stepped back a few steps, then grabbed the door, ready to close it on the predators.

Karian paused and his head turned towards the male killkon, which was still where he had landed two feet away. The animal was very still, his gaze locked on the unmoving body of his mate. Finally, taking slow, careful steps, he walked toward the downed female. As he reached her, his tongue flicked out, caressing her face and snout.

A high-pitched wail rose as the male killkon understood the fate of his mate. The sound dragged on the air, depriving it of oxygen as the pain it carried scorched everything in its wake. He turned his head to meet Karian's gaze, still howling his staggering grief. The sound pierced through, bringing tears to Rose's eyes, and as Karian's shoulders slumped, she understood he was touched by the animal's agony, too.

The male killkon didn't attack Karian. He had lost all desire to fight. Instead, he rubbed his head against her soft fur in a heart-wrenching caress, the gesture so tender it revealed feelings that were true beyond species and beyond time. It was the display of a love felt with a primal depth, all through the bones of those animals who joined their lives together. When the killkon had finished rubbing his head along the limp body of his female, he crawled over her and wrapped his limbs over her in a tender embrace, then cradled his head on her shoulders. It was as if the couple were preparing to sleep.

Karian shook his head, then closed the door on the animals.

Through the wall, the killkon's wretched, sorrowful wail still grew and grew in a variety of notes, in a staggering and terrible display of grief.

"What were you doing outside?"

Karian still had his back to Rose, but she knew how he was feeling. His shoulders were shaking and he pressed his hands onto the metal of the door hard enough that the knuckles were almost white. She didn't need to see his face to know he was filled to the brim with fury.

She didn't answer him. She was too stunned by the way events had turned out. Mainly, she was surprised to be alive. Her eyes caught a furtive movement near the house, and she turned her head to see a flutter of mother of pearl skin, black hair, and a long purple gown disappearing into the house.

"Rose." Karian's voice was falsely calm, and nearer than before. "What were you doing outside?"

Rose's head refused to snap back into place, no matter how much she wanted to look at Karian. A hurricane of emotions stormed inside her mind, laying waste to her sanity, making her blood boil and curdle in her veins.

"Rose, look at me." Hands closed around her shoulders. His voice had lost its edge, and it was filled with worry. "Are you hurt?"

A slow, deep shiver started at the base of her spine and traveled up to the top of her head. Her blood wasn't boiling anymore, the heat of the fury replaced by a frigid grasp. It was a cold kind of anger, an anger that could only be brought on by a premeditated kind of hurt. It was an arctic rage.

Outside, the male killkon's wails kept sounding, unabated.

Figures emerged from the house. First, the tall shapes of Enlon and Arlen, then the two slightly smaller ones of Arlia and Maral.

As Rose saw Arlia, unhurt, a slow, deadly certainty began to furrow inside her. Arlia had never been outside the walls. She had never lost her necklace in the grass.

Someone wanted me to get outside. It was all a set up.

They walked toward Rose in hurried steps, their faces drawn with worry. They stopped a few paces behind Karian, clearly waiting for him to speak to her before opening their mouths. Rose's eyes caught Maral's for a fleeting moment, and Maral's pupils constricted to almost nothing before dilating again. She quickly looked down at the ground, avoiding Rose's stare.

It was her. She wanted me to get mauled to death.

Rose wanted nothing more than to shred those treacherous eyes with her nails. With a supreme effort, she stayed still, and tore her gaze away from Maral.

She turned her head to stare into Karian's shocked, wide eyes. His features were drawn tight across his bones, and the corner of his mouth twitched. He was scared, scared for her.

"Maral." Rose blinked, and reality started to settle in. "It was all her doing. She wanted me to die."

A small, choked sound came from the general direction of Maral. Karian frowned and shook his head. Confusion and denial were plain on his face, and it made Rose want to scream.

"What are you talking about?" His hands on Rose's shoulders moved in a rubbing motion, like the soothing gesture would put some sense into her. Like she didn't know exactly what Maral had tried to do. "Maral holo-called all of us the instant she realized you had walked out of the enclosure. She was hysterical, saying you went after Maak."

"It's a lie." Rose's voice shook. "She lured Maak outside. She left Arlia's necklace for me to find."

Karian frowned. He didn't say it, but Rose knew he didn't believe her. She stepped away from him, shaking her head. Behind him, Enlon and Arlia exchanged a glance but remained silent.

Arlia pulled her necklace out of her dress, showing it to Rose.

"Rose, dear." Arlia took a step closer. She looked both scared and a little sad. "You knew I was going into town today, to have the fabric you chose made into a gown. You forgot."

"No." Rose shook her head in negation. "I found your necklace outside. I recognized it." But doubt insinuated itself inside her mind. She wished the necklace hadn't been lost in her escape, but there was nothing to be done about it. It was lost now, somewhere in the vast expanse of the Eokian grass. "I woke up and you were gone. I was harvesting the mushberries when I noticed the door was open."

They all looked at each other with quiet disbelief. Maral closed her hand around Arlen's arm, the long fingers like spider's legs on the deep blue of his skin.

"I was in the cleansing room." Maral spoke, her voice small and strained, her eyes wide and shining. "I saw you outside by the trees but didn't think anything of it. Then, when I looked again, you were gone, and the door was open. I closed it, afraid killkons would get in, then I went looking for you. When I couldn't find you, I called everyone. I knew you'd gotten out, but I couldn't go out there with you."

"Of course not," Arlen intervened, wrapping his arm around his mate's shoulder.

Arlia bit her lower lip, and Rose had the sickening feeling that she had lost control of the situation. She trailed her gaze over the rest of them, only to find careful, closed up expressions. They didn't believe her, either.

"We know you're under a lot of stress," Arlia said patiently. "But this was only an accident."

A few moments went by, and Rose closed her eyes. Yes, she remembered.

"Maral was there when I called." Rose shook her head, fighting the tears of frustration that came to her eyes, knowing full well they would make her seem weak and unreliable. "The door closed and locked behind me as soon as I stepped out."

"I shut the door but I didn't lock it." Maral's crystal voice rose, as sweet as sugar spiked with crushed glass. "Maybe you just didn't know how to open it from outside. The mechanism isn't easily visible, and nobody showed you how to use it yet."

Doubt settled over Rose and she fought it off. She hadn't panicked or been unable to use the lock. She had been locked outside.

"No, that's not what happened." But Rose could see in Karian's face, in the way he looked at her, that it was no use. He believed Maral. "I screamed and banged on the door. You knew I was there, and you didn't help me." She was shouting now, not caring if it only made things worse. Let them think what they wanted.

"No." Maral took a step back, hiding partially behind Arlen. "I was already inside, calling Karian, Arlen, Enlon, everyone I could think of."

"You're lying!" Rose yelled, taking a step toward Maral.

"Rose, you need to step back." Arlen talked with a calm voice but he pushed Maral behind him, using his impressive frame as a shield.

Before Rose could tell Arlen exactly where he could stick his retreat, a low growl vibrated at her back. A broad back blocked her vision as Karian put himself between Rose and Arlen, his skin rippling with aggressive tension. Arlia gasped and put both hands over her mouth, her golden eyes shining with fear and hurt.

"Do not threaten my mate, brother," Karian said.

"She's the one threatening my mate." Arlen sneered at his older brother, exposing his fangs. "You need to back off."

A vicious snarl ripped through the air. Karian stared at Arlen, his eyes shining with anger and his fangs exposed, ready for a fight.

"Both of you should be ashamed." Enlon's voice cut off the altercation, and both Karian and Arlen locked their gazes on their father. "Look at your mother, for Midnight God's sake."

Arlia's face was streaked with tears and her hands convulsively squeezed at the collar of her dress. Shame spread instantly over both sons as they took the measure of the turmoil inflicted on their mother, and they both took a step back.

Rose stared at the two males, too shocked to say anything. Karian and Arlen had been a hair's breadth away from tearing each other apart over their mates. Over her and Maral. Rose was appalled at the idea of Karian being at odds with his family, especially Arlen, who had spent the last ten years searching relentlessly for him, putting his own life on hold.

"Rose almost died." Arlia cut the heavy silence, her usually melodious voice shaking. She turned to Karian, her face pleading. "You should take her inside and help her settle down."

Karian stared at his mother, blinked a few times, then nodded. He turned his back on Arlen and Maral and locked gazes with Rose. Without speaking, he bent and swept her into his arms, cradling her like a small child against his chest.

They didn't speak until they were alone in their bedroom and he had put her down.

"Are you hurt?" He didn't wait for an answer and pulled her loose shift over her head, then inspected every exposed inch of her body with scrutiny that would make her squirm under different circumstances.

"No, I'm fine." She pulled his face up until he was staring into her eyes. "I had a good scare, and I could use some water, but it's nothing that can't be cured with a good meal and a long night's sleep. Really, I'm okay."

Karian's eyes flashed and he pulled her into his chest, crushing her in a way that spoke more than words ever could. Rose's lips began to tremble and she abandoned herself in his embrace, inhaling his scent and losing herself in the feeling of his warm skin under her cheek. His proximity stirred stronger emotions each time, and as her hands ran up his muscular back, a now familiar heat began low in her belly.

Karian pushed her away from his chest. "I can't believe you ran out like that."

She looked up to see his eyes shining with anger. His mouth was a thin line, lips pressed together, and a vein was pulsing at his temple. Now that he was reassured of her physical well-being, she realized he was angry.

"You were almost mauled. You could have died."

"I didn't run out." Rose stepped back, her irritation mixing with emotional exhaustion. This was beginning to seriously aggravate her. "Why won't you believe me? I didn't go out for a leisurely stroll. I thought Arlia was in trouble."

"You went out there with no protection, no weapons," Karian growled. "How did you expect to protect my mother from the kilkons? With your bare hands?"

"I had a knife," Rose said through clenched teeth, her anger burning like embers, low and deep. "I'm a good huntress. I track prey as well as the best of them."

Karian looked down at her, his mouth still grim, but the lines softened as the anger slowly slipped out of him. He stared for a long time, then nodded.

"All that matters is that you're safe now."

He brought his hand up and rubbed his forehead. Rose noticed the lines of worry at the corners of his mouth, the dark circles almost black under his eyes. Guilt and concern flashed inside her, and she struggled to find the strength to go to him, to stroke the tension away from those wide shoulders. In the end, she couldn't. As much as she wanted to, she was too hurt by his refusal to trust her.

She searched to find something else to say—anything—but found she was empty of words. She wasn't sure whether Maral had really locked her out, or if it was only her nerves that were frayed, but she knew the scar it had left between herself and Karian. He viewed her as reckless and without judgment. She couldn't be with someone who dismissed her, who didn't view her as his equal.

Karian's eyes left Rose to gaze out the window. Sadness and pity flashed on his perfect, hard features.

Outside, the male killkon's howls were morphing into a rhythmic, slow complaint. The sounds tore at Rose's heart, painting a picture of the animal's grief no human words could. His pain was deep and staggering, and as his voice grew in a steady staccato, tears came to her eyes.

"Why doesn't he stop?" She would give anything to be rid of that sound. It was a bottomless, dark pit of misery no animal should be able to feel.

"He's mourning," Karian answered, his face half-turned to the window, his eyes an unreadable pool of blue. "Killkons mate for life." He turned to Rose, and she was surprised to spot a veil of pain in his gaze, but it was gone too fast for her to be sure. "He'll be dead by morning."

"What?" Rose was left dumbstruck. "How?"

"Killkons do not survive the death of their mates. Their bond is too strong. He is dying as he's singing the departure of his beloved." Karian inhaled deeply, then turned away from the window to face

Rose. "Eokim is a planet where bonds run deep. Killkons and Eoks are kindred spirits in this."

Karian stepped closer, then his fingers closed at the back of her neck. He pulled Rose in and placed a soft kiss on her forehead. A fascinating, yet terrible realization lurked in her mind, just out of reach.

"How kindred?"

Her words were soft, but she sensed she was getting close to some terrible truth that had eluded her for too long. Karian stared at her, his blue eyes full of some ancient knowledge, and then she knew. His family's reaction to the bloodmating, Karian's constant obsession with her safety—it all made sense now.

"The bloodmating," she said in a breathless gasp. "It linked us the same way the killkons are linked, didn't it?"

Karian didn't reply, but the gleam in his eyes gave her the answer she needed. The implications of the true meaning of the bloodmating made her head feel light, like it was going to float away.

"Why didn't you tell me?" The words left her lips in a whisper.

"What does it change?" Karian kept his gaze on Rose with such intensity that she felt herself melting into the floor. "Bloodmating is not reversible. It's a rare occurrence, something that only happens when an Eok warrior meets his lifemate, the one he cannot live without. If she dies, he follows soon after."

"But that doesn't apply to you and me," Rose negated, but there was something stubborn and hopeful that fluttered deep inside her stomach. "You mated me to repay your debt, not because we're some kind of soulmates."

Karian watched her for a long time. All the while, hope raced around in her mind like a trapped wild animal, refusing to give up. Finally, he pursed his lips, then shook his head.

"I'm leaving for the Ring's Headquarters tomorrow." Karian pulled away and locked eyes with Rose. "The Council moved their session up. The Trade Minister is on to something."

"You're not going there by yourself." How could he think she'd allow him to go alone? "I'm coming with you."

"It's out of the question." He shook his head in negation. "You're staying here with my family, where they can protect you."

"Certainly not. I'm not about to let you go there by yourself when I'm the only proof we have. It makes no sense for me to stay behind. They'll have only your word against Minister Knut's. It won't be enough."

"I can't have you in danger." His eyes shone under the soft light. His words were as soft as his voice, but there was no mistaking the steel underneath. "I won't be able to think straight if I'm worried about your safety."

"Then protect me. I know how formidable a warrior you are. You can find a way."

"You don't understand how difficult it is to secure your safety."

"I can't live this way. I can't be with someone who's willing to crush my freedom, to impose his will over mine whenever he thinks he's right." This over-protectiveness was racking her nerves. He needed to trust her, or they could never be truly close. "Ever since we were rescued from Saarmak, you've been pushing me back. You're not honest with me."

"I'm as honest as I can be without endangering you."

"That's not enough for me," Rose replied, taking a step closer.

Karian's mouth thinned until his lips were a fine line, and his eyes gleamed, but he remained silent. He agreed, then. Rose was nothing but a female now that they were in his world. Everything they had been to each other when survival was all that mattered was gone. Rose couldn't feel the same about the Karian on Eokim as she had for the Karian on Saarmak. That Karian had been full of humor, intelligence, and had a trusting heart. The Karian from Saarmak treated her as his equal. Here on Eokim, all those things were gone.

She needed him to understand how much she needed this trust, this partnership. He belonged to her as much as she belonged to him.

"We had a deal." She lost herself in those shining blue eyes, so deep she felt as if she was drowning a bit more every time. "You promised you'd do everything you can to save my family, my people. For that, you need me at the Ring's session."

"I'm not going to put you in harm's way." He took a step closer, but nothing in his body yielded. He was unmovable, and she knew he wouldn't change his mind.

"It's not your decision to make." Rose shook her head, refusing to give in.

"Yes it is." The dominating tone of his voice transformed his words into a low growl. "You're my mate. My *bloodmate*."

Anger and protectiveness hung around Karian like a physical aura. Rose knew she should give up, but she couldn't. She needed to win this battle with him, or their life together would be a living hell, a shell of the life they could have if he just *listened*.

"That doesn't mean you get to decide for me." She stood her ground against her instinct to cower. "Bloodmate or not, you don't own me."

"I might not own you, Pretty Thing," Karian said through clenched teeth. His shoulders were tense and his entire body radiated dominating strength. "But I can order that you stay on Eokim."

"I'm their only hope," she snapped, ignoring the warning shooting through her head like fireworks. "I'm going to this session of the Ring, and there's nothing you can do to stop me."

"You won't, even if I have to lock you in."

"If I don't go and the motion is denied because of this, I'll never forgive you."

Silence fell between them. Karian and Rose locked eyes and the large warrior swallowed, his eyes going wide, then losing their usual shine. Rose felt a surge of need to touch the exposed skin of his arms, to hold him to her, but she resisted.

What she had said was cruel, but it was also true.

"I'll go wash off before bed." Karian's voice was flat and toneless.

It was clear there was nothing more to be said about the matter. He turned and walked away, but he paused at the doorway.

"I think you should sleep on the sofa tonight." Rose's voice was pinched, like she lacked oxygen.

Karian waited a few seconds, then walked away with his back turned to Rose. Not long after, the shower started, and Rose got into the bed, hot tears stinging her eyes. That night, darkness wrapped itself around her, engulfing her in its embrace, in sync with the killkon's death song.

Chapter Twenty-Six

Karian

He stood under the scorching water for a long time, allowing the heat to seep into his muscles, untangling the knots of worry that knitted his bones in place. The sheer terror he had felt came back in a flood.

Rose's words came back to his mind. She was certain the door to the enclosure surrounding the family house had intentionally been left open, and that she had been led outside. It wasn't likely, though. Even through the anger and fear he still felt when he imagined Rose running for her life in the Eokian wilderness, he couldn't blame an agent of Trade Minister Knut for it. It was too indirect, with too many chances of things going wrong. If it had been the action of a Cattelan death squad, Rose would have been captured or killed on the spot. Her survival wouldn't have been left to the instincts of wild animal.

Still, there was something there that wasn't simply a coincidence. There was something else he wasn't considering, but no matter how hard he tried, he couldn't think what. In a flash, he remembered Rose's statement.

She wanted me to get mauled to death.

No. Arlen's mate might be a lot of things, but she wasn't a killer. Maral was jealous and vain, but she knew the penalty for betrayal. Banishment and being stripped of everything she possessed. She would never risk it, not even to get rid of a rival.

Karian grunted at a sharp pain, then looked down to find a long cut along his thigh. The killkon had left his claw mark in his flesh, but the sight didn't fill him with anger. It only filled him with a tuned down kind of sorrow. The animal had fought bravely, fiercely beside his mate, but he'd lost. Now that she was gone, he had no will to live.

Karian contemplated his same fate should anything happen to Rose. That was the difference between a regular mating and a blood-mating. His life was tied to Rose's on a biological level. Her fate was his fate.

His need to protect Rose and keep her from harm was a compulsion, ingrained in his biology on the most primal level. Still, he knew he had to get a grip on it or it would smother her in the long run. Their most recent fight was a poignant testimony to that fact.

She deserves better. She's smart, and resourceful, and strong.

Rose's face, hurt and honest in her anger, came back to his mind. She was right, she had to come to the Ring session to testify in front of the Council. His testimony wouldn't be enough. All the Ring's nations would be present at the session; they would all be riveted to see and hear a human talk. Her presence was the only way to steer the balance of power in their favor.

The only problem was that Minister Knut would do everything in his power to kill Rose before she could even appear. Leaving her on Eokim while he gave his best to the Ring session was the safest option for her, but it was the worst option for the humans' cause back on Earth.

Rose would not forgive him if he caused the humans to lose the protection of the Ring. He'd know that even if she hadn't said it. She was a protector, and her heart was tied to her people in a vital way.

He might be protecting her life if he forced her to stay on Eokim, but he would kill the most important part of her. The part of her that he couldn't live without, bloodmating or not. The part of her that he loved with every fiber of his being.

A wave of exhaustion overcame Karian. He wanted nothing more than to lie in bed with Rose, lie over her body and feast on the luxurious feel of her skin. He wouldn't, though. Not tonight. Not after she'd made it clear she didn't want his presence.

He turned off the water and stepped out, glad to be clean after the fight. Outside, the killkon's song rang out, the melancholy of its melody a low-level vibration, an unshakable sadness seeping into the air around the house.

He dressed fast, then went to find his father and brother.

Karian had made his choice between his compulsion and Rose's deepest need. That didn't mean he was going to be unprepared.

Rose

Rose woke up, noticing the silence of the early morning. The killkon's song had ended sometime in the night. Her head was heavy with fatigue and the stubborn shadows of nightmares lingered in the back of her mind, just beyond the reach of her memories, casting a gloom over everything.

Slowly, she sat up in bed and turned her head to the window, from which a soft breeze flowed in. The silence was worse than the slow caress of the animal's song. She pictured the killkon outside, cradling his mate's body, seemingly sleeping in a tender embrace.

She understood why Karian hadn't rejoiced at the death of the predator.

Weariness settled on her shoulders at the thought of the task ahead. She had to go with Karian to the Ring's session. She would fight him if she had to. If only he understood how much she needed to do everything to make her family, her people safe, he'd let her come.

If he loved me, he'd understand.

She walked to the closet and drew out the sheer green gown Arlia had brought back for her from the dressmaker. It was beautiful and flowing, hinting at her body's curves instead of revealing them, with thin straps at the shoulders that showed a little more skin than she was comfortable with. It was the most beautiful piece of clothing she had ever owned. Rose viewed herself in the large, seven-foot-tall mirror set in the corner of the bedroom.

Her hair fell in a mass of curls, framing her oval face, and her collarbones drew graceful curves on her shoulders, right over the small mounds of her breasts. She looked exactly like human females were supposed to look. She looked fragile and vulnerable, made for sensuality and an easy life. She looked like that porcelain doll her mother once saw in a book and described to her, with her smooth skin and rounded lips, so red they reminded one of blood.

She looked utterly and completely human.

Rose's eyes fell on something shiny on the side table, near the bed. Her heart lurched and emotions coiled in her throat as she neared it. Reverently, she lifted it between her trembling fingers. It was a necklace, with a flower shaped pendant made of the same crystal Arlia's necklace was made of. It was beautiful and fragile, yet somehow radiated strength.

Rose swallowed through her closed throat, then fastened it around her neck. It rested on the skin of her cleavage, just above the beginning of her breasts. As she looked again at her image in the mirror, it felt like the sealing of something long overdue.

Yes. I'm Karian's bloodmate. We were fated to be together.

Steadying her resolve, Rose walked down the long hallway leading to the common portion of the house. There, she met with Arlen, Enlon and Arlia, as well as a stricken-looking Karian. The look on Karian's face was one of amazement and appreciation, in a very male way that made small flutters of awakening spark in her body.

"You're up early," Arlen stated, his eyebrows arching. There was an unsaid compliment in his gaze. "And dressed like a female, for once."

"Rose, darling." Arlia walked up to her and lifted her arms, admiring the gown. "You look wonderful."

"That's thanks to you." Rose smiled and looked at Karian, doing her best to stay both resolved and calm. "Are you ready to go?"

"We are leaving within the hour," he answered, his eyes shining on Rose, then fastening onto the flower necklace.

"Thank you... for this," she said, reaching up to touch the crystal.

His face froze and an unreadable expression passed across his face. "It's tradition for Eok warriors to give such a necklace as a gift after their mating." When he lifted his gaze to hers, there was a hunger in his eyes that vibrated along Rose's very essence.

"I'm coming with you." Rose lifted her chin. It wasn't a question or a request. It was a statement.

A pause followed her words. Karian looked at her, his unreadable alien face closed. "Yes," he answered. "You're coming with us."

"You've changed your mind?" Rose was stunned. She had been bracing for a fight, a potential screaming match, but not this. "But you said it was too dangerous."

"You will have to stay by my side at all times." Karian took a step closer, his hand closing on the naked skin of her upper arm. At the contact, a shiver of unfulfilled want traveled up her body, and when she looked at him, she saw the same need. "You're not to wander. The Minister's people will be looking for any opportunity to prevent you from testifying. There cannot be any."

"I'll do everything you say."

"Good. Because I'm not going to give you an inch of freedom."

"I wouldn't have thought any differently." Rose felt a smile spread on her lips. "Thank you."

Emotions filled her as she understood how much it had cost Karian to bend his will and bring her with him. It wasn't only his pride, although Karian was a very proud male. It was that he was putting her need to protect her family before his need to protect her.

VENOMOUS CRAVING

"Is it just going to be the two of us?" Rose asked.

"I'm coming, too," Arlen answered. "Father has to stay, as the tribe's chief, and Arlia too, as his bloodmate. I can't imagine Maral being much help either, so she'll stay here."

"I'll come with you, too." Maral's crystal voice made everyone turn with a start. "I can persuade a part of the Avonie's faction to vote for the recognition of the humans."

"Maral." Arlen frowned and looked at his mate with incredulous eyes. "The Avonies are the last faction that will vote for the human's recognition."

"Many families are jealous of the Knut clan," Maral answered, walking so softly she looked like she was gliding in her long gown. "They just need a push in the right direction. Avonies were doing just fine before they grabbed the Earth's resources. We'll do just fine after."

Maral locked gazes with Rose, lifting her eyebrows.

"You want to help me?" Rose was too stunned to say anything else. Not after the way she had accused the other female of trying to get her killed. "Why?"

"I have not been my best with you. I *am* sorry if it made you think I wanted harm to come to you." Maral pursed her lips and her pupils flashed thin, then came back to normal. "I do need the family to be as strong as it can be. Especially now." Her gaze went back to Arlen and she tilted her head, showing off the lovely curve of her neck. "I am with youngling."

"You are?" Arlen's voice became a whisper, and it was as if his knees were going to give way. "This is the best news I've gotten in a decade."

Arlen covered the distance between them in a long stride, then lifted Maral in his arms, twirling her around. He laughed, and the sound was so unlike his usual cutting tone that Rose felt her guts twist in knots. Maral smiled demurely, and accepted the congratulations flowing to her in a constant wave of happiness. Arlia and Enlon talked all at once, joy wiping away the former tension. Rose watched the happy family, feelings coiling inside the deepest, most intimate part of herself. For the first time, she wondered what it would feel like to give Karian such a gift. She longed for that happiness in a way she had never suspected.

"Maral can't come with us now, brother." Karian put an arm on Arlen's shoulder. "You can't put her at risk."

"I won't be at risk at all." Maral spoke from under Arlen's heavy embrace, her voice as sweet as her face. "Avonies look out for each other. Elvira, Willa and Illya are coming with me."

Arlen's eyes widened and a fleeting expression clouded his eyes, but it was gone in an instant. Rose watched as he grabbed Maral and started to fuss over her with all the overbearing attention of an anxious male.

Karian was standing slightly behind Rose as she studied the wonders of the Ring's main base. The mind-boggling size of it, hovering in the pitiless cold of space, made her feel slightly dizzy. The metallic alloy superstructure was larger than most medium-sized planets, and the glow of the tens of thousands of lights shining on its surface was enough to cast a glow on the nearby string of small planets used by the Ring Ministers as personal estates. It was beyond impressive. It left

Rose feeling like an ant on the trunk of one of the sequoia trees back home.

She was nothing. She was small and insignificant. She didn't matter.

"It's beautiful and terrible at the same time." Rose shivered despite the warmth. "All that power. Nobody's going to care about the fate of a few humans."

"There are good and bad people in every species. Many will be sensitive to your cause." Karian's hand closed on her own and she intertwined her fingers with his. "Two centuries ago, a very delicate and peaceful race called the Algoic was completely annihilated by the same greed that almost wiped out the humans. It created widespread outrage of such magnitude that a Genetic Preservation Board was created to make sure no other race ever met the same fate." Karian paused, his thumb tracing gentle circles inside her palm. "You have public opinion on your side."

"That's all they need?" Rose rested her head on Karian's shoulder, seeking the comfort of his strong male body. "To see me?"

"All you really have to do is prove that you were never a slave. If humans can survive without the protection of the Genetic Preservation Board, then they will be freed and will be given back their home planet." A soft kiss landed on the curve of her shoulder, just inside the side of her neck. "It's the law, and even one as powerful as Minister Knut can't change it. If not every species is protected from extinction, then all are at risk."

Rose swallowed. So much depended on her and what would happen in the next few hours.

"How can you be sure it's safe to go there?"

All the Minister had to do to make his problems go away was to destroy the Eok contingent. If she died before the session, then there was no motion. The problem was, if she died, there was a good chance Karian might die with her, along with a number of good Eok warriors. Warriors with families and younglings. She couldn't allow that, not even for her family's sake.

"We have a full contingent of Eok warriors to protect us," Karian answered, recovering his authoritative military seriousness. "But what truly guarantees our safety is that we are on board a Ring's diplomatic vessel. No one would dare attack us here, not even Minister Knut. He would get obliterated, along with his entire family."

"So we made it." The knot in her guts was still there, refusing to go away. "Nothing can stop me from going to that session?"

"Nothing."

But as she stared at the ever-growing sphere, she didn't feel safe. Behind them, the door slid open with a clean whooshing sound. Arlen stepped in, his face set in serious lines.

"We're ready to board the Ring's main base. All authorizations have been given. The warriors are ready."

Chapter Twenty-Seven

Rose

Rose stood still as the round hovering device brought herself, Karian and Arlen into the center of the assembly. Looking around at the number of people looking down on her made her vision slightly blurry, like her mind was refusing to deal with the reality. Thousands upon thousands, that was how many envoys of every nation were sitting, gazing upon her like she was an exotic animal.

The noise of thousands of voices all talking at once in the assembly was creating a buzz deep in her chest, like drums beating ten thousand times too strong. She was fighting the urge to press her palms to her eardrums to drown it out, knowing the gesture would betray weakness, and that this crowd, as curious as it was, was also cruel and ruthless. All they wanted was to see how small and vulnerable she was. They hungered for her failure.

Suddenly, the ruckus died down to a trickle, then stopped altogether.

A large hovering device shaped like an ancient throne was floating in the middle of the open space. On it sat a creature sent straight from Rose's deepest, darkest nightmares. It looked like an insect, as tall as two men standing on each other, with long, deceptively fragile looking limbs of a green so deep it was almost blue. Its head was like a mantis, with two orbs for eyes as black as the void of space, and a pointy snout flanked by a set of mandibles. The two orbs focused on Rose, full of cold calculation. No mercy, no salvation was to be expected there.

This is Prime Councilor Aarv. She's the one who has our fate in her hands.

A deep-set shiver traveled through Rose's bones, chilling the marrow within.

"We open this session with a special motion by the Eok nation." The creature spoke with a voice made of grating metal. "The motion is put forth that the human species no longer needs to be protected under the Genetic Protection Board and be given back its rightful natural habitat of Earth."

The ruckus started again, but a single motion of her long-fingered hand silenced the assembly. Rose's and Karian's hovering device floated to the center of the space, in front of the terrible creature.

"Commander in Chief Karian of the Erynian Tribe, you have the first words."

All eyes fastened on Karian. Rose watched, mesmerized, as her bloodmate stood tall and confident under the scrutiny of the crowd. He truly was a magnificent male, proud and strong. Pride churned her insides, warming the chill of her previous fears.

"We all know the decision to protect the last few human specimens was taken over a century ago. It was motivated by a desire to prevent the same tragedy that befell the Algoic nation from happening to the humans." Karian's voice was calm and strong, carrying to the far reaches of the large assembly. "The decision was a good one, and it saved the few humans who remained on Earth for the ages to come. But now, humans live free again on their homeland, they do not need the help of the Genetic Preservation Board anymore."

"Commander Karian, you will have to provide proof of the allegations." The tall, insect-looking creature leaned forward, her round, completely black eyes reflecting the light like a kaleidoscope. "Can you assure the Council that the humans can not only survive, but thrive on their homeland without the protection of the Genetic Preservation Board?"

"Yes, Prime Councilor Aarv." Karian circled Rose's shoulders. "This human female is my bloodmate. She is living proof that humans are thriving on Earth without the protection of the board."

Another ruckus shook the crowd—the news of a bloodmating, and a high profile one, causing an even greater disruption. This time it took the furious metallic hissing of Prime Councilor Aarv to silence the excited audience.

"Since her relatives are living on the free human settlement on Earth, they are protected under Eokian law. I am merely here to ask that you include all humans in the same protection."

A flurry of whispers greeted Karian's words, but tapered down quickly. A number of faces were closed off or downright hostile, but an even greater number seemed genuinely in agreement with Karian. Hope, stubborn and instantaneous, came up inside Rose, and she found herself standing straight beside her bloodmate. Let them see humans weren't weak. Let them see humans deserved freedom.

"Commander Karian speaks the truth." A familiar voice ripped the air, and Minister Knut floated to the center of the assembly. His clean demeanor had a cutting edge, and Rose knew instantly he was going to be a formidable adversary. This was an old politician, as attuned to the arena of words as Karian was to a sword. "The human female you see before you is indeed bloodmate to the Commander in Chief, but that is where the truth stops. His words, no doubt motivated by a righteous desire to protect his mate, are misleading. The specimen is property of the Human Preservation laboratories." Minister Knut sent a slow gaze around the assembly to make sure he had their full attention. "This only proves that humans are still in great danger of poaching and need the Genetic Preservation Board to protect their females, lest they become extinct."

"Minister Knut." Prime Councilor Aarv's mandible clicked and clacked a staccato beat like shears of steel ripping. "You are proposing the specimen is a stolen slave, and not a free born human, as Commander Karian swears?"

A rumble traveled through the crowd. Rose spotted a group of Avonies, elegant and composed, smiling at her with predatory satisfaction. Karian's earlier words had a new, less appealing light under the Minister's lies.

"The specimen was born in the facility. She has been marked." Minister Knut's smile grew chillingly satisfied. "All subjects born are numbered for tracking purposes."

"So, you have proof. If the mark is there, the subject was born in the facility." Prime Councilor Aarv turned to Karian. "Is the mark present on your mate?"

Karian appeared confused for a fraction of a second, then it was gone. Rose's mind ran in circles, wondering what the Minister's mark was.

"My mate bears no such mark," Karian answered, his voice assured and strong.

"We will inspect the specimen." Prime Councilor Aarv motioned, and a hovering device floated towards Karian and Rose, carrying two white-skinned creatures wearing what could only be described as lab coats. Beside Rose, Karian's entire body tensed and a deep growl escaped his throat. His arm around Rose tightened, and she had the sickening premonition that this was exactly what Minister Knut's plan was. He intended for Karian to lose his temper. In a flash, Rose was certain that to respond with violence inside the Ring's assembly meant certain death. Yes, this was the Minister's plan. Then he would be free to reclaim Rose and all the humans back on Earth.

"Medical examiners, proceed."

Karian's growl deepened and the tips of his fangs showed. Rose's stare locked with Minister Knut's, and she saw a faint glint in his eyes. Satisfaction, that was what it was. Reacting, she gripped Karian's upper arm. The muscles were taut like bowstrings under her fingers.

"Don't," she whispered. "That's what he wants."

Karian turned his blazing eyes her way and he slowly, consciously, relaxed his jaws, and soon his shoulders followed. Reassured that Karian wasn't going to rip open some Ring medical staffer's throat and sign his own death certificate at the same time, Rose watched the creatures approach. The medical examiners were of a species she had never seen or heard of before, with long, fine limbs that appeared frail and supple, with skin so white it looked transparent. Their oval, black eyes were shining under the light above lipless mouths. Their long, spidery fingers hung at their sides, moving restlessly. Revulsion and fury met side by side in her mind at the idea of those insect-like fingers running along her skin.

Rose stood still as the two creatures stepped onto the hovering device. The first one produced a rectangular device emitting a faint white light, then motioned for her to come closer and hold her arms out. After a second, Rose nodded.

"The mark is a serial number engraved in the specimen's radius bone with uranianite composite. The engraving is done in utero, a few hours before birth. It's a perfect tracking process." Minister Knut's smile turned into a sneer. "It is only visible under short wave rays."

A specimen. Not a person. An animal, to be owned and tagged.

Revulsion tapered down, to be fully replaced by the burning sensation of an all-consuming anger. The words Knut used came back and back, twirling in her mind like trapped animals.

The first creature extended its arm to touch Rose, but a vicious growl made it stop.

"I'll do the scanning." Karian extended his hand. "No one touches Rose."

"The specimen is afraid of a simple scan." Minister Knut spoke, his voice a soft, poisonous caress. "Humans can't fend for themselves. Just look at this one."

The anger broke and drowned everything, throwing Rose's caution to the wind. In a huff, Rose stepped between Karian and the creature, then yanked the device out of its hands. After she had fidgeted with it for an embarrassingly long time, the device vibrated slightly and the white light started to glow alternatively stronger and fainter. A scanning device.

Without thinking, Rose used it to swipe up and down her left arm, making a show of it for the crowd, but more importantly for Prime Councilor Aarv. She had an intuition she was powerful enough to be the real force behind most rulings. Rose squared her shoulders, then tossed her head, turning to Minister Knut. Slowly, without taking her stare off the male Avonie, Rose scanned her second arm. As she swiped the device close to her elbow, an exclamation ran through the crowd. Minister Knut's face split into a slow, hateful smirk. Karian growled, then snarled. Rose stared at him, but he wasn't looking into her eyes. No, his gaze was fastened to her arm.

"There." Minister Knut spoke, a despicable, triumphant smile on his lips. "Specimen number 35 890."

Rose's face grew numb. From the corner of her eye, she noticed the two creatures stepping back on their hovering devices, then quickly retreating. From somewhere else, a growl erupted and strong hands closed around her shoulders, pulling her to a hard, warm chest.

Rose's eyes tore from Minister Knut's face...

And landed on the outlines of a serial number, shining through her skin under the short-wave rays. Her serial number was engraved deep in the bones of her forearm.

Rose stared at the serial number, unblinking. Her mind was a gray slate, void of thoughts. She should have known. She had left the breeding facility at three years of age, when her father and several others had orchestrated the massive escape that gave her family and several others their freedom.

I should have known.

She had been marked before she was even born. Minister Knut was right about her.

A specimen. A slave.

Sensations flooded Rose's body and disappeared just as suddenly, bringing an inferno of revulsion-filled rage in their wake. She was branded like livestock.

"As you can see, Commander Karian's claims are disproven," Minister Knut said. "The specimen is indeed property of the Human Preservation Breeding Facility, and should be handed back immediately."

A ruckus exploded in the crowd. Some shouted encouragement, some shouted their outrage at the idea of a mated pair being ripped apart. Most just argued with each other.

"I am not property." Rose spoke for the first time, and was surprised to hear her voice steady and strong, reaching every ear. The ruckus stopped immediately and every eye settled on her. "It is true I was born inside the breeding facility, but that doesn't make me a slave. I'm a person. I belong to no one. Not Minister Knut's Breeding Facility, not even my mate. I am a free human."

"You acknowledge that Commander Karian does not own you?" Minister Knut's eyes shone with perverted glee. "You are but an escapee, and the safest place for you is to return to the care of the breeding facility."

"NO!" Karian roared, and his hold on Rose became painfully tight. "Rose is going nowhere. Mating law supersedes any other, and you know it."

"And yet, humans aren't a recognized free species." Minister Knut turned slightly to glance at Prime Councilor Aarv. "The mating law cannot apply."

Prime Councilor Aarv held out her hand, silencing both the crowd and the people on the hovering devices. She turned her head to stare at Rose, her multi-faceted eyes fixed in cold assessment.

"Minister Knut has the truth of the law." Prime Councilor Aarv nodded once. "Even if it is against my personal inclination, the human named Rose has to return to the care of the facility. You may proceed in reclaiming your property."

A flash of teeth and talons surrounded Rose as Karian and Arlen stepped to her sides, turning their bodies into deadly walls. Prime Councilor Aarv's mandibles clicked in outrage, and the giant creature stood up. Her size would make her a fearsome adversary, but Rose felt, deep inside her most primitive instincts, that that was just the surface of the creature's formidable strength. This was an apex predator, something that would not tolerate a single one of its orders to be disobeyed. Images superimposed themselves over Rose's vision. Images of death and violence for those who would put their lives in front of her own. Karian, as strong as he was, was only one warrior. Arlen, who was expecting a youngling.

Rose wouldn't let them die.

"Prime Councilor Aarv, you are wrong." Rose slipped through the protection of her mate and stood in front of the Prime Councilor. Black beady eyes set on her with deadly intent. "My father and forty others escaped that very facility twenty-three years ago, when I was but a small child. We have been living free of any help for all those years. Twenty-three years."

Silence followed her statement. At her side, Karian appeared baffled, then understanding came over his face. He turned to Rose and smiled.

"We have achieved independence, in spite of all Minister Knut's efforts to retrieve us. We have expanded, many children were born, and many more will be in the near future," she continued, her voice even stronger, captivating the audience. "There is no need for the Genetic Preservation Board to protect humans anymore. What we need is protection from Trade Minister Knut."

"Is there any proof of your saying? That the human village is indeed thriving?" Prime Councilor Aarv's metallic voice was higher pitched, and Rose interpreted it as interest.

"Yes, Prime Councilor." Karian stepped in. "My brother Khal located the human settlement this morning. He will give you any proof you need of the humans' condition back on Earth."

Prime Councilor Aarv nodded her assent, then looked back at Rose. "You will need a sponsoring species to ensure the humans' safety until your people are strong enough to protect themselves."

"The Eok nation will ensure their safety." Arlen spoke for the first time. "I have a seal from all seven tribes' leaders attesting to that."

"Then it is agreed." Prime Councilor turned to Minister Knut. "The human is no longer property of the Human Preservation Breeding Facility, nor is any other previous escapee."

Silence followed. Minister Knut's face contorted with hatred as he turned his gleaming purple eyes to Rose.

"The Knut family would like to put forward a temporary continuing motion." Minister Knut wiped the corner of his mouth with his long fingers. "For those subjects still living in the facility, and the exploitation of the natural resources. After that period, if the humans prove to have enough strength to protect their own species, full freedom will be returned."

"Granted for a period of five years." Prime Councilor Aarv motioned to a hidden creature waiting in the shadows of the large arena. "If, after this period, humans no longer require assistance for their prosperity, then they shall gain total freedom. The human question is henceforth closed until the lifting of the temporary continuing protection order."

And just like that, Rose was holding her freedom in her own hands.

Chapter Twenty-Eight

Rose

Rose sat in a waiting room back on the Ring's diplomatic main base. Incredulity and elation had filled her for the first few hours, but that had died down to a numbing emptiness with the passing of time. Karian and Arlen had both gone to meet with diplomats of other nations to secure as many trade and protection agreements as possible for Earth and the small human population, leaving her alone. She knew she was safe, but she couldn't help wishing she had gone with Karian. However, he had assured her that while the other nation wouldn't negotiate with her, they would gladly make an offer to an envoy of the Eok nation. It ruffled her feathers, but she knew better than to push. The humans didn't have anything to offer, unlike the Eok nation. Still, what she had gained today was a masterpiece.

She had won.

A clicking sound made her jump in her seat and she turned, her heart racing at the idea of finally being alone with Karian.

Then a pearly white face and flowing purple gown emerged into the room.

Tension gathered into a puddle at her feet as Maral entered, followed by Willa, Illya and, finally, Elvira. The Avonies walked into the room, lining up behind Maral, keeping their surreal purple eyes on Rose. Smiles stretched their lips, but alarm bells rang everywhere inside Rose's head. No matter what Maral had told her in front of Arlen, Rose knew she still wasn't a friend. Far from it. Only Elvira seemed not to want to squash her like a bug. Rose had to remind herself that she was still not an ally, merely not overtly an enemy.

"So, you secured the humans' freedom." Maral lifted her perfect eyebrows. "Congratulations."

Her face was twisted, and Rose knew she was fighting her desire to say something truly hurtful. Rose stifled a sigh. She didn't want to fight. Maral's temper tantrums were the last thing she needed.

"Thanks." Rose scanned the closed off faces of the Avonies for signs of trouble, but found only ice walls. "Karian's going to be here soon. You don't have to wait with me."

"Oh, you didn't know?" Maral talked sweetly, and the smile that pursed her lips was chilling to the bone. "Karian left for the diplomatic vessel already."

"He said he was coming back to get me." Rose tried to blink the confusion away, but didn't quite manage it. "The Ring's main base is the safest place for me."

"He's gone." Maral crossed her arms over her chest, glaring at Rose with her bird of prey stare. "Looks like we're going to go back to the diplomatic ship together. Get used to it, males forget about their mates fast outside the bedroom."

Rose locked eyes with Maral, assessing her purple stare. Her usual distaste was there, mixed with a good amount of annoyance, but Rose couldn't find anything else. There was just this suspicion at the back of Rose's throat, like an itch she couldn't scratch. Reluctantly, her gaze left Maral and slid over Willa and Illya, who watched her with a mixture of disdain and excitement. When Rose's eyes settled on Elvira, she saw pity and anger in her pretty face.

This wasn't good. Maral was up to something, all right.

"I'm tired of waiting." Maral rolled her eyes and shot a glance at Willa, whose lips twitched upward. "You either come with me or stay here. Your choice. Honestly, I don't care."

Rose glared at Maral. She was no easy prey, and the sooner the Avonie understood that, the better. Whatever unpleasantness she had planned, she could expect Rose to fight it all the way. Rose looked at Elvira again. Her face was set in stone, her features neutral, and her arms crossed over her breast. But her eyes were gleaming, the warning as plain as a bell.

"No, thanks." Rose lifted her chin. "I'll wait here for Karian to come back."

Maral's eyelids twitched under an angry tic, and she clicked her tongue with an impatient sound.

"Have it your way." Maral slid a small device from the fold of her gown. "I wanted to make it easier for you, but it seems you like to go the hard way."

The other Avonies glanced at each other, confusion spreading on their lovely faces. Confusion and fear. Whatever Maral had just decided, they weren't in on it.

"The human is making a fuss. I told you she was difficult." Maral spoke into the device. "You're going to have to come get her."

"Are you mad?" It was Elvira, shedding her indifferent façade and stepping closer to Maral. "We're on the Ring's main base. It's strictly forbidden."

"Shut up, Elvira." Maral snapped. "I'm getting rid of this... *this animal*." Maral jerked her chin in Rose's direction, looking at her like she would a cockroach on her kitchen counter.

"This isn't what you told us," Elvira persisted, looking angrier by the second. "You said you wanted to play a trick on her. I figured you wanted to mess up her hair and have her walk around the Ring base looking silly."

"Elvira's right, Maral," Willa said, her face uncertain as she kept glancing toward the door, like she was toying with the idea of running away. "I'm all for teaching the human a few lessons, but what you're talking about is serious. It's kidnapping. Our entire families will be killed if we're found out."

"Nobody will know it was us. We're only females, remember?" Maral turned her angry face to her friend, ignoring Rose. "She's going back where she belongs, as a slave."

No.

Rose had to get out of there. She didn't wait for the events to unfold, and ran towards the closest door. With a bit of luck, there would be people there, people who would recognize her as Karian's mate. Someone who would help her.

An instant later, heels clacked on the stone floor behind her. Rose was a fast runner, and she was approaching the door quickly, but it wasn't enough. A set of hands flattened on her shoulder blades, pushing her forward. Rose screamed as the stone floor rushed to meet her face, protecting her head in a reflexive gesture. A cracking sound resonated along her bone, and Rose knew her arm was broken even before the pain had a chance to settle.

A fluted voice rose behind her, high-pitched and trembling.

"She's injured." Rose recognized Illya's voice. "Shit, I broke the arm of the mate of the Commander in Chief. What am I going to do?"

"Nothing." Maral hissed at Rose's back, and another set of hands closed on her shoulders. This time, the fingers curled and a sharp pain skittered across her skin as nails dug in. Rose was turned around without ceremony, and yelped in pain as her broken arm was moved. "Nobody's going to hear about this, you understand? No one will know."

"What have you gotten us into?" Now Illya's eyes were overflowing with tears. "They'll kill my younglings, my mate, even my parents."

"We can still stop this." Elvira appeared beside Illya. Her eyes were wide and scared, but when she locked eyes with Illya, her face was determined. She looked straight at Rose. "Rose will say it was an accident, won't she?"

Rose nodded furiously, too afraid to talk.

"She's lying," Maral said to Illya, then looked straight at Willa and Elvira.

"I'm heavy with a youngling, Maral," Willa whined, tears running freely down her cheeks. "Like you are."

Maral laughed, the sound strangely distorted. "Of course I'm not," she said. "I'm not allowing any youngling of a second in command inside my body." Maral tilted her head to the side and met Rose's eyes.

"Surprised? You shouldn't be." She smiled, exposing her small, wicked teeth. "I only pretended so Arlen would allow me to come."

"You betrayed him." Anger flared inside Rose at the idea. "How could you do something like that to him? He's a good male, and he loves you."

"Love?" Maral spoke with disgust. "I don't need his love. What I wanted was a strong mate. The strongest mate, and that's not what he is. Not even after I organized Karian's disappearance. All Arlen could think of was to find his brother. Not one single time did he consider this his opportunity to seize power. Arlen is nothing but a pathetic weakling."

The revelation was too much to bear, and Rose screamed in anger and frustration. She couldn't move, not an inch, and it only made Maral more gleeful.

"You've done all this for revenge," Illya said in a trembling whisper, interrupting Rose and Maral's confrontation. "Because Karian rejected you all those years ago. Now that he's bloodmate with Rose, you figured you'll be rid of them both if she disappears."

"Shut up, or I'll sell you all with her. There's always a good price for an Avonie on the slavers' black market, even one with a youngling. They might just rip it from you and throw it to the beasts."

Willa straightened, then took a step back. Not long after that, both Elvira and Illya joined her, looking at their former friend with horror.

"You opened the gate of the house, didn't you?" Rose said with tears in her throat. "You sent Maak outside."

"And they were all so scared for you, they didn't even stop to ask how you found a necklace just like Arlia's outside." Maral's face split in an ugly grin, madness plain on her features, morphing the beautiful lines of her face into a parody of what she really was. "It was so easy. All I had to do was cut Arlia's ridiculous pet and throw him out to attract the killkons. You were so predictable. Too bad you weren't ripped to pieces then and there."

Understanding infiltrated Rose's mind as surely as the poison in Maral's words. She had been waiting for a chance to destroy Karian for ten long years. Maral was mad, rotten to the core.

The door opened and heavy footsteps sounded in the room. Maral turned to welcome the newcomer. Rose stared, wide-eyed and loose jawed, as a tall, blue-skinned male strolled in. Her breath caught as she locked gazes with Karian's cousin, Erlock. The glint in his eyes was unmistakable. There was cruelty in his expression, cruelty and lust.

"You took your time." Maral's fingers dug into Rose's flesh, making her eyes well with tears, but she didn't scream. She wasn't going to give Maral the satisfaction. "She's all yours."

Rose was still pinned to the ground when Erlock came to stand over her and Maral. His cold stare traveled up the naked skin of her legs.

"She's been damaged." Erlock squatted down at her side. "I'll have to get that arm repaired before delivering her."

Rose tore her gaze from Erlock and stared at Maral. "Don't do this," she pleaded. "All the humans, back at my village, they're depending on me." Looking into Maral's eyes, Rose realized that there was no pity to find there. She was full of bile and venom.

"Good," Maral said softly, her voice a song on the air. "That's what you all deserve."

"We have children, old people too. You know no one will escape this. They're going to either kill us or sell us."

Maral smiled, her pupils reduced to slits in the purple ocean of her eyes. She glided up, graceful and beautiful like the poisonous snake she was. Rose stayed down on the floor, her eyes rapidly overflowing with bitter tears. She had lost. She gave up everything to save her family, her people, and she had still lost. The worst part was that she'd pulled Karian down with her.

Rose's eyes left Maral and her self-satisfied expression, and went to the other Avonies. They were deserting the room, shooting furtive glances over their shoulders as they left. Elvira met Rose's gaze, and genuine hurt answered Rose's silent prayer. Then she left.

Erlock grabbed Rose's arms and jerked her up. Rose screamed at the white flash of pain, burning a hole through her vision as her broken arm was twisted.

"That's it, human," Erlock whispered closed to her ear. "I like to hear you scream."

Behind him, Maral watched, her purple eyes glinting with delight at the scene.

"You can go to your mate now." Erlock turned his head to Maral. "I have her."

"I think not," Maral said, her voice soft and sweet. "I'll wait for the payment with you. After that, she's all yours."

Erlock glared at Maral but didn't answer. Rose was relieved the other female refused to leave, for she knew exactly how Erlock had wanted to spend his time alone with her. This gave her a bit more time to plot, to think of an escape. Anything.

Her mind raced, tried to think straight, to find a way to contact Karian or any other male in the family. Physical confrontation was not the answer. She was no match for Erlock, especially with her broken arm.

"You won't get away with this." Rose turned to the traitorous Eok. "Karian will know it was you. He'll hunt you down, and then he's going to make you wish he'd allow you to die."

"That he will." Erlock smiled, and a deep chill slithered through Rose's bones at the sight. "If he finds me before the grieving sets in, that is. But rest assured that I will be far, far away from any of them until he's gone for good."

"If she doesn't betray you before that," Rose said, as softly and sweetly as Maral had done before.

"She won't betray me," Erlock said, but there was a flash of uncertainty in his eyes. "She's got too much to lose."

"What, like a big-mouthed associate who will be a constant thorn in her side?" Rose smiled, putting as much bile in her voice as she could. "My bet is you won't live long after I'm gone. She can't have you poking holes in her scheme to be the top female in the tribe. You're a threat."

Erlock squinted at Rose, but didn't answer. His gaze wandered to where Maral stood a few paces back, her face turned to the door. She was too far away to have heard, and her mind seemed to be light years away, lost in her hatred of Karian and her plans for the future. As if sensing it, Maral turned her head and met Erlock's gaze.

"They're here," she said.

The door opened and a familiar tall, mottled green male appeared. The Cattelan male walked in after casting a long glance at Maral, who stood straight, watching him with careful eyes. Arrik stopped in front of Rose, while two others of his kind stood at the back, near Maral.

"*You*." Rose bit her lower lip until blood set its coppery taste on her tongue.

"She's damaged." Arrik's gaze ran over her body, slowing at her breasts before going down. "I need to take her to medical before payment is processed. There will be a price deducted for the injury."

"You're not taking her without payment." Maral's crystal voice rang heavy with outrage. "You can inspect her here and deduct the broken arm, but she stays until I get paid."

"Fine, I'll inspect her here." Arrik's frown showed that it wasn't all right. He didn't like to be talked to like that by females.

He approached, his eyes hard and speaking volumes about revenge that was long overdue.

"Touch me and I'll be the last female you'll ever see, because I'll rip your last eye out with my teeth," Rose spat.

"It's going to be a week before I deliver you." Arrik brought his hand to his face, touching his fingers to the scar from their last encounter. "It can be a long, long time."

"Don't tell me you're still mad at me." Rose chuckled. She was surprised at her own bravado, but then, she didn't have much to lose anyway. She might as well go down fighting.

Arrik smiled, his thin, lip-less mouth curving upward, misshapen because of the scar. The eye Rose had blinded with the spear was a dull milky gray, unseeing and hypnotic. Her eyes traced the scar that pulled down the eye socket, traveled over the sharp cheekbone, and ended up at the corner of his mouth. It was darker than his skin, a green almost black.

It was ugly. It was befitting.

"You know what? I like you better like that." Rose smiled as bright and wide as she could. "It's an improvement."

The sound of the slap registered before Rose understood Arrik had hit her. Her broken arm hurt in a pulsating inferno, eating away at her sanity as pain invaded her body. She blinked, realizing she was still sprawled on the floor, the cold of the stone against her cheek, contrasting with the burning on the side of her face.

"And I like you better like that, too." Arrik's voice was shaking with anger. "On your knees. You'll be doing a lot of that from now on."

"I had a deal with the Minister." Erlock slipped between Arrik and Rose, blocking her view of the Cattelan's face. "He said I could have her first."

"The Minister is impatient to get his new pet back," Arrik answered. "He's already going to be upset the merchandise is damaged, don't go thinking you have any kind of leverage for what happens from now on."

"You asshole!"

Erlock tried to take a swing at Arrik but the other male ducked easily, then hit back with a powerful hook from his right. Arrik's fist connected with Erlock's jaw, and a sickening snap announced the breaking of bone. Erlock's howls of pain echoed, confirming what Rose already knew: Arrik was the superior fighter. In a flash of memory, Rose remembered Karian's fluid movements as he had fought the Cattelan. Karian was the best of them all, but Karian wasn't there.

"Stay where you are," Arrik snapped as Maral took a few quiet steps toward the door. "We're not finished."

Maral stopped dead in her tracks. Her beautiful face was paler than usual, as white as alabaster and twice as taut. She was scared. She had made a mistake, and was now realizing just how vulnerable she truly was. A pang of pity bit Rose, but it was soon tempered by a hateful glare from Maral's purple eyes. Her hatred of Rose was greater than her desire to protect herself.

"Take her away," Maral said. "And never come back."

Arrik turned to Rose. His face was a mask of hatred, and when he leaned down close to her, his breath was heavy with the putrid stench of sick lust. Despair drew its slimy tentacles around Rose's heart, squeezing and compressing the flow of blood until her vision was filled with tiny black dots swimming in a sea of meaningless blur.

A hand closed around her nape, fingers digging deep, immobilizing her head. Arrik brought his face close to hers and, for a dizzying second, Rose was afraid he was going to kiss her. Then his tongue slid over her cheek, raspy and slimy like a dead frog. Rose knew she should have had the courage to keep quiet, but she couldn't help the yelp of disgust and helplessness that escaped her lips.

"I'll make you wish you'd slit your own throat on the Saarmak moon."

Then an explosion of clay and dust invaded the air, and a roar like thunder itself filled the door.

Chapter Twenty-Nine

Karian

Figures came into focus as the dust dissipated. Karian's senses were sharpened by the knowledge his mate was in mortal danger, and his entire body was electrified with the burst of energy preceding the fight that was to come. He glanced over the two dead Cattelans lying on the stone floor. Blood was still gushing out of their slashed throats, but the gleam of life was gone from their eyes. It was a mercy they didn't deserve. If he could have chosen, they wouldn't have had a quick death.

A scream, female and shrill, came to his ears. Wrong... it was the wrong voice.

Karian scanned Maral's prostrate form on the ground. She was unconscious, her body lying in a heap against the wall, dust covering her exposed flesh, making her look like a statue. A wave of anger flared from deep inside his guts, instinctive and primal, but he pushed it aside. Revenge was not important for now, only rescuing Rose was.

He walked into the room, leaving Maral and the dead Cattelans behind.

Another female yelp, low and infinitely more scared. This time, his talons shot out and his muscles rippled with wrath. Rose. This was Rose.

His eyes focused on three figures near the back of the room. A male was crouched on the floor in front of two others. From the way they were lying on the floor, all wrong and twisted, it was clear the male's legs were broken. Karian recognized Erlock immediately. He hissed furiously at his cousin.

"No, wait," Erlock began. "She's lying. The female can't be trusted."

Karian didn't let him finish. Following an instinct written on the ivory of his bones, he leapt. Erlock's neck snapped before he had a chance to utter one more word.

Karian got up and turned to face the remaining threat in the room. His eyes latched onto the glare of a single yellow eye. Arrik. Karian's shoulders hurt from the tension accumulating in his muscles. He took a step forward.

"Take one more step and I'll snap her pretty neck." Arrik brought his hand over Rose's slender throat, squeezing just enough to make her eyes gleam with fear.

Karian stopped. His fists opened and closed without his commanding them to. "You kill her, and there's no money."

Arrik scowled, his face misshapen by the ugly scar. "Money is no good to me if I'm dead."

Silence fell between the Cattelan and Eok as they stared each other down. They were at a standstill. Arrik knew Karian would kill him the instant he released Rose. He was also dead if he failed to bring Rose back to her buyer. His only option was to bring Rose to his ship alive, and as intact as possible. That made him a dangerous and desperate male.

Arrik didn't care about hurting Rose, damaging her beyond repair, as long as she was alive. Karian cared about nothing else.

In a nutshell, Arrik had a leverage Karian did not possess.

"Step back slowly." Arrik kept his remaining eye on Karian. "One bad move and your bloodmate is history."

"Don't do it, Karian," Rose pleaded. "I'm not worth a thousand human beings."

"I can't," Karian said, looking straight into those eyes the color of the sky before a storm. "I can't abandon you, not for a million other lives. I'm sorry."

"I love you," she whispered. Her lips were trembling but her eyes were steady. Such strength, such courage. His heart swelled.

"I know."

Karian backed up until the path was clear between the door and Arrik. Arrik didn't wait, pushing Rose in front of him as they walked to the door. Rose stared at Karian, her storm-gray eyes tugging at his insides, tearing him apart one morsel at a time. He felt the bond of the bloodmating, pure and fierce along his veins, screaming for his mate. He understood now how the killkon had died. He wouldn't survive if anything happened to Rose, either. The will to live would slip out of him one agonizing second at a time.

Behind him, a furtive movement attracted his attention, but Karian didn't dare look away from Arrik.

"Kill her." Maral spoke from somewhere behind Karian. "Kill that bitch now. It's what he'll do anyway."

"Shut up." Arrik's eye traced frantic glances from Karian to the door. "I'm not giving up on the human."

A creeping chill invaded Karian's mind. Maral was right. Karian should have thought of it sooner. After she had touched so many hearts in the Ring's session, Rose's death would make a compelling case. All Trade Minister Knut would have to do would be to show Rose's tortured, abused body to prove that humans still needed protection from the Genetic Preservation Board. It was the perfect set up.

Minister Knut was a very cunning male.

"She's a loose end." Maral got to her feet, wiping dust off her ruined gown. Her purple eyes shone with a cold resolve. "She has to die."

"No." Arrik changed his hold on Rose, sliding his hand from her throat to her shoulder. His other arm wrapped around her waist, pulling her in to his body even more. "The human female is mine."

The words resonated in Karian's body, across his ribs and into the depths of his guts. Rage flowed, unabashed and unrestrained along his veins, spreading a fire that burned his flesh, leaving behind only an iron red wasteland.

Karian roared, his wrath pouring out in a white flash. A female screamed at his back, the sound shrill and grating. Arrik's single eye grew wide as he realized his mistake. He had let go of his grip on Rose's throat, and his life had slipped through that small moment of inattention. Rose dove to the ground, understanding Karian's intention without needing any additional instruction.

In the split second it took Karian to act, he reveled in the knowledge that she was his half, connected to him in everything. It wasn't surprising his blood had reacted the way it did. She was his mate, the one inside whom his life essence ran. She was his life.

A wet sound reached parts of Karian's awareness as his talons dug deep into Arrik's throat, cutting the soft tissue, veins and arteries. The Cattelan's blood splattered his face, its warm salty taste spreading on his tongue. His warrior instinct surged with the knowledge that the wound he'd inflicted was fatal.

Arrik's single eye latched onto Karian, its yellow iris swirling with fear and understanding as his hands went up in a futile attempt to stem the flow of blood. It gave Rose enough time to jump out of harm's way, and she landed on a heap of debris as Karian's talons shredded through Arrik's chest, ripping through his ribcage as if through the most tender meat. Arrik's eye shone with surprise as his hearts were stabbed, stopping the life force from flowing into his body. The awareness of life shone, brief and bright, then a cloud settled over his face. Karian's enemy was dead.

Suddenly Rose screamed a warning.

"Karian, behind you!"

Karian turned, his talons at the ready, but he was too late. Purple eyes bright with ancient hatred shone in his field of vision, and a blade played a red dance as it slid into his chest.

Rose

Rose tried to scream but there wasn't enough air in her lungs. She felt as if she were watching the universe through an ever reducing tunnel, and she could only stare helplessly as events unfolded.

As Karian watched, Maral's twisted face broke into a fierce smile. The small, wicked blade she pulled out of Karian's ribs was covered in bright red, and she stared directly at Rose as she stabbed it into Karian's powerful chest again. And again. And again.

"No!"

Rose heard herself scream, then she was on top of Maral, her hands around the Avonie's tiny neck. The two females tumbled backward while Karian's heavy weight hit the floor with a sickening sound. It was the sound of a dead weight. The sound of a body which didn't have enough life left in it to absorb its fall. Rose's heart shredded into pieces. As she fought with Maral, a separate part of her mind registered Karian's fall, the way his life spilled out faster than the pool of blood spreading under him on the stone. He was facing away from her, his head flat on the ground.

Maral screeched and hissed under Rose's heavier weight. Finally getting the upper hand, Rose sat on Maral's delicate chest, holding her hands above her head. Rose pummeled Maral's hand to the stone floor, still holding the blade soiled with Karian's blood. The Avonie twisted and writhed like a snake, tiny fangs trying to dig into her wrist. Rose continued hitting Maral's hand on the stone as hard as she could, trying to loosen Maral's hold on the only weapon in the room.

The pool of blood from Karian's body spread to them, creeping under Maral's hand as Rose banged it on the floor. A sob escaped

Rose's lips even as she screeched in fury. Karian's blood splashed and droplets landed on her face. The contact made her resolve even stronger, but Maral was not easily defeated. She was surprisingly strong for such a fragile creature. Rose finally managed to make the Avonie's hold on the blade falter, and as the knife fell to the floor, she reached for the weapon with both hands.

Tiny fangs dug into Rose's flesh, at midpoint in her upper arm, like a million needles. Rose screamed in pain but didn't let go of the blade. Maral twisted under her, then kicked her straight in the chest. Rose lost her balance and rolled away, still clutching the blade.

"I'll kill you." Rose held the blade in front of her like a promise. "You twisted, sick bitch."

Maral got to her feet, wiping blood from her lips. Her purple eyes shone with madness, but there was no defeat in them. She laughed, the sound insane and terrible, penetrating Rose's body like a cold wind.

Cold, she was so cold. Something was wrong.

"I'm sorry," Maral said between two burst of hilarity. "It's just so funny. You made this *so* perfect."

"What are you talking about?" Rose took a side step toward Karian. Her teeth chattered and her muscles were stiff. "What did you do?"

"You let me bite you." Maral's mouth opened in a wide grin, revealing tiny fangs stained with Rose's blood. A drop of white, pearly fluid fell on her lower lip. "Avonies are poisonous. And you know what the best part is? We only produce poison when we're scared for our lives. You couldn't have made this better if you'd tried."

The cold seeped to Rose's legs, and she fell to her knees beside Karian.

"They'll kill you for this." Rose managed to get the words out, but her jaw seemed to be moving through mud. "Arlen will never forgive you for killing his brother. He'll hunt you to the end of the universe."

"How will he know?" Maral brushed her hair away from her face, leaving a long trail of red on her cheek. "All he will see is that a crazy, violent human female conspired with those filthy Cattelans to murder his brother. Even worse, it's going to cause me to lose our poor, poor youngling. Why, you even killed Erlock, who came to Karian's rescue. After that, who will care for a bunch of slaves? They deserve nothing more than to be treated like the animals they are."

The cold invaded the rest of Rose's body and she fell, her head hitting the already cooling pool of blood beside Karian. Rose could see his handsome, strong face now. His eyes were closed and his lips parted. Dead. Karian was dead. Pain tore at her, savage and deep. He couldn't die. He was too fierce, too proud, and too passionate. Rose wanted to scream and kick, shock him back to himself, the strong lover who had kept all the world's threats away. She wanted to stroke his cheek and kiss him until life returned to his hard, kissable lips.

"You won't get away with it." Her words were as hollow as her body was becoming. The cold was reaching higher inside her ribcage. She could feel it enclosing her heart, slowing its pace.

Maral lay down beside Rose, bracing her head with her hand. A perverted, sweet smile stretched on her lips as she watched Rose.

"But I already have." Maral was so close to Rose that her lips brushed her cheek. "And I'll make sure your precious family follows you to the grave."

Anger flared inside Rose's numb chest, warming it just enough so she could clutch the wet handle of the knife between her frozen fingers. Her arm was a lump of wood encased in ice, but it answered Rose's order.

The blade flashed and Maral's eyes widened as it was embedded in her throat. Rose locked eyes with the Avonie as understanding dawned in her shining purple gaze. Her pupils dilated and shrank furiously as a gush of blood flowed from the wound in her neck. Maral brought two long-fingered hands up to her throat and jerked the blade out in an instinctive gesture. The knife clattered to the floor in a wet splash. Blood poured freely from the open wound, and the Avonie fell on her back in the pooling red, gasping helplessly.

Rose closed her eyes on the image of Maral dying. She should be glad her enemy was getting what was coming to her, but she simply wasn't. She was no weakling, but she didn't have it in her to hate the other female. Mostly, she didn't want hate to be the last feeling she would take with her.

With a supreme effort, Rose turned her head toward Karian and opened her eyes again. His face was slack and peaceful, unmoving. Despair washed over her, but she couldn't sob anymore. Everything was over. Her family was dead, or would soon wish they were. Karian was dead because of his love for her. She understood it now, understood it all. Everything he had done for her was because of love. He hadn't tried to own her. He'd sacrificed everything for her, even his life.

How blind she had been.

Maral's gurgles stopped, but that registered as a meaningless fact in Rose's mind. All she cared about was the feel of Karian's blood under her cheek and the warmth of his flesh where their bodies touched. She fought to keep her eyes open as the cold made her eyelids heavy, blurring everything. When she couldn't fight the heaviness anymore, she closed her eyes and summoned Karian's features, the way she remembered him on the Saarmak moon when they had both stood outside the pod, watching the stars in the strange sky. Strong, male and warm. Her Karian.

She wanted to die with his smile etched in her mind.

I love you.

Rose thought the words, hoping she had been able to show him that weeks before, when it had still mattered. What a mess she had made of things. She did love him. She had loved him ever since the first time those hands had comforted her in the escape pod, so warm and full of strength. She had just been too focused on keeping her freedom to realize her loneliness was just another prison. There were so many things she wanted to tell him, so many words he needed to hear.

Too late; it was all too late.

Somewhere far above, a loud noise erupted. Shouts and screams, familiar voices.

Too late.

A flash of sapphire blue invaded her vision, but Rose couldn't focus anymore. There was more shouting, and more movement filled the blur of her vision. Someone talked into her ear but the words were lost. Hands closed around her shoulders, lifting her from the cold of the stone floor. Rose couldn't feel Karian's body anymore. They had taken her from him.

She whimpered, fighting them futilely.

Let me die with him. Please.

With Karian's presence gone, the cold closed around her, invading her last refuge. A darkness filled with ice drowned her thoughts and she let go, accepting the silence that blanketed everything.

Chapter Thirty

Rose

A hand on her forehead, petting her damp skin. The feeling of a warm cloth, washing cold sweat away. A hot glow coming from both under and over her body, wrapping her in the embrace of sunlight. Cold... Rose was still so cold.

Funny, I didn't picture death like this.

The feelings melted together in time as she lay unmoving in a sea of darkness. Eons passed and went, until the darkness changed from an all-consuming ink into a thick fog. There were people on the other side of that fog—so close, Rose knew she only had to reach out to touch them.

This is more like it. I shouldn't be alone, it's too cruel.

Rose hoped against all hope that Karian wouldn't be waiting for her on the other side of that fog. She had thought him dead before, but now, she wasn't so sure. Yes, his injuries had been severe, but Karian was so strong, he might have pulled through with the will to survive. Even through the grieving of the bloodmating, she hoped. She smiled inside, imagining him walking in the tall grassland, hunting. He belonged there, with his family.

Voices called from the other side of the fog, familiar and full of promises. Encouraging her to come to them, to open her eyes—only they were wide open. She fought, wanting to go to them, tired of the boredom of the darkness.

"Pretty Thing." That voice, Rose knew it so well. She would recognize it amongst millions of others. Pain pinched her heart. He hadn't survived, then. "Wake up. Rose, come back to me."

She pushed the fog away, tired of its weight. Her eyelids weren't open like she had thought. Concentrating so hard it hurt, she lifted them, then closed them again. Voices erupted, a commotion as people talked and called for things that made no sense in the afterlife: medical equipment, doctors and nurses. They were drowned by the sensation of the hand cupping her cheek, a rough thumb caressing her with unbearable tenderness. With another supreme effort, the world appeared.

The colors were too bright, and the light too harsh, but Rose kept blinking until her vision adapted enough to focus on a male face with skin the color of midnight. Karian's blue eyes shone bright as stars, and when he swallowed, she had the impression he was unable to talk. It made no sense. You didn't swallow your emotions in the afterlife, did you?

"I'm so sorry." She croaked the words, surprised that her voice sounded so broken. She had always envisioned the afterlife as being perfect, but what did she know about it after all?

"What can you be sorry about, Pretty Thing?" Karian smiled, his impossibly handsome lips curving upward. So kissable, so masculine. He was a dream, even dead. "Hush now, don't strain yourself."

"I'd just hoped you hadn't died, that's all." Rose smiled, but pain morphed it into a grimace. It was so strange, she shouldn't hurt anymore. "The afterlife is greatly overrated. It sucks."

Karian frowned, confusion plain on his face. Another person entered the room, and Karian glanced up briefly before returning his gaze to her. He seemed even more concerned now.

"The doctor is going to be here any second now." A familiar female voice, warm and melodious. "How is she?"

"I'm not sure." Karian held her hand, his touch so hot, so real, it brought tears to her eyes. "She's talking nonsense. She thinks she's dead."

The reality of the words penetrated her mind, and Rose widened her eyes in shock.

"I'm alive?" She tried to turn her head to face the owner of the familiar voice, but it was too much to ask. All she managed was to send a shockwave of pain all the way to her toes. She grimaced at the agony.

"Yes, Pretty Thing, you're alive." Karian laughed, the sound more beautiful than anything. "You're alive."

Rose let that sink in. Confusion rode side by side with a giddiness bordering on euphoria as she progressively became aware of Karian's hand in hers, the intermingling of their fingers. She tore her eyes from his face and looked at the room she was in. Definitively a medical pod, with equipment lining the walls and a clean, antiseptic white all over. Her body was in a strange bubble, white and opaque, and as she wiggled, she realized it was some sort of jelly. It generated heat, enclosing her in a steady cocoon of warmth.

Memories of Maral and her tiny, wicked fangs rushed through. Her laughs and her jibes about the venom Avonies were able to produce when they were scared for their lives. Then her purple eyes clouding as her life slipped away.

Arlen will never forgive me.

"Maral—"

"Don't worry about it," Karian cut her off, his eyes blazing with an anger that verged on savagery. "You did what you had to do. It was only by luck that Elvira was able to alert us fast enough."

"Maral's dead?"

Karian nodded, and a silence like red velvet descended over the room. Rose had done it, then. That she'd acted in self-defense was little comfort. Taking a life left her feeling hollow and dead inside, as though she'd killed a part of herself at the same time. Rose blinked, and wasn't surprised to feel a tear sliding down on her cheek, unchecked.

"Arlen?" That was all she could get out before her throat constricted and her voice broke.

"He's grief stricken." Karian shook his head, the pain plain on his face. "She was as bad a mate as can be, but the link was deep, even if she wasn't his bloodmate. He doesn't blame you for it, you need to know that."

Rose nodded, biting her lower lip. There was too much she needed to know, and her tired body was already pulling her under, dragging her mind back into the fog. She fought the urge to close her eyes, but it was getting harder by the second.

"The humans, my family…" Her words got lost in the wave of fatigue that washed over her body. "The Trade Minister will want to erase them all."

"Don't worry." Karian bent over and kissed her. His heat scorched her lips, dulling her senses, pulling her under even faster. How badly she longed for his arms, his warmth and his passion. "Khal has already taken command of a garrison to protect your people. They're safe."

The relief that washed over Rose was like a liquid tide of joy. Her family was safe. Karian had kept his promise; through everything, he had kept his promise.

"I love you."

Rose managed to keep her eyes open just long enough to see his eyes shine and his lips curve in the most heart-wrenching smile.

"I love you, too, Pretty Thing. I've loved you since that first time in the pod."

Rose allowed the darkness to take her again, surrendering to its embrace like a lover.

Chapter Thirty-One

Rose

It took a few weeks for Rose to fight off the deadly Avonie poison, but she was eventually allowed to leave the medical pod and go back home with Karian and his family.

They were on the transport, riding slowly under the midday sun while she enjoyed the feel of the wind in her hair. It had been so long, it seemed, since she'd simply enjoyed being. Karian's hand reached out, stroking hers in a tender caress.

"Any news on my family?" Rose watched as a family unit of killkons ran in the tall grass. Mother and pups followed the father in apparent bliss. She remembered the killkon's grief and death as his mate had died, and her heart pinched. Rose understood, now, the link between the mates. She didn't think she'd survive without Karian for long, either.

"Your mother and brothers are safe and cared for," he said, looking straight ahead. "There is still no news of your father. We have found the breeding facility thanks to the location tips you gave us, but by the time we arrived, it had been emptied."

"Emptied?" The warmth of the sun deserted her skin and Rose felt as if she were under the spell of the poison once again. "Are they dead?"

"We don't think so." Frustration was clear in Karian's voice and face. "The trade is worth too much money, even if the Prime Councilor declared the trade illegal. In all probability, Minister Knut had them moved to another world."

"So, it's over? I'll never see him again."

The face of her father, with his steel gray eyes and easy smile, imposed itself in her mind. He gave up everything to save his people, and in the end, Rose knew he would have been proud of her. It was little to quell her grief, but it was a comfort nevertheless. The faces of her loved ones appeared in her memory, one after the other. They were safe, but how many more were still being kept in a hellish life? Too many. Even one single human living like that was one too many.

"Not quite." Karian gave her a fierce smile. "These humans are family members of Eok warriors. They are Eokian by law. And Eoks do not tolerate their own being enslaved."

"You'll wage war on the bastard?"

"So to speak." Karian chuckled, and when she frowned, he nodded. "There is another one who's under attack as we speak."

"Who?"

"Your cousin Aliena gives my brother Kamal the hardest of times." Karian broke into a heartfelt laugh. "She insisted on being part of the team leading the search for the remaining humans."

"Aliena will give him hell."

"That's what I hope."

Karian stopped the pod over the sea of grass and turned to Rose. There, alone under the three suns, he grabbed the back of her neck and pulled her to him. His lips took possession of her mouth and she surrendered, opening it and kissing him back with passion. After a long time, he released her, and they both panted, looking into each other's eyes.

"Do you like it here?" Karian waved at the general area.

Rose looked around and saw what he meant. They were on top of a rounded hill, and on all sides, they could see a different part of the Eokian landscape. The rolling hills spread to the north, smooth and moving like the sea, while to the south, the jagged teeth of the cliffs broke the grassland into a breathtaking landscape. All around, the flow of the river sparkled in the grass like a diamond necklace.

"It's the most amazing view I've ever seen," she said truthfully. "Where are we?"

"We're home." He squeezed both her hands between his.

"I don't understand. We already have a home, with your mother and father."

"This is where I will build our own house, our own enclosure, with a garden and fruit trees. Where our own younglings will be born."

"We could start by making a youngling here." Rose smiled, then kissed him.

"My thoughts exactly."

His voice was already husky as his hands ran over her body, spreading fire and need. He pulled her to him again, and this time, he didn't just kiss her. He lifted her, as easily as a child, and set her down over him. Rose gazed into his blazing eyes, as full of hunger as her own.

Her bloodmate. Her life. She truly had everything she ever needed.

MARY AUCLAIR

The End

ABOUT MARY AUCLAIR

Mary Auclair is a lover of romance novels of all genres. She likes to write everything, from science fiction to fantasy, passing through paranormal and historical, but always with a dark, sexy twist. She spends too many hours to count daydreaming about adventures and hot, dominant, alpha male heroes. When she's not writing, she's busy being a full-time mom, as well as caring for her many pets.

Visit her website here: www.maryauclair.com

Find her on Facebook: www.facebook.com/authormaryauclair/

Find her on Instagram: https://www.instagram.com/maryauclairbooks/

Find her on TikTok: https://www.tiktok.com/@authormaryauclair

Find her on BookBub: https://www.bookbub.com/profile/mary-auclair

Don't miss these exciting titles by Mary Auclair and Deliciously Dangerous Books

OTHER TITLES FOR MARY AUCLAIR

Eok Warriors Series

Venomous Craving - Eok Warrior Series Book One
Venomous Hunger - Eok Warrior Series Book Two
Venomous Heart - Eok Warrior Series Book Three
Venomous Lust - Eok Warrior Series Book Four

Dawn of Dragons Series

Touch of Ice – Dawn of Dragons Book One
Caress of Fire - Dawn of Dragons Book Two
Kiss of Night - Coming Soon...

Printed in Dunstable, United Kingdom